For John Weatherall, who loved Dorset.

PROLOGUE

Scriptorium, Cathedral Church of Sherborne, Wessex. Spring A.D. 707

Wite was deep in concentration. With her head bowed and eyes fixed on the parchment, she was only vaguely aware of the sound of the wind as it swept through the branches of the yews that circled the churchyard. The other scholars had finished hours ago, yet Wite remained willingly, even as the light had started to fade into early evening. She took a few minutes to stretch her aching back and cocked her head to scrutinise her work. The manuscript was her best yet, similar in style to the old Gaelic books she had been shown with wonderful illuminated texts in vivid blues and greens, finished with gold. Bishop Ealdhelm had told her this was a very important script, one that would contain a hidden message only to be deciphered by those who have the gift of sight from God. Wite had been thrilled to be chosen by Ealdhelm from among the other male scholars to do this work, although within her heart she always knew this had been her destiny.

Wite dipped the pen into the precious blue pigment and then paused. The flame of her candle was dancing wildly as if someone had walked by. Resting the pen in its cradle, Wite became very still and closed her ears against the strengthening breeze that whistled beyond the shuttered windows. She could hear it now, the sound of creaking wood like somebody had eased themselves down at one of the writing desks. Were they here again, the ghosts from her past? Wite scanned the room with wide eyes but there was nothing. The door remained closed and the triangular-headed windows sealed.

'Who is here?' Wite called, the echo of her voice bouncing off the empty writing desks. There was no reply. Frowning, Wite retrieved her pen to continue her work.

'I'm over here!' The shrill tones of the voice sliced through the air like a sharpened blade. Wite spun round, her heart thumping. To her horror she could just about make out from the increasing darkness the figure of a woman, slumped against the writing chest. As she approached Wite noticed that the woman's cheeks were hollowed and her eyes sunken, yet her clothes were well cut and trimmed with fur. At first Wite did not recognise her, but slowly she began to find familiarity in the distorted features. Biting her lip, Wite stepped forward a little further and bravely extended her trembling hands in greeting. The woman instantly recoiled.

'Don't touch me!' She croaked. 'Can't you see? I am sick.'

In an instant Wite now understood what had caused the change in appearance and realised that sickness alone was not to blame for the lines etched on the woman's face. The passing of time had played a significant part. Ignoring her plea, Wite reached out and clasped the woman's hands in hers. They were clammy and cold.

'You will have my help and prayers. I will not cower from you because of your sickness.'

The woman flicked a strand of greying hair from her face and Wite noticed her forehead was beaded with perspiration.

'I didn't want to come here and put you in danger, but you are our last hope. The healing spring has run dry and now many in the village are falling victim to this pestilence.'

The woman's voice trailed off into a fit of coughing that seemed to last for an age. Wiping her bloodstained mouth on the back of her hand, she tried once more. 'If you can make the healing water appear again, then perhaps there will be a chance for those who are not yet too sick.'

Wite felt a rush of sadness as she recalled those she had once shared her life with being no more. This pestilence was severe. It was most certainly beyond her help but she had to remain positive, she had to try.

'The spring is dry at West Lytchett.' Wite replied. 'It has been for many years, but be glad, for at least I still have some of the water. I shall ask Bishop Ealdhelm to bless you with it, but first come, I will find you a room and bed where you can rest.'

Wite's stomach turned over as she helped her friend down from the chest. She was so thin and weak, no more than bones underneath the layers of her clothes. To see her in this state in contrast to her former beauty was shocking. Once Wite had settled her in the bed of the cell opposite her own, she fetched bread and a draught of weak ale and went to look for Ealdhelm.

It was a long, torturous night. Wite kept vigil, praying for the fever to relinquish its grip. When the patient cried aloud with distress, Wite stroked her brow and applied the healing spring water. Bishop Ealdhelm too gave his blessing, but by the first light of dawn they could see there was nothing more to be done. The patient's chest rattled in protest for a final time and Wite slumped against the wall of the cell, exhausted in defeat.

'The water of the spring can have the powers to heal, but this fever is too strong, its grip too severe.' Ealdhelm whispered. His kind face was sorrowful, his voice apologetic. 'Come now, Wite. You have done all you can. We must give her a decent burial, one that is befitting of her status, but not here in the churchyard. I fear this pestilence could be dangerous after death.'

Wite nodded wearily in agreement. She was already thinking of a special place, a beautiful wilderness where the land met the sea and all that could be heard was the cry of the gull and the rushing of the wind and waves.

CHAPTER 1

South Dorset.
June 2009

Suzanne Brookes narrowed her eyes and focused on the road ahead. She wasn't used to driving on country roads, the speed limit seemed far too fast for all the dips and bends. Looking in her rear view mirror she noticed with annoyance that the car behind her was still tailgating, the driver so close that she could see his agitated expression. Spotting a layby a few metres ahead, she flicked the signal and pulled in.

'Okay you win,' Suzanne said through gritted teeth, feeling the driver's eyes boring into her as the silver car raced past. Pulling on the handbrake she sat back with a deep sigh. It had been a longer journey that she had expected, but she knew it was totally necessary. It would be worth it just to remove herself from the office and take stock, even if it was only for a week. Suzanne reached over to the passenger seat to retrieve Melanie's hand-written directions. All around the Dorset countryside had opened out like a soft green patchwork, mainly pasture divided by pale grey limestone walls and the occasional rooftop flecked with orange-yellow lichen. The early evening sun was illuminating the road ahead, and further still in the distance, Suzanne could see the deep blue of the English Channel, the promise of the coast drawing ever near.

Taking a gulp of tepid mineral water, Suzanne reviewed Melanie's directions once more before setting back out onto the road. She figured she must only be a few miles away from her destination as she approached Corfe Castle, the thousand year-old beacon ever watchful over the Isle of Purbeck. As she drove the remaining few miles Suzanne found she couldn't help but think about the first and last time she had visited West Lytchett.

It had been twenty six years ago, a week before her seventh birthday. Suzanne replayed the scenes in her mind and was surprised at how vivid they were given the length of time that had passed in between; the heat of the sun on her bare arms and legs, the feeling of excitement as she'd ventured down to the duck pond on her own. Looking back now, she felt guilty for taking advantage of her mother's distracted state and wished she had instead remained close by and helped with the search for unknown ancestors among the village gravestones.

It had all gone terribly wrong. One moment she had been standing in the heat of the sun, fishing net in hand and feet cooled by the gentle lapping of pond water, the next she was sat in the murky coldness with a twisted ankle and a burning pain shooting through the palm of her left hand. It was only a few minutes later when raising her bloodied hand to show her frantic parents, that it became apparent the offending object was still embedded in her flesh.

Suzanne glanced down at the white scar as if to verify her memories, and in doing so cursed as she nearly missed her turning. Taking a sharp left by the side of the Cock and Bottle pub, Suzanne snapped herself from her thoughts and slowed the car to a crawl. Passing the neatly manicured green on her right, she found an involuntary smile was forming on her lips as she drew up in front of the quaint terrace of traditional Dorset limestone cottages.

'This must be it.' Suzanne said to herself as she recalled Melanie's enthusiastic description of her late uncle's cottage. The terrace comprised four cottages in total, each finished with pastel coloured window frames and matching front doors. According to Melanie, Tilly Whim cottage was the third one from the road. Suzanne brought the car to a stop in what looked to be a suitable spot by a low wall and retrieved her hold-all from the back passenger seat.

Approaching the front garden, Suzanne was delighted to find Tilly Whim as Melanie had described. Although it formed one of a terrace, the front of the cottage felt private and tucked away with geraniums, forget-me-nots and foxgloves adorning the small front garden. Suzanne breathed in the heady scent of the sun-warmed flowers as she picked her way through the greenery that was threatening to invade the garden path, and marveled at how lucky her work colleague had been to inherit such a gem of a place. Inserting the key in the lock, Suzanne pushed at the pale blue front door which creaked open with a wonderful noise that could only be expected from an old building.

On entering, Suzanne found that the cottage was small but not cramped by any means. Downstairs, she found there were only two rooms, a modest sitting room which came straight off the front door, and a country-style oak kitchen with a window that faced south onto the enclosed rear yard. The overall appearance was clean and airy and the smell of fresh paint in the sitting room prompted Suzanne to think about how many times Melanie had complained that her weekends had been taken up by the 'project'. At the time, Suzanne remembered she had not wanted to be in Melanie's shoes at all, but now seeing the finished product, she could not help but feel a pang of envy.

Taking her hold-all Suzanne began to ascend the short but steep staircase. Although there wasn't exactly much to explore, she found that upstairs had been renovated to the high standard she had seen on the ground floor. To her delight she found the main bedroom had a wonderful view towards the village green, and paused a moment to open the tiny sash window and let the scents of the front garden overcome the fresh paint odours. Across the landing, she found a spare room with a single bed and lop-eared toy rabbit sitting on the quilt; surely Melanie's way of making younger holiday guests feel welcome. It was just like Melanie to go the extra mile and think about how her guests would appreciate such things Suzanne reflected, and wondered somewhat negatively, if given the same project she would have done quite so good a job.

Just over half an hour later, Suzanne had unpacked her clothes and small quantity of kitchen provisions and sunk down onto the welcoming softness of the floral sofa with a mug of tea and mobile phone ready to call Melanie. It had been good of her friend to let her stay here at such short notice, especially when she could be letting it out to paying guests. Suzanne had offered to pay the going rate but Melanie would have none of it, insisting that it was the least she could do under the circumstances.

Under the circumstances. Suzanne replayed Melanie's voice in her mind. It was a delicate figure of speech that described nothing, but encompassed everything that mattered. The phone rang several times before going on to the answerphone and Suzanne left a short message. On disconnecting the call her mind inevitably drifted back to the problems at work. If only she hadn't agreed to meet up with Jed that night, things would be fine now. She should have told him that she was busy, she had to work late but as she reluctantly admitted to herself, part of her hadn't given up on Jed and despite everything, she had been more than eager to see him again. Suzanne stared absently for a moment and chewed on a ragged finger nail, her mind a whirlwind of regret and trepidation when something caught her eye through the kitchen window. She blinked a couple of times to focus her vision, frowning in disbelief. Feeling her pulse quicken as her eyes focused in on the dark shape in the back yard, she found herself taking slow, deliberate footsteps which led her from the sitting room into the kitchen. When she was there Suzanne cautiously peered out on to the small yard, her eyes fixed in the same spot.

The hunched shape had not moved. Suzanne's heart hammered in her chest as she strained her eyes against the failing light of dusk. To her surprise she could just about make out the body of a man, his right arm twisted at an odd angle, the face hidden from view by the upturned collar of his jacket. Suzanne's instincts told her to get the hell out of the kitchen but she found that her own curiosity had her rooted to the spot. After a few seconds of staring, Suzanne found she had gathered enough courage to move closer, as near as she could to the kitchen window. Placing both hands on the edge of the Belfast sink, Suzanne leaned forward and was immediately startled when movement came. An over-fed tabby cat appeared on top of the garden wall and jumped onto the stiff torso, carefully placing its paws as it slinked down the body towards the flagstones. Still, the body did not move. That was enough. Suzanne was about to turn on her heels when a face suddenly appeared on the other side of the garden wall.

'Oh my God!' She said aloud in shock. It was only a few moments later, once she had recovered her senses that she realised the face must belong to the next door neighbour. Suddenly grateful of another living soul, Suzanne's fingers trembled as she struggled with the back door latch, bracing herself as she opened the door to the back yard. Unfortunately the man had disappeared from view, but she hoped he still might be in ear-shot.

'Hello, is anyone there?' Her voice sounded feeble and attracted no reply. She looked around the yard and noticed an ancient looking garden hoe lying to one side near the flower beds. An idea formed in her mind, and picking up the hoe she used it to gently prod the crumpled figure on the back. It remained deathly still. In her peripheral vision Suzanne became aware that a light had come on behind her.

'Are you all right there?'

Suzanne spun round, clutching the garden hoe in self-defence. An elderly man was leaning on the boundary wall staring at her. Recognising him as the presumed neighbour she had seen a moment ago, she lowered the garden hoe and managed to stutter a reply.

'Yes, I think so.'

The man was more agile than he looked. In a flash he sprang over the wall and landed on the other side with a jump. 'What's the matter?' He asked. 'You look shaken.'

Suzanne pointed at the figure. 'What on earth?' She started and found that the need to swallow meant she could not complete the sentence.

The man looked in the direction she was pointing and his thin lips started to curl upwards in a wry smile. 'Ah. He won't be bothering you at all!' He sniggered. 'Why, he has a turnip for brains.' To demonstrate, the man pulled the hunched figure up with one arm and showed him to be nothing than an innocent, redundant scarecrow.

Feeling both relief and foolishness, Suzanne laughed awkwardly. 'I'm sorry. It looked like a real person, the way it was sat, I mean, positioned. I feel such an idiot now.'

'Not to worry. It's the half-light. Plays tricks with your eyes. No problem at all. I'm Edward by the way. As you've probably guessed, I live next door.'

Suzanne took a breath in and tried to compose herself. 'My name is Suzanne. I'm here on holiday for the week. My friend Melanie, she owns the cottage, she....'

'Yes I know Melanie.' Edward interrupted. 'A hard working lady she is. She inherited Tilly Whim when her uncle Elias died and she's done wonders for the place. I tell you I had doubts that she could bring it back to life but she did it, all credit to her. Done a marvelous job with restoring it, and hardly any workmen used, it was all her graft.'

Suzanne nodded in agreement. 'Melanie thrives on a challenge, I remember her saying how difficult it was trying to manage the project whilst holding down a demanding job and bringing up two teenage children.'

'Indeed.' Edward smiled. 'Anyway, now you are okay I'd best be off. I'm sure I'll see you round and about the village during the week.' He turned away and was just about to climb over the wall when Suzanne thought of something she needed to ask of him.

'Sorry before you go could I ask you a question, about the village church?'

Edward turned around to face her. 'Certainly, I've lived here in West Lytchett all my life. What is it you want to know?'

'I came here many years ago when I was a child and I remember looking round the churchyard with my mum. She thinks that one of our ancestors from the 19th century is buried there but hasn't had any luck finding her. I wouldn't mind researching it while I'm here. Do you know if the records are kept within the church?'

'They are. Records have been kept at St. John's since the earliest of times, and might I add if you are interested in history then I recommend that you pay a visit to the church anyway. I'd say it's worth looking at both outside and in, fascinating gargoyles and a Saxon doorway, if you are into that sort of thing. Otherwise I recommend the village pub, you will get decent ale in there or white wine and soda or whatever you ladies like.'

Suzanne laughed. 'Ale will do just fine. Thanks for the information. I studied history at University so I am generally interested in old buildings. I will head to the church tomorrow and have a look round.'

'Right then, now that you are sorted I must be off. It was good to meet you Suzanne.' With the agility that would be expected from a much younger man, Edward scaled the wall and dropped back onto the other side, before closing the backdoor behind him.

For a moment, Suzanne remained alone in the back yard admiring the scent of the small cluster of herbs growing close to the kitchen window, but quickly found herself staring at the expressionless face of the scarecrow, its crooked mouth nothing more than a knife slash into the flesh of the turnip. Perhaps she should have asked Edward what on earth it was doing in Melanie's back yard, she didn't know Melanie was in the habit of homing retired scarecrows. Suzanne let out a little laugh which was louder than expected now she was alone and the night was drawing in. The odd thing was she was sure that the scarecrow hadn't been there when she had first arrived, but had she really paid that much attention to the back yard? Suzanne shivered as a chilly breeze embraced her bare arms. It was getting late.

When Suzanne returned to the living room she noticed her phone was flashing, its green pulsing light indicating a missed call. Checking the number she immediately recognised the area code and prefix as belonging to work. Suzanne sighed to herself, immediately concerned why someone in the office had been calling her so late in the evening. There was no chance it could be Melanie, she would have phoned on her mobile, besides Melanie was a stickler for 5pm finishes. Whatever it was about, it couldn't be good news, she thought morosely. Pressing the redial button, Suzanne waited several seconds before disconnecting the call. Glancing at her watch it was almost 10pm, and whoever it was had done the sensible thing and left the office. She would have to wait until tomorrow to find out who had been putting in extra hours and why they needed to speak to her.

Locking the back door, and pulling down the handle to make sure it was secure, Suzanne considered that given her fragile frame of mind tonight, she would sleep with the bedside lamp on.

CHAPTER 2

West Lytchett, Dorset.
June 1325

Blanche Myddelton had been wide awake for most of the night. Noticing the subtle change in light that heralded the dawn, she pushed back the thin woolen blanket and stretched her bare legs towards the end of her pallet. Blanche did not usually need to be up so early, but this morning was different. The restless night would be worthwhile so she would not miss this last opportunity. Securing the russet tunic around her waist and quietly dabbing her face with cold water from the pail, she took care to step around her aunt Fleta who was still snoring on her pallet, her rotten teeth protruding from her mouth like broken grave markers, and ducked her way out of the humble dwelling.

Had it been winter, it would still be the night time, but this morning the late June sun had already started to appear on the horizon. On leaving the enclosure that housed the seven straw and stick homes of her neighbours, Blanche picked her way carefully through the woods that encircled the grounds of Martravers Manor. The dew on the long grass clung to her slender ankles and refreshed her as she walked at pace. Hidden under her mantle was the book which Lady Philippa had told her to return this morning. The instructions had been clear if not a little odd, she was to double wrap it in linen and hide it within the hollow of the Mayflower tree. Blanche knew exactly where that was located, the Mayflower was well known as the place where lovers met for their trysts. It was far enough to be out of sight of the Manor, but near enough to retreat should the advances become unwelcome.

Blanche could not help but think it was strange that Lady Philippa should choose this spot for the book to be returned, but had thought best not to challenge it. As she came to the fork in the dusty track she hesitated; one direction led to Martraver's Manor, the other to the quarry and headland. Blanche was surprised to find that she was in two minds about what to do next. If she returned the book early she could head home and make a start on her daily chores, leaving ample time to visit her cousin Mary. But this hadn't been the reason for her pre-dawn awakening. Had she not set out especially early so she could have another try? This was the best time given that no-one was around and, after all, her last chance. Checking on the sun's low position in the eastern sky, Blanche found her feet to be taking the southern path, the one that led in the opposite direction to the Manor.

The walk did not take too long, but Blanche was glad once she had reached the cool sanctuary of St. Alban's chapel where she could not be seen. The tiny chapel was quiet and lonely and these reasons had meant it was the perfect place for her to look at the ancient book without the disturbances of her daily routine. Closing the door behind her, Blanche located her usual bench, the one reserved for the sick and elderly and settled upon it.

Opening the book to its central illuminated pages, she marveled again at the illustrations. The colours were so vivid, even though they were centuries old. The emerald green of the scaled dragons, the strange man who seemed to be sheltering under his own giant foot. Blanche had attempted some of the text but found it was in a strange tongue, not the Latin or French that she had been taught by her late father. Regardless of the script, Blanche had come to realise there was more to this book than its text. It had other properties. She closed her eyes for a moment, hoping to conjure the same sensation she had experienced a few days before. She waited in silence with just the sound of her own breathing for a few more minutes, but nothing happened.

Closing the book she cleared her thoughts and tried to remember exactly what had happened the first time, but she hadn't really been paying attention then, and it was difficult to recall what had been the cause. It seemed that she had just slipped from one world into another as simple as waking from a dream, but this morning nothing was happening. Blanche was about to give up and reluctantly head towards Martravers Manor when she noticed something odd about the central column that held up the vaulted roof of the chapel. As she narrowed her eyes in curiosity, it started to happen. Blanche remembered now, and felt waves of panic and excitement for she knew what was to come. First her hearing started to fade, it felt as if she was about to faint, but the sensation wasn't too unpleasant. Next came the black and white dots appearing in front of her eyes, making everything blurred and slowly, willingly, she began to succumb to the lure of the other place. For a brief moment she teetered on the threshold, her consciousness divided between two worlds and in that same moment she became aware of the presence of another. Someone was watching, she could feel his dark eyes staring at her in bewilderment, but Blanche knew she had already gone too far to return.

CHAPTER 3

2009

Drawing back the vintage-style curtains Suzanne looked out of the window across the village, catching site of the copse of trees that shrouded St. John's church from view and the glint of sunshine reflecting back from the murky waters of the duck pond. In the pleasant light of the new day the memory of being frightened out of her wits by a scarecrow the night before, now only succeeded in making her laugh.

Suzanne showered, dressed and applied a touch of make-up before heading downstairs for breakfast. As she sat at the kitchen table munching on over-done toast, Suzanne considered Melanie's advice. She did need to put some space between work and personal life. Her career had been her main focus now for too long, especially since her split with Jed over six months ago. Suzanne knew in her heart of hearts she hadn't got the balance right, she would all too often take the problems of her colleagues on and solve them without fanfare, but without taking the necessary credit either. However, lately the pressure of taking everything upon herself had gotten too much and she had made errors of judgement. Taking a deep breath and easing down onto the sofa, Suzanne decided she would phone the office, remind them she was on leave and then do her best to try and forget about work for the rest of the week. This was after all, her holiday.

She stared at the number on her phone a few moments before making the call; half hoping that no one would answer so she could pretend that in this world of the quaint country village the metropolis of Birmingham did not exist. To her disappointment after a few seconds her call was answered by a chirpy receptionist with a strong midlands accent.

Suzanne swallowed, her palms were sweaty and she could feel her pulse racing. 'Hi its Suzanne Brookes, someone phoned for me yesterday on this number?'

'Can you repeat the extension number Suzanne?' Came the clipped reply.

Suzanne gave the number that was on her phone. The receptionist confirmed that it was a Human Resources number and would put her through. There was a short pause followed by the on hold music which was a crackly piano medley. At last someone answered;

'Suzanne? Hi it's Greg Jones here, HR.'

Greg Jones. Suzanne remembered Greg. They had spoken briefly at the office party a couple of Christmases ago. She recalled that the conversation had been work focused, and peppered with awkward pauses. Perhaps Greg had been tasked with delivering bad news.

'Oh hello Greg, you phoned me yesterday?' Suzanne asked assertively, trying to mask her nervousness.

Greg wasted no time and went straight to the point. 'Well it's about the situation with the lost data. You are aware that the Management Team is meeting today to consider how to proceed with matters?'

Suzanne's heart sank. 'I had no idea that the Management Team were discussing it, I hadn't realised it had got to that level.'

'Hmmm that's the problem, I'm afraid it has. The loss of a significant amount of client data is a very serious matter and the Management Team need to be briefed so they can consider how to mitigate the impact.' Greg paused, Suzanne heard him draw in a breath. 'If this gets out to the press, then the team have to be prepped with the right things to say.'

'Yes of course, I suppose you are right.' Suzanne agreed sullenly.

'I have a letter here for you, although I realise that you are away at the moment so you won't receive it until next week.' Greg went quiet for a few seconds before coming back in hushed tones. 'Hang on a minute, I'll just put this call through to the meeting room and speak to you from there.' The line clicked a couple of times and there were several minutes of silence before she heard Greg's voice again. 'Suzanne? I thought you might want me to read the letter to you over the phone so I'm in here for privacy.'

'Thanks Greg. Yes I suppose you'd better read it to me.' Suzanne's heart was pounding, her legs shaky. Greg proceeded to read the letter to her. His words continued to ring in her ears long after he had finished speaking them; *serious misconduct, disciplinary hearing, suspension pending further investigation.*

'Right, I see.' Suzanne was trying hard to suppress the fear in her voice. She found that she couldn't say anything more, the words had dried up.

When Greg spoke his tone was remorseful. 'I'm sorry the call wasn't to bring better news.'

Suzanne bit her lip. Her eyes were hot and prickly with tears.

'Oh it's not your fault Greg. You are just the messenger. But thanks for giving me advance warning of the letter. I suppose it gives me more time to prepare my case.'

'Yes, that was the purpose of my call really. You should get yourself some advice and representation as soon as you can. I know someone who......' Greg's voice trailed off before he completed the sentence.

'Yes?' Suzanne prompted.

'I was just about to say that perhaps you should contact the Union if you are a member, before you do anything else.'

Suzanne sighed. 'That's the problem I'm not in a Union. I suppose I'll have to get some advice from elsewhere.'

There were voices in the background and the clatter of chairs being moved.

'I'll have to go now.' Greg said suddenly. 'I'm not supposed to be in here, people are starting to arrive for a meeting.'

Suzanne thanked Greg again and the call was ended. Standing with the phone in her hand, Suzanne felt numb, like this was happening to someone else. At the back of her mind she had clung onto the outlandish hope that the data had been found, and things weren't going to be as bad as she'd thought. Although admittedly, losing the computer memory stick in a city centre pub while trying to patch things up with her ex was not the most favourable of scenarios she could have confessed to. An image went through her mind of the Management Team discussing the issue while drinking coffee and secretly feeling smug that this hadn't happened to them. Suzanne knew most of them had at some point breeched company rules on taking data away from the office.

Suzanne dabbed her eyes on the sleeve of her cardigan. *So much for forgetting about work* she thought, feeling quite alone. What she really needed was to hear her mum's reassuring tones, telling her not to worry about the situation. Her mum had a way of trivialising work related issues that made her feel as though they weren't the be all and end all. She decided she would call her mum later, when at least she had worked out a plan of action. Strangely, the thought of confessing to mum that she had seen Jed again seemed far worse than explaining the work predicament.

Suzanne shook her head in disappointment at herself, her long dark hair falling around her sorrowful face. Draining the last of her instant coffee she thought about what Greg had suggested; to seek professional representation. The trouble was she didn't know of anyone who could provide such advice. She would have to do an internet search at Swanage library and find someone suitable to represent her. Roughly pushing back the kitchen chair as a way of venting frustrations, Suzanne realised at once that she needed to do something else to take her mind off things. Perhaps a walk in the village would help to clear her mind and prove a suitable distraction? Pulling on her black slip-on shoes, Suzanne grabbed her bag from the kitchen table and eagerly made her way towards the front door.

CHAPTER 4

The first thing that struck Suzanne was that the village seemed much smaller than she'd remembered from childhood, which was somewhat perverse as she could see that it had grown modestly judging by the newly built stone cottages on its periphery. Suzanne began her walk by heading towards the duck pond. As she approached, a solitary mallard swam up, his head craned forward inquisitively.

Suzanne crouched closer and whispered 'Sorry boy, I've not got any bread, perhaps tomorrow once I've been shopping.' The mallard was not deterred as it waddled out of the pond flicking water from its tail feathers. As she stared at the ripples of the pond water, her thoughts went to the strange object that had become lodged in the palm of her hand all those years ago. Before she'd left her flat the day before, Suzanne had taken time to retrieve the object from her collection of childhood things and packed it in her hold-all. She couldn't quite explain why she had done this; only that it had seemed the right thing to do, seeing as she was returning to West Lytchett.

The church bells of St. John's began to chime for midday and roused Suzanne from her daydream. Remembering the conversation she had with her neighbour Edward the night before, she made her way towards the churchyard, the sound of the bells drawing her nearer to the ancient church like a welcome pilgrim.

When she arrived outside the church she realised that Edward was right, the place was captivating. Above the windows of the south wall were a series of carved heads, both animal and human, all with different expressions, some mocking, others grimacing. Venturing closer still Suzanne could distinguish that not too far from the present entrance, a small doorway had been blocked up many years ago. Old buildings had always fascinated her. There was something mysterious and powerful about a place that had seen the passing of time; a silent witness to the coming and going of many seasons, people and ages. At the entrance, her hand connected with the cold smooth metal of the latch and she lifted it gently. The wooden door started to move inwards and she followed its lead.

Inside the church Suzanne was immediately greeted by the familiar musty smell that was characteristic in such places, a mix of time worn wood, candle wax and dampness. What caught her eye immediately was a magnificent semi-circular chancel arch with bold zig-zag patterns. She remembered when she had studied history that these were a Romanesque design brought over to England by the Normans.

Suzanne was pleased to find a leaflet on the history of the church in a nearby stand and tossed some coins into the donations basket. Choosing one of the pews at the back, she sat down and began to read. She learned that the church had been built in the early 12th Century and was a very good example of Norman church architecture. The leaflet also said there was a sister church, a chapel located on the headland to the south of the village and that this was the topic of many a myth and legend. Suzanne's eye was drawn to a pencil sketch of the chapel and more description beneath. It appeared there was even some question over the original purpose of the building, given its odd shape and orientation. Reading on, she learned the chapel was perfectly square in shape with its corners orientated to the points of the compass. This was unusual as Suzanne knew that most churches were aligned east – west. Intrigued, Suzanne turned the page and was about to continue reading when she heard the church door creaking open.

Turning in her pew she noticed an elderly lady with neatly coiffed white hair had just entered with a greyhound dog at her side. She carried a large cardboard box in her arms and set it down on the floor beside the dog. The confident way in which she had handled the heavy door and its cumbersome latch told Suzanne that she was no stranger to this place. Spotting Suzanne, the lady offered a welcome.

'Good afternoon and welcome to St John the Evangelist church.' Her upbeat voice carried all the way down the nave. 'I can see you have found our leaflet about the history of the church. Are you visiting the area?' The lady asked Suzanne, her eyebrows disappearing inquisitively under her hair line.

'I'm staying here in West Lytchett for the week' Suzanne replied.

'Lovely, well do feel welcome to have a good look around, and when you are finished if you would be as kind to sign the visitor's book?'

'Yes, of course. I'm just reading about the history of the church, and the chapel, out on the headland - St. Alban's Suzanne gestured to the leaflet in her hand. 'It's very interesting. I'd like to find out more about the chapel in particular, it sounds captivating.'

The old lady was now standing next to her, the greyhound had obediently followed. 'Indeed. Our vicar put that leaflet together, with the help of a few local boffins' she explained and winked in a mischievous manner which reminded Suzanne of her late Nan.

'On holiday are you?' she asked.

Suzanne nodded. 'Yes I'm staying at Tilly Whim cottage.'

'Oh yes, I know the one.' The old lady smiled approvingly. 'Have you met your neighbour, Edward yet? Ed Suthermount is one of those boffins I mentioned earlier.'

'I met him last night, in fact he told me to come here as there is some research I'd like to do while I'm staying in West Lytchett. Perhaps you might be able to help?' Suzanne explained briefly about her ancestor being buried in the church yard and if she could help her locate the headstone.

'Of course.' The old lady's pale blue eyes flashed with interest. 'You will find that we have quite an extensive graveyard here. Some of the headstones date back to the 1630's. What era are you looking at?'

Suzanne thought carefully. 'It must be the mid 1800's I think.'

'Well there are many graves and tombs from that time, mainly over in that corner of the churchyard.' She pointed towards the back of the church. 'What's the name?'

'Sorry?' At first Suzanne didn't understand the question and then she realised somewhat foolishly the lady was referring to the name of her ancestor. 'Oh, actually, I don't know. I need to speak to my mum. What I do know is that it's a female relative, on my mother's side, but as you suggest, I really do need to find out her name first!' Suzanne could feel her cheeks getting hot with embarrassment and at the same time she noticed that the lady's greyhound was observing her with sorrowful eyes.

'Your dog is lovely' Suzanne said, glad of the distraction as she stroked the animal's velvety fur. 'What's his name?'

'Jasper. He's a rescue dog. He used to run in the greyhound races and when he injured his leg his original owners didn't want him anymore. Looking at him now, one would not think of him as a racing dog, he has put on a bit too much weight. Haven't you my lad?' She directed the question at Jasper who looked up at his owner, his thin rat-tail wagging, clearly enjoying the attention.

Suzanne wouldn't have exactly described the dog as being overweight, but he was probably less lean than other greyhounds she'd seen. The old lady affectionately patted his head and fished out a brown biscuit from her jacket pocket.

'I'm Margaret by the way,' she said. I'm doing some preparation for the church garden party on Saturday afternoon. You are welcome to come if you are still on holiday. I've got a few boxes to bring in from the porch.'

'Do you need a hand? Suzanne offered 'I'm not in a rush to be anywhere. My name is Suzanne, Suzanne Brookes.'

'If you don't mind dear. The boxes aren't heavy, but there are quite a few of them so it would be helpful. I'm not as spritely as I used to be.'

Suzanne followed Margaret into the porch area where several small boxes had been stacked and waited as she tethered Jasper to the end of a bench. Stooping to pick up one of the boxes, Suzanne noticed that it was surprisingly light. Margaret was quick to explain its contents.

'Corn dollies.' She exclaimed. 'I make them myself. They are always popular at the Garden Party. After last year's stock sold out, the vicar suggested that I make more for this year. I don't think he is too worried about their connections with pagan belief, so long as they bring some revenues in for the church.' The mischievous grin had spread across her face once again. 'They are an ancient tradition which some country folk still believe in round here. Hang one in your home and it will keep the corn spirit happy all winter.'

Picking up another box and stacking it on top of the first, Suzanne followed Margaret down the nave and into the tower where a church organ was suspended above them in the gallery. When they had finished relocating the boxes, Margaret opened one and handed a corn dolly to Suzanne. 'There you go, a reward for your efforts!'

Suzanne examined the corn dolly in the light from one of the southern windows. It had been formed into horseshoe shape rather than a doll and tied with a red ribbon 'Thank you, that's very kind.'

'Not at all dear. When you've found out the name of your ancestor let me know. I have access to the parish records you see, and they are a good starting point. You'll find me here at the church most days for a couple of hours in the afternoon.' She paused and then added 'Ah, but not tomorrow. Come to think of it I'm taking the Friendship Club on a tour of the village and a ramble up to St. Alban's chapel. You are most welcome Suzanne, to join us on our ramble if you like. I mean you will bring the average age down by about thirty years but they are a pleasant enough bunch!'

Caught off guard, Suzanne automatically tried to think up a polite excuse so as not to upset Margaret's feelings. She was not expecting such an invitation and would normally decline any such offer, but Margaret's easy manner made her feel strangely at ease.

'Actually, that would be great. I'd really like that.' Suzanne said, genuinely grateful.

'Good. We will be meeting outside the Cock and Bottle pub at half past one. Be sure to wear some decent walking shoes.'

Suzanne said goodbye to Margaret, stopping on her way out to sign the visitor's book, and headed across the village to retrieve her car.

Sometime later when she had returned from Swanage with bags of groceries, Suzanne took time to re-examine the object that had been stuck in her hand all those years before. She never had got round to finding out exactly what it was, although her uncle who was an archaeology enthusiast suggested it could be a piece of scrap metal from the Victorian era when the quarrying industry at West

Lytchett was in its heyday. Un-wrapping it from the checkered handkerchief, she startled when a piece of rust fell away and rolled down her lap. When she looked again, a bright yellow hue could be seen in amongst the dull brown of the encrusted metal. Suzanne gasped, for in the place where the metal shone brightly, she saw the crude outline of a face with eyes like pin pricks staring back at her.

CHAPTER 5

St. John's Church, West Lytchett, Dorset. June 1325

Opening the heavy oak door to St. John's Fr. Eldrith stepped into the dim light of the church and closed it firmly behind him. There was still some time before Mass to survey the book which he grasped in both hands. He hurried into the south chapel, a mix of nerves and anticipation surged through his body as he cleared the trestle table of its clutter. Setting the book down, Fr. Eldrith could immediately see its value. The quality of the leather binding, the intricate saintly figure inlaid onto its cover. It was clearly an ancient work.

He had been surprised to see young Blanche that morning at the chapel. Setting out early to make the preparations for the feast of St. Peter and St. Paul, he had expected to find the chapel empty, yet, there she had been; Blanche Myddelton with the book on her lap staring trance-like before quite suddenly she had disappeared before his very eyes! When she had reappeared, on the far side of the chapel seconds later she has seemed dazed and nauseous. He had asked her about the book in her possession but she had stammered, saying something about returning the book to the manor. Fr. Eldrith had seen his chance and had grabbed the book. He fled from the chapel before Blanche could even focus her eyes, taking the book to the relative safety of his church.

Fr. Eldrith wasn't sure what he had witnessed. He wasn't even sure if he believed his own eyes, but one thing he was sure about was the bitter winters, the wet harvests and hungry common folk. These episodes were happening all too frequently and the people of the village were starting to suspect that this must be the work of the dark arts. Fr. Eldrith could feel the veins in his temples throbbing and his head was starting to ache.

Wasn't it true that witches used holy places and objects to unleash their wrath – to make them more powerful? 'Witchcraft' He affirmed under his breath as he cautiously turned a couple of pages of the beautifully illuminated text.

Having made his decision, the priest closed the book and went to locate the key. 'I'll be doing Lord Martravers a duty in keeping this book out the little witches' hands.' He assured himself as he closed the lid of the strong chest on the new found treasure.

CHAPTER 6

Martravers Manor, West Lytchett, Dorset. June 1325

Lady Philippa Martravers sat alone in the window of the Solar watching as her father's falcon circled the woodland, swooping every now and then for its prey. As her green eyes focused on the middle distance, her brow furrowed. She noticed her servant Gwen returning through the woods, empty handed once more. Earlier on that morning Gwen had reported that she had found no parcel under the Mayflower tree as expected. At first, Philippa couldn't help but giggle to herself as she recalled Gwen's reaction when she had mentioned the *Mayflower tree.* Her maid must have thought that the parcel was a gift from a lover. This would be another test for Gwen, to see whether she could refrain from gossip, and thereby prove herself to be a trustworthy servant.

Philippa closed her eyes for a brief moment as she thought of the handsome Thomas Beaufort, riding his chestnut horse through the estate, dismounting to collect the flower she had thrown to him from her window. Thomas had been chivalrous, stooping to collect the flower and kissing it's petals before tucking inside his jerkin- a sure declaration of his feelings towards her. Despite these thoughts of Thomas, Philippa felt a sense of unease. It was odd that Blanche had not left the book as instructed. Blanche was reliable and had always returned books punctually on previous occasions. She considered their secret friendship, one that had been borne out of mutual benefit at the time. Philippa's cheeks coloured as she recalled Blanche stumbling across her and Thomas kissing behind a wall along the Priest's Way. From that point, Blanche had agreed she would deliver covert love notes between her and Thomas in return for access to a collection of books within the Manor. At first Philippa had been concerned about the common girl's motives, but she soon discovered Blanche had a talent for reading which was exceptionally rare among the common folk. In fact it was Blanche's intelligence and determination that fascinated Philippa and she found that she had a strange admiration for the girl who was in her sixteenth year, just a year younger than herself.

Philippa turned away from the window and paced back and forth, pondering what could have happened. Perhaps Blanche had been taken up by preparations for St.Peter's fair and had simply forgotten to return the book? Perhaps she had been waylaid by her brute of a step-father whose demands could simply not be ignored? Philippa flicked her long dark red hair over her shoulder. No matter, it was only a decrepit book, no one had read it for years judging by the amount of dust that had gathered around it in the library, and besides she was confident that Blanche would return it before anyone noticed it was even missing. Pausing with her ear to the Solar door, she heard footsteps and the voice of her mother getting louder as they approached the Solar. She needed to be alone. Rising from her crouched position Philippa smoothed her gown and slipped out of the door, down the stairs and out through the hall to take some morning air before her music tutor arrived.

CHAPTER 7

It took a long while for Blanche to regain her senses, longer than the previous time. Part of her had wanted to stay in the *other place*. She had been welcomed and treated with respect there. She leaned against the cold wall of the chapel and took several deep breaths. To her dismay the book was nowhere to be seen. She recalled seeing Fr. Eldrith as she flittered on the brink of two worlds, but she didn't remember anything else. Desperately she took a few steps forward, trying to focus on one spot on the dusty chapel floor, before staggering sideways, like her step-brother did after too much ale. Steadying herself on the door arch, she realised that she had to get to St. John's church quickly as Fr. Eldrith may have wrongly assumed that she had stolen the book. Blanche didn't even want to think about how much he had witnessed, or how she was going to explain what happened. She just needed to be able to put one foot in front of the other and she would somehow get back to the village.

Once outside the chapel she embraced the morning light with invigoration and gasped at the fresh salty air of the headland. The breeze sobered her and she managed to quicken her pace and run away from the headland, down past the quarry and back into the village almost without stopping. She knew that at a later hour she would have to explain to Philippa that she no longer had the book, that is – if she could not retrieve it beforehand. A plan was forming in her mind as she passed the strip lynchets with some of the small holders out already harvesting their pea-crops. Blanche waved to say hello, but also to indicate she could not stop to talk. She had to get to St. John's before Mass.

Breathlessly, Blanche at last found herself in the cool darkness of St. John's church. With no candles burning, it took a while for her eyes to adjust to the gloom but she was grateful that the church was empty. Without hesitation, Blanche headed directly towards the Sanctuary, the most sacred part of the church, where the mystery of the Mass was celebrated. She treaded quietly through the Nave, the light through the stained glass windows was reflecting off the earth floor, colouring the dust blue, red and yellow.

Once behind the rood screen Blanche's eyes darted around in panic. She must not be found here, it was strictly off limits to anyone other than priests. The Sanctuary was heavily decorated with images of the saints and apostles which had a luminous quality compared to those in the main part of the church. A statue of the church's patron, St John the Evangelist stood in one corner, the saint's eyes appeared watchful, following Blanche as she slowly walked around the altar. Blanche gently lifted the heavy white and gold altar cloth to peer underneath. She flinched as the spider she had disturbed scuttled across the floor towards her feet. *No book.* Other than the Tabernacle, which was clearly too small, there was no place that the book could he hidden away within the Sanctuary.

Smoothing the altar cloth back into its original position Blanche strained her ears. With the exception of the faint rustle of the trees outside all was quiet, if Fr.Eldrith was administering to the sick it would be quite a while before he returned. To her left a small arched door leading to the south chapel beckoned her inside. She listened out again before trying the door and then cautiously, twisted the handle. The door which was hung in a crooked manner plunged forward, the handle slipping out of Blanche's grip. Like lightening, she reached out and managed to catch the door before it could make too much noise and stood for a few moments, her heart beating wildly. Regaining her composure, Blanche entered the south chapel – the room used as Fr. Eldrith's private chapel, where he prepared for Mass. She noticed on the far wall directly in front of her a couple of the priest's vestments were draped over a wooden stand. In front of these stood a small stool partly tucked under a table, upon which sat two candles and quill pen. Blanche gingerly touched the candles. The wax was still warm. She shivered at the thought of Fr. Eldrith who had been sat there moments earlier. Had he been reading the book? Perhaps writing an account of what he has witnessed at the chapel?

It was then that Blanche noticed the strong chest, lying on the floor and partially obscured by one of the priest's cloaks. Hurrying towards it she pulled at the lid, as she had suspected it was locked. Blanche knelt down by the chest and peered through the key hole. It was too dark. Perhaps if she could pull the chest out a little, near the window, there might be enough light to see.....

'Is it this you are looking for?'

Blanche spun round. Fr. Eldrith was stood in the doorway, holding a large iron key. She stood up quickly and felt dizzy from the motion. Blanche opened her mouth but no words came.

'Have you come to confess your sins before Mass?' Fr. Eldrith prompted with a measure of cynicism in his voice.

'I saw you Father, earlier on this morning, up at St. Alban's.' Blanche spoke quietly, trying to remain calm. 'I think you have taken the book that was in my care.'

The priest raised his eyebrows 'I have no idea what you are talking about. I spent the whole morning in this very church praying for the soul of Alwyn Smythe. He died of the sweats during the night'.

'But, you were there, at St. Alban's' Blanche was indignant. 'I was looking after the book for Lady Philippa you see, it belongs to the Manor.'

'Who are you to question my authority?' Fr. Eldrith snapped. 'Blanche – Gerard Myddelton's daughter is it not?'

'Gerard Myddelton is my step-father.' Blanche carried on. 'I know you have the book Fr. Eldrith. I don't know what you want with it but I'm sure that Lady Philippa would be pleased to lend it to you if you are interested in the writings of St. Aldhelm, but I really must return the book today otherwise she will no longer trust me as her servant.'

Fr. Eldrith clasped the key in his gnarled hands and sighed. 'What puzzles me Blanche, is why a simple girl like yourself would be interested in a book such as this. Surely you cannot understand what is written within, the wise, poetic words of St. Aldhelm?'

Blanche felt the colour rising to her cheeks. 'My father gave me the gift of words. He was a monk before he married my mother. I can read both Latin and French and I understand what St. Aldhelm is saying in his manuscript.'

Fr. Eldrith sneered. 'Maybe you can read a little Latin, taught by your way-ward father. I have heard that much. So what if you can? I do not think that you or indeed anyone at the Manor appreciates the value of this book. It is a holy work, one that can only be interpreted by a holy man.' Fr. Eldrith gestured towards the strong chest.

'Have no fear Blanche, for the book is in a safe place and when I have finished with it, it can be returned to the Manor. Now go. Tell Lady Philippa you need it for a few more days'.

'With respect, Father I have no desire to lie to Lady Philippa, especially when she has been so trusting with me.' Blanche's voice was shaky, she could not believe she was challenging Fr. Eldrith in such a way.

'You have no choice'. The priest hissed. 'You seem to be forgetting that if you don't play along with my game, I can't play along with yours. In my version of events I was here all morning deep in prayer while you skulked on your pallet. In your version, you took this holy book to a sacred place and abused its powers disappearing like a will' o the wisp - in a way that only a true witch would know.'

The harsh sound of the word resounded in Blanche's ears, *witch!* The mere mention of that word had changed everything. 'I'm no witch, Father. I swear it!' Blanche said, horrified.

'And I am to take your word on this?' Fr. Eldrith asked, a crooked smile playing on his lips. 'For you do not offer me any explanation for what happened at St. Alban's chapel.'

Blanche lowered her gaze. She found she could no longer look the priest in the eye. 'I cannot explain what happened Father, but I know I am not guilty of witchcraft – it just happened, one minute I was in the chapel reading the holy text and the next I was..' Blanche hesitated, feeling nervous. How could she explain it? How could she convince Fr. Eldrith that she wasn't guilty of practising witchcraft when she wasn't even sure herself?

'Yes?' Fr. Eldrith prompted. His devious smile hadn't reached his eyes which were remained cold and serious.

Blanche was stunned into silence.

'I'll tell you what I'll do.' Fr. Eldrith sighed. 'I will give you a chance. I will give you the benefit of doubt in this case.'

Blanche picked her gaze from the stony floor of the church, her face lighting up in hope. 'Thank you Father! I am grateful I mean, it is right that you should do so for I am innocent! May I return the book to Lady Philippa now that this is settled?'

'Ah, no no no..' The priest shook his head. 'I think you must realise that I cannot let you have this back unsupervised. In fact, in order to settle my mind that you are indeed innocent of practising the dark arts, we must return to the chapel.'

There was something in the priest's tone of voice that unnerved Blanche.

'Return to the chapel?' her heart pounded in her chest with confused panic.

'You said before that you understand what St. Aldhelm conveys in his manuscript. I, for all my learning cannot read the text in that book, let alone know that it was written by St. Aldhelm himself.' Fr. Eldrith twisted a small yellow-gold ring around his middle finger. 'If you say you understand the text in the book, then you must prove it. We will meet at St. Alban's chapel after Mass. Tell no one where you are going, slip out quietly.'

Blanche considered what has been said and then nodded in unhappy agreement. It was clear that Fr. Eldrith was trying to set a trap, but if she could satisfy his questions, refrain from venturing into the *other place* there was a chance she may be all right. Rising from her knees, Blanche made the sign of the cross and headed towards the door, reverently bowing towards the Tabernacle as she did so.

After she had gone Fr. Eldrith mused to himself. *St. Aldhelm.* He had heard about the lost writings of St. Aldhelm, the story of the lost crowns of the Wessex Kings. If the girl's claims were true, and she could read the text, then she may prove very useful indeed. Fr. Eldrith smiled to himself as he prepared for the Mass, tucking the key out of sight within his chasuble.

CHAPTER 8

2009

Suzanne awoke suddenly, aware that something was not right. She had a vague recollection of being awake, yet not awake; memories, of reality or of dreams? She looked around in confusion. Melanie's cottage, the living room; everything was as she had left it. But what time was it? Fumbling with her sleeve to check her watch, she suddenly became aware that she was very cold. Her nightshirt was damp with perspiration and her watch was missing. Squinting at the clock on the mantelpiece, it read was a quarter to four. Suzanne could tell that it was almost dawn from the chinks of light visible around the thick floral curtains. She must have been sleep-walking, that was the only explanation. Rubbing her eyes, Suzanne sat down on the sofa to gather her thoughts.

The dream had been so real, she could not separate what she had felt a moment ago from the reality of the present. Blood. There had been so much blood, gushing from her mouth, suffocating her nostrils. She could still recall the hot metallic taste on her tongue as she licked her dry lips. Feeling anxious, she padded into the kitchen, taking care not to look through the back window and filled a mug with tap water. Taking a gulp, she tried to remember other details of the dream before it eluded her.

There had been a struggle, a brawl. She had struck out in self-defence but her fist had not come into contact with anything, it had simply thrust into thin air. It was then that her attacker struck her on the head, and a delay of a few seconds before she felt the gushing of the blood and the scent of damp earth as she collapsed face down to the ground. Finally, and worst of all, came silence. The feeling that everything around her had stopped, that Suzanne herself had stopped, her heart, her breathing, her senses. She had known then with a terrible realisation that she was dead. What a nightmare. Suzanne shivered violently and looked around the room for something she could wrap around herself. Locating a crocheted blanket on the back of a chair she pulled it tight around her body, rocking herself like a small child being comforted by its mother. It was only then when she became aware of a strange weight in the pocket of her nightshirt. Slipping her hand in, she gasped as she drew out the metal object from the pond that she had been examining the evening before. As she looked at it in the half-light a little bit more of the rusted encasement had come away revealing a set of hands with long slender fingers together as if in prayer. Suzanne felt a wave of confusion for she could not recall putting it in her pocket. Perhaps she picked it up subconsciously while she was sleep-walking? Putting the object back inside her shoulder bag, Suzanne slowly drew the curtains so as not to startle herself with the morning sun which was beginning to climb in the eastern sky. There was no point in trying to get back to sleep, instead she headed back into the kitchen to make a strong coffee.

* * *

Standing outside the Cock and Bottle pub, Suzanne wondered if she had remembered the meeting arrangements correctly. It was a 1:40pm and she had been waiting for at least fifteen minutes with no sign of anyone joining her for the ramble. Suzanne reached into her bag and checked her mobile phone out of habit. No messages. Returning the phone to her bag she was startled when she felt a cold hand touch her arm.

'Excuse me dear, are you joining us for the walk today?'

The hand belonged to a woman in her mid-sixties with short blonde hair, wearing walking attire.

'Yes, I am' Suzanne replied in a way that sounded too enthusiastic. 'Although I'm not exactly wearing the right gear.' Suzanne looked down at her fashionable jeans and trainers and wished she had thought to pack her walking boots.

'Don't worry too much about that. The walk we are doing today isn't far anyway. Only five miles or so. We will be back in time for afternoon tea in my orangery if you are interested.' The lady spoke assertively and Suzanne felt she could only agree and accept the invitation.

'I'm Gracie.' The woman extended her hand and gave a firm hand shake.

'Suzanne. Nice to meet you.'

The noise of chatter was coming from behind them and Gracie turned, 'Ah, Margaret is here now' Gracie announced.

Margaret was stood in the entrance to the pub. She caught Suzanne's eye and beamed. 'Afternoon dear!' Her voice rang out cheerfully like small bells. 'Have you just arrived? A few of us have been in for quick drink before we start the ramble.'

'Oh, I didn't realise people were meeting *in* the pub. Well I've not been here too long. I've just been speaking to;'

Suzanne hesitated and looked around to see where the blonde haired woman had gone to, but she couldn't see her. 'A lady named Gracie, but I can't see where she has got to.'

Margaret's eyes narrowed. 'Oh. Well never mind. She sometimes turns up for these walks but she struggles.' Margaret lowered her voice. 'She has health issues you see.'

Suzanne detected from Margaret's tone that the health problems were a delicate matter and she should not enquire any further. At that moment a tall middle-aged man spoke up and addressed the gathering.

'Ladies and gents, or ladies and *gent* as I should say.' The man gestured towards the only other male in the group and polite laughter resonated. 'In case you don't already know me, I'm Tim and I'll be giving Margaret a break today and leading the walk on her behalf.'

Margaret waved her hand to acknowledge thanks to the new volunteer. Tim carried on.

'We are going to be covering about four and a half to five miles today, starting here in the village and then over to the chapel at St. Alban's head. From there we will follow the coastal path back round, taking in some beautiful scenery, passing Sealand Pool and eventually linking up to the footpath of Randall Lane. It should take us about two hours if we go at our usual leisurely pace'. Tim grinned before adding 'Before we set off, I'd like to welcome any new people who are with us today.'

Tim looked over in Suzanne's direction and she smiled back shyly. 'Okay then, without further ado and before it starts to rain, let's set out.' With much enthusiasm Tim stepped forward and the remainder of the group followed on. As Suzanne fell into step with group which was moving at a surprisingly brisk pace, she scanned around looking for Gracie, but there was no sign of her. She was about to mention this when Margaret spoke.

'Did you remember to ask your mother about the name of her ancestor who lived in the village dear?'

'Yes, I spoke to mum last night. Our ancestor's name was Eleanor Taylor. She is my great, great, great grandmother. Mum is sure she is buried in the village.'

'Taylor, that's not a name that I can connect with the village, but then again I don't know everything about this place, that's the job of your next door neighbour, Edward – he's written a lot of books you know, about local history and the like.'

Suzanne recalled the conversation she had with the elderly gentleman on her first evening. He did seem knowledgeable, but he hadn't struck her as a busy-body. The group of ramblers were now out of the village and heading west to meet the southerly path that would take them towards St. Alban's head. There were grassy fields on either side of them dotted with traditional limestone cottages and farm buildings. Suzanne took a deep breath in, enjoying the scents of mid-summer, a mixture of drying hay, meadow flowers and dust. At that moment she felt pleased that Margaret had invited her along, that she was taking the trouble to make conversation. Margaret told her about her own family history, and how, with much research she had managed to put together a family tree dating back to the fourteenth century. It seemed that her family had lived in Dorset in the medieval times but had moved to London in the sixteenth century. Margaret herself had been born in London, but married a West Lytchett man at the end of the second world war which brought her back to her ancestral county.

'He was a marvelous man was my husband.' Margaret sighed. 'We had so much in common, it was destiny that I met him.' Margaret looked ahead into the distance where St. Alban's chapel was beginning to appearing on the horizon. For a moment Suzanne thought that she was trying to suppress a tear. 'That is, if you believe in destiny. He is at rest now and has been for the last twenty six years.'

Suzanne felt a wave of compassion for Margaret 'Oh I'm so sorry to hear that. Your late husband, is he buried in St. John's churchyard?' Suzanne immediately regretted asking the question. It somehow sounded intrusive and inappropriate. She tried to explain her train of thought to Margaret. 'I mean, is it must be comforting to be near him when you are at the church.'

Margaret's head snapped up. 'No. He is not buried at St. John's.'

Suzanne was surprised at the force of her reply and the sudden sternness of her tone. She hoped she hadn't upset her by the crass comment. She was about to try and make amends when Margaret changed the subject. 'Ah, the chapel! Nearly there now, although its further away than it looks. I have to say I know quite a bit about this place, I've lead many a walk down this path.'

Suzanne looked ahead at the tiny Norman chapel perched on the headland. She could see that the group leader Tim, and a couple of others were already approaching its curtilage. It was an austere little building with no exterior decoration with the exception of a small stone cross perched on top of the roof. As she and Margaret finally caught up with the rest of the group, Tim who was waiting patiently welcomed them before starting his resume. Suzanne who had a love of historic buildings listened attentively, straining her ears against a strengthening easterly breeze. Tim explained that St. Alban's chapel had been constructed during the second half of the 12th century, although the site itself was possibly pre-Christian judging by the earthwork embankment that surrounded the chapel. He went on to say that the shape of the building and its north-south orientation had given rise to many legends, as neither were characteristic of a typical church built at that time. Suzanne recalled the leaflet she had read in St. John's the day before which had referred to the chapel's odd shape and pondered whether the building had been constructed for another purpose.

Tim looked around his windswept gathering to make sure he was holding their attention before offering what he considered to be a plausible theory.

'One explanation for the locating a chapel out here on the headland, is that it is a memorial. Legend has it that around 900 years ago, a young bride set sail with her new husband off the coast near here. Unexpectedly, a storm whipped up and the father of the bride could only watch in horror as the little boat was tossed about by the waves and eventually swallowed up by the sea. It is said that the devastated father commissioned the chapel to be built in memory of his daughter and her husband, and with a candle burning at all times, it could act as a beacon to warn passing ships of the proximity of the headland.' Tim eyed Margaret for approval.

'How am I doing Margaret – did I remember all that correctly'

'Spot on Tim. Spot on.' Margaret beamed in approval.

'For those of you that aren't regulars, Margaret is our resident expert on the chapel so please do not hesitate to ask *her* if you have any further questions!' Tim smiled at Margaret. 'Now then, let us get inside out of this wind.'

Suzanne crossed the threshold into the tiny chapel. It took her eyes a while to adjust to the gloom, but when they did she was surprised to see how much work had gone in to the construction of such a small building. It comprised of four vaulted compartments supported from a large central column. A number of Victorian pews were arranged in rows facing a simple stone altar, upon which were two tea-light candles, their flames dancing wildly. Looking up Suzanne realised why the building had been over-engineered, the vaults were supporting a solid stone roof. Across from where she stood was a single narrow lancet window which offered the only natural light. Even in the company of seven others, the chapel seemed sombre and lonely.

Once they were all inside Tim started to say something about the services held at the chapel when Margaret nudged Suzanne.

'Have a closer look at the central column' she whispered.

Suzanne moved nearer towards the centre of the chapel. From a short distance it looked like the column had been beaten and ravaged with age, but on closer inspection, she could see that it was covered in scratch marks and etchings.

Little gaps in the stone appeared here and there and where they did they had been filled with silver objects, coins and pins that caught the meagre light. She looked over at Margaret with an inquisitive frown.

'I'll explain in a minute' Margaret offered.

The group jostled round the small building, some sat down in the pews to rest their legs while others lit candles and placed them on the altar. Suzanne wondered if Margaret would light a candle in memory of her husband, but she didn't. Eventually, the ramblers started to filter outside. Suzanne was about to follow on, but Margaret gently held her back. When it was only them that were left in the chapel, Margaret began to explain.

'Tim didn't mention this, but I thought you might find it interesting' Her eyes glistened in candle light.

'It is believed that the central column has special powers.' She paused for effect before continuing. 'It is said that if you insert a pin and make a wish, your wish will be granted! Why don't you try it?'

Suzanne looked at Margaret and tried to establish if she was serious or having a joke with her. She decided that it was the former. 'Urmm, okay but I don't have a pin. Shall I take one of these?' Suzanne was about to reach out and take one that was loosely wedged in the column.

'No, leave it be! It's someone else's wish. Best not interfere with that. No a silver coin will do, five pence would work.'

Suzanne went to her bag and quickly found her purse which was bursting with loose change that she hadn't got round to spending. Picking out a five pence coin she held it up in front of her.

'Go on, close your eyes dear then make your wish and find a niche in the column to leave your offering.'

Feeling slightly silly, Suzanne closed her eyes and made a wish. Her mind automatically focused on her main worry, the lost data at work. She wished that the memory stick would turn up in some mundane place, and no harm had been done, and most of all she could be happy and get her life back on track again. Opening her eyes and blinking a couple of times Suzanne reached out for the column. Her hand made contact with the ancient haggard stone. Finding what looked to be a suitable niche, she inserted the coin before stepping back a pace.

'Okay it is done!' Suzanne exclaimed. 'Let's hope the chapel works its magic.' She looked up and suddenly felt disorientated. She was sure that the lancet window was on her left at minute ago. Now it was directly in front of her. Her head began to feel fuzzy and she instinctively reached out to steady herself on the column. That's what happens when you wake up too early, Suzanne thought. A scene from her nightmare flashed before her eyes and made her feel pure panic for a brief second before she swayed and then staggered over. The last thing she recalled before the darkness enveloped her was the smell of damp earth and voices around her fading into silence.

CHAPTER 9

St Alban's Chapel, 1325

Fr. Eldrith's rheumy eyes were studying the six hundred year old text with its beautifully illuminated lettering, still rich with colour. His brow wrinkled with frustration. He stood up and went to light another candle which he set in a small niche in the chapel's wall. He spoke gently as he lit it.

'I was educated in Poiters. French is my first language, and Latin is the language I learned as a scholar. English is secondary to me but in this form it is almost illegible. How is it Blanche, that you are able to understand this text?'

Blanche was kneeling on the floor, nervously scratching at the dust with her index finger. The air was getting cool and she shivered noticeably. Fr. Eldrith was asking too many questions, becoming too inquisitive. She had to find the right balance – tell him something, but not everything. That way she might just escape his accusations and she could return the book to Lady Philippa. Perhaps, one day, when things had settled down she could ask to borrow it again.

Her thoughts were interrupted by the priest who was beginning to pace around the small chapel impatiently. Blanche hurriedly rose to her feet and moved nearer so she could see the text. 'I don't understand all of it.' Some of the words were unfathomable, but others she remembered learning in the *other place.* Clearing her throat Blanche started to explain. 'The chapter speaks of true gold, to be found at the southern point of the headland. That is the only part of the chapter that I understand.'

'And have you not tried to find this gold yourself?' Fr. Eldrith asked sharply, raising his eyebrows.

'No. I mean, yes - yes I have tried to find it but it was not where I looked.' Blanche lied. 'I simply can't translate enough of the text to understand exactly where it is hidden.' Blanche looked at the floor before making eye contact with the priest. She had always found lying difficult. As she was speaking she noticed the chapel door had come away from its latch and was open an inch or two. Perhaps she could take a chance and run for it, ask Lady Philippa for protection. However, Blanche remained fixed to the spot and decided to carry on. 'In earlier chapters, the book talks of treasures of heaven and of earth. I have come to think that perhaps Aldhelm was not concerning himself with earthly gold, but with spiritual treasures. That is what I understand from the text.'

Blanche looked down at the floor, wondering if she had done enough. There was a short silence where Fr. Eldrith seemed to be pondering what Blanche had told him, before he spoke again in his authoritarian tone.

'Treasures. Of heaven and *Earth*, Exactly. Is that why you find the manuscript so enticing? You and I have both heard of the legend of the lost crowns of the Wessex kings. Many people believe there is a missing chronicle that offers an explanation of where these treasures lie hidden.' Fr. Eldrith continued to study the girl with hard eyes. 'You are hiding something from me. You say you cannot find the treasure, but your eyes tell me otherwise. Suppose you have found the gold. What would you do with it? Perhaps it is hidden back at your hovel? I think not!' The priest turned his back on Blanche and was pacing around the vaulted columns. He continued his tirade. 'Why would you risk hiding it there when you could flee and escape serfdom forever? Sure, you would not want your good-for-nothing step-brother or step-father finding it.'

Blanche felt a wave of panic at priest's accusations. A gust of wind suddenly picked up and the chapel door swung inward. Seeing her chance, Blanche grabbed the book from the altar and lunged forward towards the open door. Fr. Eldrith leaped after her with surprising speed. Realising that she was out of arms reach he flung his foot forward, his leather shoe making contact with the back of Blanche's knee. Blanche yelped at the force, both her legs giving way from under her, the book still cradled in her arms like a precious child. Scrambling to get up, she realised that her escape out onto the headland had been thwarted. Fr. Eldrith was now closing the door of the chapel and to her horror, locking the door behind him.

'There.' He said breathlessly, brushing his hands together. 'I think you will find that it is very much in your interest to co-operate with me Blanche Myddelton, especially since I witnessed your devilish disappearance in this very place this morning!'

'Father, I can explain what happened.' Blanche had already prepared her words. 'You may not have seen correctly in the half light of dawn, but I did not disappear. I had dropped a ha'penny and I was on the floor scrabbling in the dust to find it. It rolled over there, and I crawled to retrieve it, that is all.'

'Silence!' Fr. Eldrith's voice boomed. 'You talk too much for a woman. Now hand me the book, and we can try again.'

Blanche reluctantly handed the book back to the priest who was stood with his arms extended.

'Now, where were we? Yes. The lost crowns of Wessex. I want you to translate exactly from this page here.'

Blanche looked over the priest's shoulder at the page he was pointing to. The illuminated letter J was guarded by a two headed dragon, painted in vibrant green and gold. She remembered looking at this page earlier. Suddenly, the text seemed to shimmer and swim before her eyes – she could feel it was happening again! Oh no, she could not let it happen, Fr. Eldrith would certainly have her burned as a witch if she disappeared once more.

Blanche quickly turned away from the book and shook her head, partly to regain her senses and partly to indicate she could not understand. 'It's no good Father. I do not understand this. The words are too abstract. Perhaps I am tired. I will come tomorrow and try again then..'

She was cut short by the priest. 'No, tomorrow will not do. It is the feast of St. Peter and St. Paul, I will not have the chance. Try again now Blanche, focus on the writing. Focus properly..'

Blanche felt her eyes reluctantly rest back on the dragon heads, instantly they were hazy and shimmering. She could not let this happen.

'Fr. Eldrith, I am tired, hungry and thirsty! I need to go home and rest. I cannot do anymore. Now, if you would be so good as to unlock the door and let me pass. You have my word that I will return at a time of your choosing, after all, you have taken this book from me and I shall need to return it to the Manor.'

To Blanche's surprise, the priest grabbed her by the wrists and shook her firmly. 'You, my friend are not going anywhere!' Fr. Eldrith hissed, flecks of spittle flying from his mouth. 'You think you are superior, don't you? The daughter of an unholy monk and a temptress whore!'

Blanche stared at the priest unable to speak; she could not understand why he was so mad.

'You think you have power over me, a learned man, because you can read this text!'

Blanche was quick to respond. 'No that is not true!'

'Well, we shall see who has the power, when the wisps of smoke curl around your toes and the whole village is baying for your blood, thanking me for culling the witch in their midst!'

That was enough, Blanche could take no more. She spat with force in the priest's face. 'How dare you slander my family! How dare you accuse me!'

For a few seconds Fr. Eldrith was stunned into silence, Blanche took her opportunity and grabbed the book once more, but then Fr. Eldrith snapped. He lashed out at the girl once, and then again, and once more. A fountain of blood poured from her nostrils. Blanche stumbled forward, her head striking the central column with considerable force. She landed face down, a torrent of blood running down her forehead, pooling into her eyes.

Fr. Eldrith immediately stepped back, horror shrouded his face. He stood for a few moments not knowing what to do. Eventually he uttered her name. 'Blanche?' He drew closer, still she did not move. It was then that her body started to twitch violently. *As though possessed by demons!* He could feel stomach acid in his throat. The priest backed away and turned to mutter a short prayer before the crucifix on the altar. He had not meant for this to happen - he had not intended to harm her, but rage had taken over. When Fr. Eldrith turned back around, he could not believe what lay before his eyes. Where Blanche's broken body had lain a few seconds earlier, a spring of fresh clear water now rose, bubbling from the ground and spreading across the floor of the chapel, washing any trace of blood. Of Blanche and the St. Aldhelm manuscript, there was no trace.

'Witchcraft!' Fr. Eldrith cried out loud, and with that, the priest gathered his cloak and ran out from the chapel onto the wild headland. He did not stop running until he reached St. John's where he bolted the door of the south chapel, locking himself away until the first light of dawn began to filter through the stained glass.

CHAPTER 10

2009

'There you go. Get that down you.' Margaret put the Irish coffee on a beer mat in front of Suzanne. The pub was quiet, with the exception of a couple of locals at the bar they were the only people there. Before sitting down Margaret went straight to the Jukebox and to Suzanne's surprise she selected record from a rock music compilation.

'So you like this type of music?' Suzanne enquired with uncertainty as Margaret returned to her seat.

'Not really, it was too quiet in here and walls have ears, especially in village pubs!' She glanced over towards the direction of the bar, where a barmaid briefly met her eye, smiled and went back to stacking clean glasses. 'You had me worried before.' Margaret said concerned. 'I was just about to go and get the others when you started to come round.'

Suzanne felt slightly embarrassed. She had attended the ramble as an inconspicuous guest of the Friendship Club, the last thing she wanted was to have caused a scene.

'I'm sorry, I don't know what happened. One minute I was making a wish and the next my vision started to go black and white. Like an old television with no signal'.

'A good way to describe it' Margaret said almost under her breath. She continued. 'Now then, do you remember any more about what happened to you at St. Albans, I mean what you saw when you were out cold?'

Suzanne sipped her coffee, enjoying the warmth of the whiskey and silkiness of the cream as it slipped down her throat. She still had slight headache but it was fading fast.

'Yes. Yes it is coming back to me, slowly.'

'Well take your time dear. You must be shaken after collapsing like that'. Margaret drank some of her whiskey and ginger. 'On the way back to the village you mentioned a girl's name. You said you were worried about her, that she had hurt herself. Do you remember?'

Suzanne frowned. She did not recall much of the walk back to the village, only flashes that formed stills in her mind, mainly of the dusty path, the cornfields and the soulless grey sky. There was something familiar about what Margaret was saying though. She rubbed her eyes out of tiredness and as soon as she closed them an image appeared in her consciousness. Two people stood in the chapel with her, a teenage girl and a man, a priest. The atmosphere had been dark.

Her eyes snapped open.

'I remember!' Suzanne said with certainty. 'There was a girl. She wanted to escape from the chapel but the priest wouldn't let her go. I tried to reason with the man but he just ignored me.'

Margaret was silent. Her eyes urged Suzanne to continue.

'They were both studying a book, it was on the altar, but the altar was different to how it is, and there were no pews, only one bench set against the wall.' Suzanne was surprised at all she had managed to retain. She closed her eyes again.

'The girl wanted to take the book and escape, yes, the book was greatly important to her.'

'Did she tell you that? Did she speak to you, this girl?' Margaret enquired.

Suzanne suddenly felt puzzled. 'No, she didn't. I could just tell what she was thinking, like in a dream.' She paused for a minute to take a long gulp of her coffee which had cooled down to the right temperature. 'I sensed her desperation so when the priest had his back turned I opened the door so she could escape.'

Margaret's eyes sparkled with renewed interest. 'You opened the chapel door? It actually opened for you?'

Suzanne wondered why Margaret was picking up on such a small detail.

'Yes, only a few inches, just off the latch so it would give her a better chance. The girl noticed straight away and she smiled at me.'

'Amazing! Go on please tell me what happened next, if you can remember.'

Suzanne closed her eyes again. There was nothing else. She could not remember anything beyond opening the chapel door.

'No. That was it. I'm pretty sure something bad happened though, but I can't remember the detail. After that all I remember is waking up and seeing you were standing over me, looking worried'. Suzanne slumped back in her seat and drained her coffee. She could not help but notice a look of disappointment cross Margaret's face. After a few moments of silence, Suzanne spoke again.

'Did I tell you any more, on the walk back, or just after I came round? Is there something I've forgotten? Didn't you say earlier that I mentioned the girl's name?'

Margaret looked into the distance. Something appeared to be troubling her. 'You told me quite a bit when you came to, but it was garbled. The account you have just given me makes more sense.' She smiled and patted Suzanne's hand. 'Let's leave it there for now. It's probably best that we both go home now and have a rest. Do you want me to walk you to your cottage?'

'No I'm perfectly fine now. My headache has completely gone. I just need a bath and an early night. Thanks for looking after me so well.'

Suzanne gathered her bag and jacket and was about to say goodbye when Margaret pulled gently on her arm.

'If you have any more flashbacks or anything at all is worrying you, then you must come a see me. Talk it through.'

'Okay, will do.' Suzanne suddenly realised she did not know where Margaret lived.

As if reading her thoughts again Margaret piped up 'Encombe Cottage, immediately opposite the Vicarage. Remember, tomorrow I'll be at the Garden Party till 4pm.'

Suzanne noted that the last comment was more of an invitation than anything else. 'Of course, the famous corn dollies! I will see you there.' With that Suzanne said good bye and commenced the short walk back to Tilly Whim Cottage. Although she had sounded upbeat, she only planned to show her face at the Garden Party the following day. While it had been far from her mind earlier on in the day, the realist in her told her had other things to do, particularly as she had neglected the search for a suitable HR representative. She needed to follow up the leads she had gathered at the library yesterday and set the ball rolling before the weekend. After all Greg had said it was important to get advice sooner rather than later.

The main road running through the village was quiet and Suzanne crossed over, taking the shortest possible route back to the cottage. The late afternoon sun had finally broken through the clouds and its strong summer rays felt warm and energising on Suzanne's face. She pondered the sequence of events that had unfolded earlier. What exactly had happened to her back there at the chapel? She had not had the chance to analyse it properly yet herself. As soon as she'd placed the coin into the ancient stonework she felt it. First her vision went, then her hearing started to fade too. She recalled being ten years old and almost passing out following a blood test at the doctors, although what had happened today was different. It was strange because Suzanne had not been feeling the least bit faint before she made the wish, in fact quite the opposite, the exercise had felt good, invigorating. Still, factors such as pressures at work and lack of sleep the night before could have played a part. 'That is what this break is for.' Suzanne whispered to herself as she rummaged in her bag for the front door key. Something else was odd though. Why did Margaret seem so interested in what had happened to her, in what she had witnessed? Sure, she had a right to be concerned about a guest of the Friendship Club going unconscious on one of their outings, but what had been her words? *Come and see me if you have any more flashbacks.* But why? Was she just saying this out of politeness, to offer friendly support because she somehow felt responsible for what happened?

Suzanne pushed the door open and immediately spotted a small white envelope lying face down. On retrieving it from the mat she was surprised to see that it was addressed not to Melanie, but herself. A wave of curiosity came over her. Who knew she was here besides work colleagues and her parents? Could it be Jed? Her heart thumped in her chest as she threw herself down into a chair and tore open the envelope. Her eyes immediately looked to the bottom of the hand written letter. It was from Greg Jones in HR.

Dear Suzanne

I hope you don't mind me writing to you while you are away on holiday. I have a good friend who studied alongside me at University. I'm sure he'd be able to provide you with some good advice, given the circumstances. I've enclosed his details below.

I have written this note to you as a friend, and not in the capacity of HR Officer. Therefore for obvious reasons, please do not mention this to anyone at work.

Take care,

Greg (Jones).

At the bottom of the letter Suzanne found an office address and mobile number for a Peter Doyle. She glanced at the clock. It was 5:45pm, possibly still time to contact the HR specialist before he finished for the weekend. Wearily, she reached for her mobile and tapped in the number Greg had supplied.

CHAPTER 11

Edward Suthermount was sitting in his small but neatly ordered living room busily tapping away at the keys on his laptop. He did not often get the urge to write these days, so when he did he would make the most of it and put everything else to one side. Today was such a day and the words were flowing freely with little effort. Like the old days he thought, a wistful smile playing on his lips. His current work was a biography of King Alfred the Great. Edward had spent most of the previous year researching the Saxon king, gleaning as much as he could from text books, historical novels and journal articles. A melting pot of fact and fiction was what he was in the business of creating, to fill in the blanks using artistic license. It was his forte. Some days when particularly engrossed in his ideas, Edward could feel the boundaries beginning to blur. At such times, it seemed like his real life was merely a façade. Perhaps he had been in the game for too long.

Edward clicked on the save button and backed up his work on another drive. He reclined in his straight backed chair which had been made comfortable by the introduction of two cushions and scanned the bookshelf in front of him. Thirty eight titles over the last forty years. That was an achievement he should be proud of, except; it wasn't over yet. There was a title missing from his collection, his life's work incomplete, and it was a story that had nothing to do with a Saxon King. He stood up and stretched his arms out in front of him, his shoulder cracked painfully.

'The pains of a writer' he muttered to himself as the clock on the mantelpiece began to chime the hour.

CHAPTER 12

She had allowed her tea to go cold again. Margaret pulled her face in disgust as she swallowed a mouthful of the cold brew before pushing the cup aside. She had more important things to do than worry about cold tea.

The plastic storage box was heavy, and Margaret struggled to get it down through the loft hatch. Rather than try and carry it down the ladders, she had allowed the box to drop onto some pillows on the landing floor. It had made a loud thud, tipping onto its side, the contents eager to escape.

Ten minutes later Margaret was sat at the kitchen table, riffling through a clutch of local newspapers. The earliest dating from 1951, and later editions from the 1980's. She did not know why her husband had kept them, on cursory inspection certainly nothing out of the ordinary seemed to jump out. Putting the newspapers to one side she went back to the storage box. More newspapers, an empty ring bound file, and then at last what she was looking for; a two-tone blue notebook with the velvety flock fleur-de-lys pattern on its cover.

Although aware of its existence, Margaret had never wanted to read her husband's diary. Diary keeping was a habit Lance had indulged throughout their married lives and Margaret felt that reading his diaries would be betraying his trust. Given what had happened today though, she knew she had no option.

Margaret sat for a few seconds in a state of inertia. *Lance would want her to do this.* She took a deep breath before turning back the front cover.

CHAPTER 13

It was around midday before Suzanne was ready to leave the cottage the following day. Waking later than expected, she had nursed a dull headache and been unable to stomach the thought of breakfast until the painkillers had kicked in. Pulling on her jacket, Suzanne still could not fathom what had happened at the chapel the day before, although in the light of a new day she was beginning to conclude that stress and worry had taken its toll, manifesting in a fainting fit.

As she strolled into the village Suzanne replayed in her mind the conversation she'd had with Peter Doyle, or 'Pete' as he insisted on being called. It turned out that Pete had been relaxed and easy to talk to, but at the same time confident and knowledgeable about the world of employment law. During their half hour conversion she had shared her account of what had happened; the growing and unreasonable pressures at work, the expectation to meet targets above anything else, the fact that she had felt compelled to take confidential information home to work on and then had lost it. As she'd recanted the story to Pete, Suzanne recalled feeling strangely distant from it, as though it was merely a tale about someone else. The conversation had ended by Pete promising to write up Suzanne's version of events as she had explained them, and also draft a letter to her employers, explaining that all further correspondence should be c.c'd to him. Pete had said he could not work miracles, Suzanne clearly had made a mistake, but there were certainly grounds for 'mitigating the damage' as he'd put it.

Suzanne crossed the quiet road to the churchyard. The morning was still and humid, but the grey clouds looked as though there were slowly moving eastwards, revealing streaks of pale blue on the horizon. Good news for the organisers of Garden Party Suzanne thought as she entered the churchyard between the sturdy limestone gate posts. Once inside its curtilage, Suzanne slowed her pace, scanning headstones as she went. *Eleanor Taylor. Where are you?*

After exploring the south side of the church yard with no luck, Suzanne skirted round the east end of St. John's to continue her search. The easterly part of the church yard was enclosed by a number of trees, some yews, others deciduous. She could see from a distance that a few stones lay under the trees, although some were barely detectable due to the overgrown vegetation. She decided to venture off-piste and parted the branches of a nearby silver birch tree. When she was within the tree's lair she paused by a small headstone and read it out loud to herself. 'Edmund Carroll' b. 25th March 1833, d.14th May 1833'. At the top of the headstone was a cherub, its empty eye sockets gave her a hollow stare. Just a tiny baby, Suzanne thought sadly before moving on.

She noticed that the cluster of headstones under a birch tree were about the right era. Most were ornate in style, celebrating the cult of death as the Victorians did best. As she investigated the larger headstones, she noticed a surname which kept cropping up again and again; Willows. Margaret had said that her husband was originally from West Lytchett so it was no surprise. What was strange perhaps was that he himself hadn't been buried here if his ancestors were? Suzanne's attention was diverted to a stone which rested below her feet. She hadn't noticed the graves below her feet, her eyes had been looking for headstones, and this particular flagstone was almost totally covered over with grass. She respectfully tried to remove the carpet of grass with her shoe and noticed that it had immediately uncovered a date; August 1886. Suzanne crouched down and tugged at the grassy cover. A clump came away in her hand revealing a number of insects that squirmed and scuttled about the stone slab. She recoiled for a moment before regaining her composure and pulling the rest of the vegetation away. She could clearly see that the name on the headstone was Eleanor Jane Taylor.

'Found it then?' A man's voice rang out from beyond the birch tree. Suzanne looked up, suddenly feeling like a trespasser guilty of uncovering the graveyard's forgotten secrets. Through the foliage she could see the outline of a tall slender man. His voice seemed familiar but she couldn't place him immediately. She straightened and parted the drooping branches of her leafy hiding place. It was only when she was out in the open that she recognised him properly. The man dressed in a pale blue short sleeved shirt and beige corduroys was Edward, from the cottage next door.

'I'm sorry?' Suzanne uttered.

'Your ancestor's grave. You said you would be looking for it while you are staying here.'

Of course. Suzanne remembered now. She had mentioned to Edward about her possible ancestral connections with the village on the night she'd arrived.

'Oh yes. I'm pretty sure it's over there.' She gestured towards the birch tree. 'Eleanor Jane Taylor, Died 4th August 1886. My great times three grandmother apparently.'

Edward nodded. 'Very good. What else have you found out about her? Suzanne considered the question. 'Not much else really. I was speaking to Margaret Willows yesterday, she said that Taylor isn't a name that connected with the village. I haven't come across any other grave stones with that name yet either.'

Edward appeared deep in thought for a moment. 'Well there was a farmstead by the name of Taylor, contemporary with the grave stone you've found. I seem to think the original farmhouse was destroyed in a fire in the mid 1800's. It was outside the village – a few fields to the west.'

Suzanne felt a wave of excitement rise within her. She needed to find out more. 'Are there records of this somewhere?' she asked.

'At the Dorset Records Office.' Edward informed her. 'Saying that, I've written a number of books on local history and I'm pretty sure that I covered the Farmhouse fire in one of those. I will have to check for you, I'm afraid my memory isn't what it used to be.'

Something in the way Edward delivered his final comment led Suzanne to believe that he remembered a lot more than he was letting on. Nevertheless she was intrigued by the story and was eager to read what he had written on the subject. 'Yes please, I would be really interested to learn more. I didn't know you are an author, I mean you didn't mention it the other day.'

Edward smiled. 'Well I'd say that I'm a historian first, and author second. Of course you are more than welcome to browse my library, after-all we are neighbours for the time being aren't we?'

Suzanne was about to reply when she noticed a thick-set man approaching them. He was carrying two folding tables, one in each hand. As he got nearer, Suzanne saw that he was out of breath, beads of sweat trickling down his forehead.

'Ah, afternoon Terrence.' Edward exclaimed. 'Let me help you with one of those.'

As Edward took the table from the beleaguered Terrence, he turned to Suzanne.

'I'm just setting up for the Garden Party. It's worth your while coming along if you are free. I've got a stall myself this year, perhaps I could interest you in my publications? Half of the proceeds go to the village hall maintenance fund.' Edward looked at her expectantly.

'Yes I will be dropping by, I shall see you later.' Suzanne confirmed as the two men made off in the direction of the field beyond the church.

In the near distance Suzanne could hear a Brass band tuning their instruments. Glancing at her watch she was surprised to see how time had flown - it was only ten minutes to go until the Garden Party opened. The sun started to appear for the first time that day, evaporating the dew from the churchyard and warming Suzanne's cheek. Smoothing her hair to remove any trace of tree debris, Suzanne made her way through the churchyard, and headed towards the direction of the increasing hubbub.

CHAPTER 14

1325

The peace and quiet of St. Alban's chapel was welcome relief to Roger Cheney. It was a place he could seek sanctuary from his raucous siblings. Roger closed the door behind him and went to his usual place. Dropping to his knees he crossed himself before a simple triptych that hung on the wall. It was the day following St.Peter and St.Paul, and the Wareham Fair would soon be drawing to an end. Roger was glad, the fair was always a busy time for him and this year had been no different. Lord Carringstone and his entourage had arrived late at the Manor on the eve of the celebrations and the additional stabling duties had been left to Roger and his younger brother Edwy. Tomorrow it would all be over and everything should be back to normal, except it wouldn't. That was the problem.

Staring hard at the tryptic, Roger implored the help of St Mary and the infant Jesus. Blanche had been missing for two days without a trace. What made matters worse was that he had been one of the last people to see her, in the stable yard at the manor. Roger thought the worst had happened to her. He had known Blanche since they were tiny and her disappearing like that was out of character for her. He uttered a simple prayer, focusing on the sacred images as he spoke.

The best he could hope for was that she was still alive, being held captive somewhere. As he prayed he vigorously scratched his left forearm and immediately felt the warm trickle of blood running down it. He found his skin always got worse whenever he was ill or worried. He dabbed at the blood with his sleeve. He would have to use his balm sparingly now, it could be the last that Blanche would make for him, Roger thought desperately.

The young man's lips moved in quiet prayer as he reached for his purse, an offering to St. Aldhelm was customary. In his mind he cursed as he remembered that he'd given a farthing to Edwy earlier on that day - a piece of scrap metal would have to do. Selecting a piece from his purse, he slid it between two stone blocks within the column in the chapel's centre and backed away, his head bowed reverently.

Completing his prayer, Roger was about to leave the chapel when he stopped in his tracks. He could hear the sound of water. Turning around, he gasped in surprise. Bubbling up from the ground near to the column was a small spring of clear water. *The work of St. Aldhelm? Was it a sign that his prayers would be answered?* Curiously, Roger moved towards the spring and reached a hand out towards it. It was cool, but not too cold. Refreshing. He first let his arms be cleansed, the water soothing his raw skin, then his feet and ankles as he stepped near to its source. As he stood there in the clear coolness with the sound of water echoing around the chapel, Roger could not recall a time when he had felt so at peace.

CHAPTER 15

2009

Suzanne idly let her flip flops slide off her feet as she pushed herself back in the sun lounger. The back yard of Tilly Whim was small but it was certainly a sun-trap. A bumble bee dozily buzzed about her before settling on a nearby hydrangea, the plant's flowers were as blue as the sky overhead. She had not had the chance to speak properly to Margaret at the Garden Party. In fact every time Suzanne had looked over to her stall, she had been surrounded by people. The Corn Dollies were clearly a resounding success once more.

Suzanne tilted her face towards the sun and closed her eyes. Edward's pamphlet on Walking the Priest's Way was lying open next to her, she had read only the first page but now in her mind's eye, she was starting the walk not alone, but accompanied by a good looking stranger perhaps, she hoped, someone she might meet whilst away this very week. Pushing away any thoughts of Jed, Suzanne indulged her imagination; and for once was pleased to find that this mysterious man wasn't anything like Jed. He was taller, with kind eyes but a roguish smile. His was holding her hand as they walked together, chatting away with ease like nothing else mattered but only that very moment. In her mind the two of them walked a little further before spotting a suitable place to stop. The tree was in full bloom, with white blossom petals cascading down. She lay down, he did the same. He reached for her face and touched her cheek and as he did so, Suzanne noticed the unusual colour of his eyes, they were amber and had a mesmerising yet tranquil quality to them. She wanted to continue staring into those hypnotic eyes but found she couldn't, her own eyes were closing - she could not keep them open. The heat of the sun compared with the shade of the tree, Suzanne was caught in a world where both existed simultaneously. The drowsiness was enticing and Suzanne found herself drifting into a slumber. The voices came quietly at first, muttering and laughter. Suzanne tried to block out the sounds, she wanted to stay, not to wake from the dream just yet. *Voices again.* Suzanne's eyes opened slowly, adjusting. She was pleased to find she was still under the tree in her dream. Something was odd though.

As she looked up, she noticed all the blossom had vanished. Suzanne was just considering what had happened when somebody caught her eye. A tall girl with dark red hair tied up in a coif was stood close by, speaking to the amber-eyed stranger.

'Thomas, let us be gone! If people see us here tongues will be set a-wagging.'

The red haired girl shot a playful look at the young man that was both flirtatious as well as serious. Suzanne felt pangs of jealousy as she realised the two were lovers.

'I know where we can go my love. Buck's Meadow has the tallest grass, we will not be seen if we lie there together.' Thomas suggested.

The red-haired girl seemed pleased. She looked around cautiously before drawing closer to him, planting a quick kiss on his lips. Thomas's hands immediately moved to the waist of her side-less gown and slid them around her slender back, pulling her towards him. She drew away quickly.

'No. Not here. It's the first place people would look. Come, I do not have long. Let us make for Buck's meadow.'

Thomas let her out of his grasp 'Something is wrong, isn't it.'

The girl glanced at him. A worried look flickered across her face. Thomas continued;

'Has your father been speaking of marrying you off to Lord Carringstone again? I've seen the way old Carringstone preens himself when you are in his company, and his wife is not yet cold in her grave. He has no shame, the old goat!'

Despite Thomas' wicked humour the girl did not laugh. 'No, it's not that.' She paused. 'A friend of mine has gone missing. No one has seen since yesterday morning. The Fair has brought new people into the village, not just merchants but all manner of folk; brigands, vagrants, and other outlaws. I'm worried Thomas. She wouldn't just disappear like this. It's not like her.'

'What are her family doing about the matter? Has the Bailiff been informed?'

'She is a commoner. Her mother is sick and her step-family do not really care for her. In fact her step-father only reported she was missing when she wasn't there to put food on the table.' She paused a moment to smooth a loose strand of hair back in place. 'I have little confidence in them. As for the Balliff, Roger, our stable boy went and told him this morning. It seems that Roger was with Blanche before she disappeared.'

Thomas raised an eyebrow. 'And Roger, is he not under suspicion?'

The girl shook her head vehemently. 'Absolutely not! Roger was very fond of Blanche. He is as worried as me if not more so. Let us make tracks now before I have to return home.'

The pair turned away from Suzanne and walked quickly, hand in hand. It seemed they did not know she was even there. It was at that moment when the memory came back from the depths of her mind. Blanche! The girl at the chapel - her name was Blanche! Suzanne suddenly felt compelled to run after the couple and tell them what she had seen at the chapel. She pushed herself up onto her feet. Looking ahead the couple were moving hastily, but still just in view, if she ran she would easily catch up to them. *Ping. Piiiinng Piiinnnngg.* Her phone was ringing. Not now, Suzanne thought. Let it go on to voicemail, nearly there. Breathless, Suzanne slowed as she drew closer to the couple. The grass was getting longer and it was getting increasingly difficult to pick her feet up. It seemed the grass was actually pulling her down, deliberately trying to delay her. Piinnngg. *Damn phone.* Suzanne stopped. Something was tickling her feet.

Suzanne bolted upright in the lounger. The large tabby that she had seen on her first night shot away across the yard in fright. It scampered up the wall and down into Edward's yard.

Her heart pounded as she tried to make sense of her surroundings. It had just been a dream. *Another vivid dream.*

'Blanche.' Suzanne said the name out loud. It seemed to bounce off the four corners of the yard. Hadn't Margaret said that she'd mentioned the girl's name when coming round from her fainting spell? This was all very strange. *She had to do something,* she felt compelled to act like she had done moments before when trying to catch the handsome couple as they moved through the tall grass. The feeling remained with her. Raising the lounger to an upright position, Suzanne scanned the yard for her trainers. They were where she had left them, by the back door. She hopped towards the backdoor, the heat off the flagstones surprisingly hot on her bare feet. Once her trainers were tied, she made for the shed. She had spotted the push bike earlier when searching for the lounger. it was an old thing, clearly Melanie's spare, but it would make the journey quicker. She locked the backdoor and pushed the bike towards the gate. It was years since she had ridden but after a short practice on the lane in front of the cottages, she was ready to set out, taking the same path as she'd done the day before, in the direction of St. Alban's chapel.

CHAPTER 16

Margaret emerged from her kitchen carrying a tray of various sandwiches and cake and set them down on the dining room table. Suzanne weighed up the selection before choosing cheese and pickle and ham with coleslaw. Her legs were twinging from the speedy bike ride and she had only just noticed how hungry she was. The pair ate the first few bites in silence, the grandfather clock ticking steadily in the background. After she had poured herself a cup of tea from a rather delicate looking teapot, Margaret spoke.

'So nothing happened this time?'

Suzanne shook her head, swallowing huge bite she'd just taken.

'No. It was silly I suppose. When I got the idea to ride to the chapel I must have been half asleep. It seemed like the right thing to do at the time, but now I feel a bit of a fool.'

Margaret took another sandwich and pushed the plate in Suzanne's direction. 'Go on, have the last one. If I have it I won't have any room for the cake, and besides you seem hungry after all that dashing about.'

Suzanne did as she was told and took the proffered sandwich. It was egg and cress, not her favourite but she wolfed it down anyway. She noticed that Margaret was studying her and she suddenly felt self-conscious. Looking down she nudged the crumbs on her plate into a tidy pile.

'Do you think I'm being silly? I mean, what I did today, racing off to the chapel on the back of a dream I'd had.'

Margaret was quiet for a while.

'Not at all. Sometimes it is wise to follow your instincts, to listen to the inner voice within you.' She paused a moment as she sliced the small lemon sponge into quarters. 'We spend too much of our time these days analysing things in a scientific way, using our heads rather than our hearts. Looking back over my life, when I've chosen to listen to the voice of instinct or conscience or whatever you choose to call it, everything has always worked out for the best. Conversely, when I've ignored the voice and tried to put reason before instinct, bad things have happened.'

A haunted look flashed across Margaret's face. Suzanne wondered what the 'bad things' were but she wasn't about to ask. Margaret continued;

'What is your gut feeling about the visions and dreams you've been having? Do they make sense to you, is there a message that you can glean from them?'

Suzanne sighed, her head cupped in her hands. Remembering her manners, she removed her elbows from the highly polished table and sat back in the chair. 'I think something happened at St. Alban's chapel. Judging from the dream I had this afternoon, it happened a long time ago. The people were wearing old fashioned clothes and their speech is almost illegible. I'd say from their dress, they were medieval.

Margaret topped up both tea cups and remained silent, urging Suzanne to continue.

'The girl, Blanche is her name. She has gone missing and people are worried about her, it was her I saw at the chapel yesterday, it came back to me whilst I was dreaming! I mean, that is strange in itself isn't it?'

Margaret didn't comment.

'I know that she was badly injured, perhaps even dead. In my dream I tried to catch up to Blanche's friend, tell her what I'd seen at the chapel, tell her that she was being held captive.'

'And did you tell her?' Margaret asked.

'No, I was following them, running in the tall grass but they didn't even hear me approaching. Then I heard my phone ringing and a cat tickled my foot and I woke up.'

Realising how it all sounded, Suzanne laughed. 'It sounds crazy doesn't it? It was then that I went off to the chapel to see if I could witness the vision again, perhaps get a better look at the priest who was holding Blanche captive. Suzanne took a sip of her tea before adding 'Perhaps I've been a bit under pressure lately and it's all catching up on me, in fact, I must ring Melanie back, it was her who was phoning me this afternoon.'

Suzanne briefly explained about her friend who had lent her the cottage for the week, due to the problems she was facing at work. Margaret offered some sympathetic words while she was clearing away the plates. Suzanne offered to wash the dishes, but Margaret was not having any of it.

'You are a guest, and guests should not have to do the chores. Besides, there are only a few plates and cups.'

Suzanne thanked Margaret for the afternoon tea and was heading to the front door. Jasper the greyhound was sleeping in the hallway, he didn't move when Suzanne stepped over him.

'He is a lazy excuse of a dog, but he keeps me company now that Lance is no longer around.' A pair of morose brown eyes looked up, as Margaret patted the dog's head. 'Perhaps what you needed was a catalyst.'

Suzanne turned around to face Margaret, 'I'm sorry?'

'Something that you had with you yesterday, that you didn't have today.' Margaret explained quietly. Maybe that is why you couldn't see the vision at the chapel.'

Suzanne was just about to enquire further when the phone on the hallstand began to ring, the shrill tones making them both startle.

'I'm sorry I'll have to get it.' Margaret headed back down the hall towards the phone.

'Of course.' Suzanne made for the front door, the evening sun was beginning to filter through the art nouveau style stained glass.

'Have a think about what I've said - about the catalyst'.

'I will. And thanks for the tea, it was lovely.'

With that the door was firmly closed and Suzanne could hear Margaret answering the phone on the other side, her voice fading into the background as she carried the receiver into another room. The abrupt ending to their meeting left Suzanne feeling more confused than when she had arrived. It was all very cryptic. If Margaret knew more about the visions, why wasn't she letting on? A number of questions began to circle in Suzanne's mind as she made the short walk back to Tilly Whim. A catalyst. Something she had with her yesterday but not today. Was Margaret referring to herself? It was a possibility.

The cottage was dark when she got back. Its north-south orientation meant that there were no windows to let the evening sun in. It was a stark contrast to the bright airy feel of Encombe Cottage with its large windows, high ceilings and well-proportioned rooms. Suzanne immediately switched on a couple of table lamps in the sitting room and flopped onto the sofa. She turned the television on with the remote and flicked through the channels, looking for a programme which required little concentration. She finally settled on an episode of a period drama, it was one she had seen before, but that didn't really matter her mind was on other matters. *A catalyst? Just what did Margaret mean?* Unable to focus Suzanne riffled through her handbag. It contained all her usual things, purse, mobile phone, make up, a packet of mints, a pen. She moved her attention to the front zipper compartment, noticing the flat shape contained within. As she slipped her fingers into the bag Suzanne recalled the night she had slept walked and had placed the strange metal object in the bag whilst in a state of confusion. It had been in her bag ever since.

Suzanne's thoughts were disturbed by the ringing of the doorbell. It was more of a buzzer than a tuneful ring, certainly not Melanie's choice. Making her way towards the front door she cautiously peered through the bevelled glass panel. It was Edward, and she could see that he had some books under his arm. Pulling the latch down, she opened the front door and greeted him.

Edward held out the thicker of the two books for Suzanne to take 'I've found the book I was referring to earlier. The complete history of a Dorset Village - West Lytchett, E P Suthermount' he announced without any introductory greeting.

'Thank you.' Suzanne said as she took the book from him. She could see that his hands looked a lot older than the rest of him, they were crinkled and spotted with dark pigment.

'You will find reference to the farmhouse fire in there. In 1853 it was razed to the ground. A tragic incident. Anyway, I'll leave you to read it for yourself.' Ed took a step back as though he was about to leave. Suzanne was curious about the other book which was still tucked under his arm.

'Does that book have a similar account within it?' Suzanne enquired, pointing towards it.

Ed looked down, he almost looked like he had forgotten the second book.

'What? Oh yes, of course. This one,' he said, passing it to Suzanne, 'It takes another view on the disaster. I didn't write it. I wanted to give you both accounts, it is for you to decide which one is the more convincing story.'

Ed grinned to himself, as though he knew there would be no competition. Suzanne thought.

'Well, thank you for bringing them round.' Suzanne uttered although Ed was already down the short path, he waggled his fingers in the air as a goodbye and then he was gone. 'What a strange character.' Suzanne exclaimed quietly to herself once she heard Ed's front door close behind him.

CHAPTER 17

The church bells of St. John's were ringing jauntily as Suzanne rode the bike out of the village. It was a bright but fresh Sunday morning, the breeze strengthening as she headed into the open countryside. Suzanne had toyed with the idea of going to see Margaret first thing, but in the end she had decided against it. She was probably at church now anyway.

The books that Ed had lent her had proved to be an interesting read. Suzanne had stayed up beyond midnight reading, and even then she had wanted to stay awake for longer and read more, particularly of Ed's fascinating accounts. Suzanne had immediately flicked through to the part that interested her the most; the Taylor farmhouse fire. Ed had included a pen and ink impression of the farmhouse, a large double fronted stone building with two tall chimneys at each gable and multi-paned windows which were typical of the Georgian era.

Ed's version of events had told her that the farmhouse had been constructed on the site of the abandoned Martravers Manor, which somewhat ironically, had also been destroyed by fire back in the 1530's. She had learned that the Taylor family were successful crop farmers, their wealth ensuring a good standard of living for Amos Taylor, his wife and their seven children, but that was until the great disaster. In 1853 the farmhouse caught fire and claimed the lives of six of the children and their mother. The only survivors were Amos and his eldest daughter – Eleanor. Suzanne had then been fascinated by the next part; for it specifically concerned her great times three grandmother, Eleanor. She'd read that the fire had been subject to much local speculation; that Amos himself was responsible, with the intention of wiping out his entire family. When questioned however, the thirteen year old Eleanor would not speak out against her father, in fact she became a mute following the tragedy and had never spoke to anyone again. Ed's account of the story explained that if Amos had been responsible for the fire, then he certainly got his comeuppance the following year as he was killed in an agricultural accident.

Suzanne was disappointed that Ed had not gone into any more detail, but was nevertheless interested to learn that going forward some 30 years in time, villagers of West Lytchett must have been somewhat surprised when Eleanor gave birth to a daughter in her early forties and then swiftly moved away from the village, possibly due to the disgrace from having a child out of wedlock. It was only when Suzanne's eyes started to close that she reluctantly had given in and put the book on the bedside table.

Now in the crisp light of day, Suzanne considered the finer details in comparison with the other much thinner book Ed had lent her. Although Ed's account was fascinating, Suzanne did wonder where he had got all his information and whether or not it was accurate. Flicking through the second book earlier that morning, she had found that it corroborated on the key facts of the story, but mentioned nothing of the scandal that then followed. There was something else bothering her too. If Eleanor had left the village in disgrace, why had she been buried in the churchyard at St. John's only a few years later? Suzanne made a mental note to address these niggles with Ed when she returned the books, tactfully of course, his pride could be at stake.

Taking one hand from the handlebar, Suzanne checked her jacket pocket to ensure the curious metal object was still within. The idea had come to her the early hours of the morning when she realised what the 'catalyst' could be. The object had been in her bag all along, but in her haste to cycle to the chapel the day before, she had only taken her phone and wallet.

Pressing down on the pedals hard, Suzanne found she was enjoying the acceleration as the flat yellow cornfields passed her by on both sides. It was years since she had owned a bike herself and she had forgotten how exhilarating riding one could be. As Suzanne drew near to the chapel, adrenalin started to flow within her, it was a fearful excitement, she reflected, the kind of feeling one would get prior to embarking on a theme park ride. She hadn't felt the same yesterday, but then she had been dazed from her dream, but now, in the sober light of day and the outline of the chapel black against white clouded sky Suzanne wasn't so sure. *No one knows you are here.* The little voice nagged as she pulled up with the chapel now on her left. Part of her wanted to turn the bike around in the direction she had come and head back to the safety of the village.

Putting her fears to one side, she dismounted and hesitantly wheeled the bike up to the chapel, bringing it to rest against the ancient wall between two crude looking buttresses. Her hand went once more to her jacket pocket, her fingers tingling as they closed around the cool metal of the Brass. Strangely it seemed to give her courage and she found herself boldly opening the wooden door, creaking on its hinges in a way that Suzanne now found to be familiar. The darkness engulfed her as she stepped inside. She focused her eyes in one spot for a while to become accustomed to the lack of light before making her way to a pew, the bench groaned a little as it took her weight. She examined the Brass in the light of the chapel. Since the rough pieces of corroded metal had fallen away Suzanne was certain the object was an engraving of a person, and strangely enough, this seemed to be clearer now in the half-light of the chapel as she suddenly noticed for the first time two slender hands with elongated fingers drawn together, as if in prayer.

Suzanne thought about what she had attempted the day before with no success. Perhaps she could try the same again, now she had what was hopefully the catalyst. A wave of fear and excitement surged through her and she shivered as she reached into her pocket for a coin.

As the coin made contact with the worn stone she became aware of movement around her. Her stomach started to clench and the woozy feeling embraced her like it had the first time. Panicking at the reality of what was happening and her vulnerable solitude, Suzanne pinched her fingers together and removed the coin. It was madness, she shouldn't be dabbling into the unknown! She drew her hand away from the column and to her relief the sickly feeling subsided and everything became still.

The coin had vanished. Frowning, Suzanne looked to examine the small niche in the column where she had placed it only seconds earlier, but that too was no longer there, in fact, the column itself was different. Gasping in shock, Suzanne stared at what was before her. The haggard ancient stone was now painted deep red and edged in green. In a moment of confusion Suzanne wondered why she had not noticed this before and at the same time she *remembered.* Red, gold, blue and green, the gaudiness of the chapel's decor was beginning to dazzle her. She closed her eyes for a moment and when she opened them the colours were grainy, now black and white and there was a humming in her ears too. Her senses were fading like the last time. She made a last grab for consciousness and cried out for help before she allowed herself to be seduced by the bright flags, the laughter and the sweet taste of honey mead on her lips.

CHAPTER 18

1325

The banners of St. Peter and St. Paul were flapping directly above her head, the brightly coloured depictions of the saints and lettering reflecting against the strong sunlight. Close by Suzanne noticed a group of children, their clothes ragged and hair tangled. One of them wore a sackcloth hood over his head and was walking with his arms outstretched.

'Hoodman blind is coming to get you.' One of the boys shouted. The other children squealed as they got as close as they dared to their hooded companion before skittishly diving away.

Suzanne felt slightly tipsy. Looking down, she remembered why. A small clay mug containing only the smallest drop of liquid was in her hand. She brought the mug to her nose, and sniffed recognising the smell of honey mead. Gingerly she sipped at the last drop, enjoying the taste of sweetness mixed with the heat of the alcohol and then shook her head a few times to try and sober herself. Was this a dream? If so it was extremely realistic, the sounds, tastes, scents were all too vivid. Suzanne placed the mug down with others on a wooden bench beside her before walking on, underneath the banners towards the main stalls. The enclosure was packed with people, the smell was pungent – a combination of rotting hay, and human perspiration. Canvas tents were arranged in a haphazard manner, the vendors displaying their produce on trestle tables. The meats and game sellers seemed to have only just arrived and were busily hanging their bloodied wares from hooks arranged on the tent frame. The atmosphere was up-beat as lots of people, some apparently wealthy judging by their clothing, and others not so mingled and jostled around the stalls. It was becoming clear to Suzanne that what she was witnessing was a medieval fair. She had briefly studied these at university but nothing from a text book could have prepared her for the vibrancy of the event. Looking down at her twenty first century clothing she suddenly felt vulnerable and wondered why no one had noticed her.

Suzanne was abruptly roused from her thoughts when she was pushed aside by two large women who did not seem to even notice she was there. Perhaps that answered her question. Regaining her balance, Suzanne detected their excitement as they approached a nearby stall vendor. She observed that he must be a spice merchant, his dark complexion spoke of journeys to faraway lands. As the women approached they ignored the display of ochre powders and focused their attention on the piles of dried and fresh fruits.

'A penny for 4 ounces.' The vendor gestured by nod of the head towards a small pile of figs. The more slender of the two women shook her head and instead pointed to slices of fresh orange, her expression curious as though she had never seen such things before. Just as the vendor was about to explain a loud drum was beaten and everyone turned towards the source of the noise where a large crowd was beginning to form. Suzanne was plucking up the courage to ask the spice merchant where everyone was going, when a loud booming voice made her jump. Spinning around she saw that the voice belonged to a short bearded man with a scarred face and missing teeth.

'Prize Ram Wrestling! Gather round, ha'penny seated, farthing standing.'

Suzanne stood on her tip toes. Above the sea of heads about twenty metres away was a wooden cage, not much bigger than the curly horned ram that was enclosed within it. In the distance she could just about see that two sinewy young men stripped to the waist were beginning to jostle. One quickly lashed out with his fist, hitting his opponent square on the cheek. The man reeled back in pain but then quickly recovered and pounced upon his attacker, locking his head under his arm. The crowd let out a loud cheer and the pair continued their brawl. Suzanne sank back down onto the flat of her feet. Something about the gratuitous pleasure of watching others fight reminded her of the scraps she had witnessed in the yard at high school and it made her feel uncomfortable. Looking around she was conscious of making the most of her time and seeing what else she could witness and learn about this strange place. It was then Suzanne spotted her. Standing by a cloth merchant's stall just a short distance away was the girl with red hair who she had seen the day before in her dream. Suzanne approached quietly, unsure if she could be seen at all. The girl with red hair began to speak to the cloth merchant.

'I love it. I will arrange for my maid to collect a measure of both the green and the blue. Look, here she is now.'

A mousey-looking girl had appeared from round the far side of the stall. She had an exasperated look about her and was trying to catch her breath.

'Lady Philippa, I thought I'd lost you. Your mother was enquiring of your whereabouts and I had to admit that I knew not of where you'd gone! Shame on me when I'm supposed to be your chaperone.'

The last remark was said respectfully, and yet Suzanne detected a hint of annoyance, as though the maid had lost patience with her spirited mistress. So the red-headed girl was of high status - the maid had referred to her as *Lady* Philippa.

'Gwenny, you do not have to stick to me like tallow to a wick.' Philippa laughed. I am quite capable of looking after myself.' Philippa's eyes quickly darted about before readdressing her maid. 'Now that we are alone, you can tell me what you found out from your investigations this morning. Has Blanche been found safe and well?'

Gwen shook her head. 'I spoke to her step-brother. She still hasn't returned home.'

'And what of our priest, Fr. Eldrith? Has he seen her? Has she been to him for spiritual guidance recently?' Philippa enquired.

'He wouldn't tell me at first. He said he would be breaking his covenant of privacy. So I explained that I'd been sent from Martraver's Manor and that Blanche had in her possession a book from the library, which has not yet been returned.'

Philippa interjected 'Gwen I thought I told you not to mention the book unless it was absolutely necessary?'

The maid didn't seem put out by her mistresses disappointment, instead she answered smugly 'Fr. Eldrith said that he thought he might have seen Blanche yesterday evening, heading off along the Priest's Way towards Swanage. Carrying a thick book under her arm.'

Philippa gasped. 'No! Why would she do that? She wouldn't leave the village without telling anyone. How certain was Fr. Eldrith that it was Blanche?'

'He was quite certain it was her.' Gwen retorted. 'Although I had thought it myself my lady. When you told me that she had one of the books from the library the first thing that came to my head was that she had made off with it. They are worth a lot, and common folk know that.'

Suzanne had edged closer and now stood within touching distance of the two young women, but neither seemed to know she was there. She was observing the conversation closely, listening carefully to every detail, waiting for the right moment. Philippa looked subdued.

'I wouldn't have thought.' She began.

Quickly picking up on her mistresses mood Gwen tried to offer some comfort.

'I know, I'm sorry to bring the news my lady. People aren't always what they seem.'

But Gwen's comment did not soothe and in fact clearly agitated Philippa.

'Do not lecture me on judging people dear maid! I for one do not believe that Blanche is a thief. She is a kind, intelligent girl who would not double cross me. Besides, she has had plenty of opportunity to steal from me before. She would have do so already, if such were her intentions'

Gwen retained an uncertain silence.

Philippa explained. 'I have been lending her books from the library for many months now. Each time they have been returned perfectly and at the time I requested.'

'With respect my lady, she might have been gaining your trust, and waiting for the right opportunity. Many people from all over England and even further afield are in the area at the moment. She could quite easily become hidden within a crowd and leave with them. She is probably heading north now as we speak.'

Philippa ignored Gwen's final comment.

'I shall go and see Fr. Eldrith for myself. I want to make sure that it was Blanche who he witnessed.' Philippa paused before speaking in a softer tone. 'Oh and Gwen, be sure not to mention to anyone else about the missing book. My father does not know any of this, and I want to keep it that way until it is found.'

Gwen nodded and lowered her eyes with deference. 'You can trust me, my lady.'

Suzanne had been busy assimilating the thoughts in her mind. Had the priest lied to Gwen? He had only mentioned that he had seen Blanche heading along the Priest's Way after Gwen told him about the missing book. It seemed probable that he was the guilty party in all of this, that it was the same man who had been holding Blanche captive at the chapel.

Philippa had turned back to the merchant to discuss her cloth purchase. Her conversation with Gwen about Blanche was clearly over. Suzanne felt the same compulsion to do something, as she had done each time she had seen visions of this past world. She waited until Philippa began to move away from the stall before she approached.

'Lady Philippa.' Suzanne's voice was croaky, and quieter than she had intended it. She tried again.'Lady Philippa, can you hear me?' As Suzanne suspected, Philippa could not even see her, let alone hear her talking. It was now clear to her that she was merely an invisible witness to these events, there was nothing she could do. But why was she being shown all these visions if she was unable to practically do anything to help? It seemed obvious to her now, the thread was easy to pick up. Blanche had been abducted by the village priest, she had accidentally suffered injury and died whilst in his captivity, and now Suzanne was seeing the aftermath, the cover up. Blanche, was not happy to rest with this injustice. To die young was one thing, but to have your reputation tarnished by a man who supposed to be a man of God, a trusted authority in the village, was another matter altogether.

She gathered more courage and this time she rested her hand on Philippa's arm, the sheer fabric crinkled under her touch 'Lady Philippa. Please, I have news about Blanche.'

There was still no acknowledgement, and Philippa picked up her pace, asking Gwen where they were to meet her mother and the rest of her entourage for the journey back. The lady and her maid were heading towards the exit of the enclosure,

Suzanne could see that a small group were waiting by the flag poles with their horses ready for the ride back. In a desperate last attempt Suzanne stepped out a few paces in front of them and grasped Philippa with both arms, shaking her. 'Philippa. Can you hear me?'

Philippa abruptly stopped in her tracks and stared directly at Suzanne. Suzanne's heart missed a beat. Had Philippa seen or felt her at last? She had to pull herself together now that she had her attention.

'I have some information, about your friend Blanche. I think I know what has happened to her.' Suzanne tried to keep her voice composed but it had an unmistakeable wobble to it.

'Lady, what is the matter? Is something wrong?'

Gwen looked across at her mistress who had drawn to a complete halt. She was as still as a statue and staring straight ahead. A look of confusion in her deep green eyes.

Gwen tried again.

'My lady what it is? Are you feeling faint with the heat? Come let us rest a moment in the shade of a tent.'

Philippa drew her arm away as Gwen tried to manoeuvre her towards a nearby tent. Suzanne stepped back, suddenly fearful of her bold move, but she drew the courage to speak again, this time more softly.

'Do not listen to Fr.Eldrith. He is lying! He was holding Blanche captive.'

'Blanche?' Philippa whispered, uncertainty in her voice.

Excitement surged through Suzanne's veins. She had communicated with Philippa. Gwen on the other hand was clearly puzzled by her mistress's behaviour and annoyed that the conversation had moved back on the peasant girl.

'What about Blanche?' Gwen said curtly.

All of a sudden Philippa snapped out of her trance, her gaze moving away from Suzanne to the middle distance. Disappointed, Suzanne stepped away and let the two young women pass as Philippa endeavoured to explain.

'Oh nothing. The heat was getting to me, that's all.' Philippa took a few breaths to demonstrate the point and then changed the subject.

'Father has a seamstress from London visiting at the end of next month. I plan to ask her to make for me two fashionable gowns in the style that is worn there. The cloth that we have just bought will be perfect. Can you make sure you awake early tomorrow to receive it? The merchant told me he is staying one more night and then leaves first thing.'

Gwen obediently agreed and the pair stopped at the Mead stall and took some refreshment before mounting their horses. Suzanne felt a mixture of emotions as the horses trotted away. Philippa had heard her. That was something - she wasn't completely without influence in this world. Perhaps she just needed some practice.

‘What now?’ Suzanne asked herself looking round. Some of the stalls were already packing up for the day. The crowds had started to thin out and she was beginning to feel increasingly lonely in this alien world where nobody could see her. She needed to get back, to confide in Margaret – tell her everything.

The Brass. Suzanne was pleased to find that it was in the pocket of her jacket, although she did not remember putting it there. As she held the object in both hands a worry crept into her mind, she had no idea where she actually was. How could she find her way to the chapel if she wasn’t able to ask anyone? But no sooner than the worrying thought had appeared she could feel the familiar churning in her stomach. The sun disappeared behind a cloud and the background drone of voices started to fade. The flapping banners became still. Instinctively, Suzanne increased her grip on the Brass though it was her life line and closed her eyes. Doing her best to retain consciousness she sank to her knees as the rush of air circled around her. The dizziness came and went, then all became still.

Suzanne was afraid to open her eyes, afraid she was still within the Fair enclosure and trapped hundreds of years in the past, but all was silent. Hesitantly, Suzanne peered through the tiny gap in her eyelids and sighed in relief when she saw the familiar grey of the chapel walls that surrounded her once more.

CHAPTER 19

The front door of Arne Cottage was painted pale blue like Tilly Whim, but was adorned with heavy looking door furniture which looked out of place on the traditional Dorset cottage. The knocker had been cast in the image of a fox scooting down towards the ground. Suzanne lifted the fox's head and rapped twice. Having returned from the chapel she had immediately called on Margaret but had been disappointed to find that she was not at home. Feeling restless, she had decided to return Ed's books and perhaps pick his brain about the finer details of the farmhouse fire story.

It was a few moments before the door was opened. Ed was wearing an apron, his shirt sleeves where neatly rolled up to his elbows. His expression concealed something what Suzanne read as irritation at the prospect of visitors.

'I'm sorry if I've disturbed you' Suzanne began. Ed's expression changed to a mask of pleasantness, but behind it Suzanne could still see mild annoyance in his eyes.

'I'm just returning the books you lent me.' She held them out towards Ed. She could tell it wasn't a convenient time so she would save the questions she had about Eleanor for another day. She was about to say good bye and leave when to her surprise Ed opened the door wider and stood aside.

'Do come in.' He invited, a smile now extending further across his gaunt face.

Suzanne suddenly felt uneasy and she wasn't sure why. She couldn't think of any excuse to refuse, so reluctantly she stepped over the threshold and followed Ed through the porch door and into his living room.

'I was just making some tea. Would you like a cup?'

Suzanne didn't really want to linger but she accepted out of politeness. 'Yes please, milk, no sugar thanks.'

While Ed was in the kitchen making the tea Suzanne scanned her surroundings. Her neighbour's cottage was laid out the same as where she was staying, which was hardly surprising as both formed part of a terrace. She noticed an unusually large number of clocks in the room; she must have counted at least nine, all ticking away with slightly different rhythms. On one side of the room there were three bracket clocks each made in a different style set on a dark oak dresser, two skeleton clocks with their delicate inner workings on display were set on either side of the fireplace, and a number of smaller carriage clocks were dotted about the room wherever space permitted.

'Do have a seat, the tea is almost done' Ed called from the kitchen. Suzanne choose a firm looking wing-backed chair by the wood burning stove and sat down, placing the books neatly on the floor beside. It was at that point that she noticed it; a stick-like arm protruding from a hiding place underneath the stairs. It was the scarecrow that had given her a fright on her first day. Blood suddenly rushed to her head and pounded in her ears – it belonged to Ed?

'I rescued him from your backyard!' Ed was back in the living room and had followed Suzanne's horrified gaze to underneath the stairs.

'What was it doing in my backyard in the first place?' Suzanne asked. Her was voice sounded accusatory and she immediately tried to make amends. 'I mean where did it come from originally? I checked with Melanie, and she hadn't left it there.'

Ed shrugged his shoulders and began to untie the apron he was wearing. 'There are lots of them round here in case you haven't noticed. One of your predecessor holiday guests had probably taken it and left it in the backyard for future guests to enjoy.'

On reflection, Suzanne considered that Ed was probably right. Melanie had said something to her about a number of irksome guests she had had to deal with since letting Tilly Whim, and the cleaner she hired wouldn't have bothered going out into the back yard.

'I guessed that a young woman staying alone might be perturbed by that thing in the backyard so I took the initiative and removed it for you. It had after all given you quite a fright when you first arrived.' Ed set the tea cup and saucer down on a table near to Suzanne's chair and sat himself down in a straight backed chair opposite her.

Suzanne blushed. She wasn't good at playing the damsel in distress. 'Well thank you for being so thoughtful. I had forgotten about the whole thing until now.' She almost went on to say how busy she had been since, but at the last minute she pulled herself up short. It wasn't necessary to discuss anything about her daily trips to St.Alban's with Ed.

'Good, and I trust you are having a pleasant break here.' It was more of a statement than a question, Ed took a quick sip of steaming tea before settling the cup back on its saucer. 'Now then, how did you get on with those books I lent to you.'

Suzanne leaned to pick both books from the floor. 'I prefer your account of the Taylor's farmhouse fire. The section in the other book is very light on detail, it just states the basic facts whereas your book gives so much more information, about the murder conspiracy and Eleanor becoming a mute. It is very interesting story, I can't wait to tell my mother about what I've learned about our ancestral history. She will be fascinated.'

A satisfied grin appeared on Ed's face. 'I aim to please' he smirked, drumming his fingers on the wooden arm of the sofa.

Suzanne could see that Ed was very responsive to compliments about his writing. However, since first reading the accounts of the fire, she could not ignore the questions that had been circulating round her mind, the parts of the story that did not seem to add up. Suzanne finished the last of her tea and put both cup and saucer on the table next to her. 'One particular fact that interests me is that the farmhouse was built on the site of Martraver's manor, which was also wrecked by fire.'

Ed nodded. 'That is true. Some people in the village regard the site as cursed, although Wolvercote, the house that Amos Taylor built after his first house burned down has stood there for over 150 years with nothing untoward happening. Have you been to see Wolvercote?'

Suzanne thought for a moment. 'Not intentionally, but I think I might have passed close by the other day. Is it the farmhouse just off Randall Road, near the public car park?' Suzanne enquired.

'Yes that's Wolvercote. I know the Cohens who live there, nice people. Perhaps if you have time you could call in. I'm sure they would be good enough to show you round, especially if you mention that it was me that has sent you.' Ed winked.

Ed's self- importance was beginning to grate on Suzanne a little. She decided without further ado she would try and get some answers to her questions and then head next door. 'I was wondering, if the Taylor farmhouse was built on the same site as Martravers Manor, is there any connection between the two families?'

Ed smiled knowingly, his crooked front teeth catching the light for a brief moment. 'Yes, my belief is they are one of the same, although I have never researched it in any significant detail. You see while the great manor was destroyed in around 1536, I'm sure the land would have remained in the Martraver's family and be passed down through the centuries. One can only guess that at some point there was a female heiress who married a chap named Taylor.'

'Or another explanation is that the Martravers family had to *sell* the land and it then was passed down a different genealogy altogether?' Suzanne proposed.

Ed looked at her for a moment, he seemed surprised that someone was challenging his authority on local history. He shook his head. 'Unlikely' was all he said before changing the focus of the conversation. 'I suppose you are wondering why your great great great grandmother is buried in St. John's church yard when she moved away following the birth of her daughter?'

Suzanne was taken aback by Ed's accurate guess. 'Yes, I was wondering that actually. I thought perhaps she might have requested it in her will, to be buried at St. John's I mean.'

The knowing smile had returned to Ed's face. 'Ah no, not exactly. When I was doing my research I found that she moved back to the village in around 1884, just a few years after she had left, and sadly just two before she died. I couldn't find out the reason for her doing so, which I why I didn't mention the fact in my book.' He quickly got up from his chair, took the books from Suzanne and began to slot them into a large built in bookshelf next to the chimneybreast.

'Perhaps you didn't mention it because you could find no juicy conspiracy to report!' Suzanne suggested, but instantly regretted the tone of unintentional mockery in her voice. Ed stopped what he was doing and looked at her for a moment, an expression that was halfway between anger and frustration flashed in his eyes.

'You will find that did not mention it because I genuinely did not know the reasons for her returning to the village. When writing about historical events I try to create a balance between.' All of a sudden Ed stopped. He was staring at Suzanne, his mouth opened as if he was about to say something but instead he continued to gape with a look of amazement. Following Ed's stare, Suzanne realised that he had noticed the Brass which had edged its way out of her pocket was threatening to slip down the side of the chair. She fumbled with her pocket and carefully zipped it away.

'Do you mind me asking *where* you found that?' Ed asked inquisitively.

Ed's reaction had made Suzanne nervous. The voice of instinct was warning her not to tell the truth, and she suddenly realised that she did not have an alternative story for how it had come into her possession. She would need to make one up, and quickly at that.

'My uncle.' Suzanne started. He was an amateur archaeologist. 'He collected antiques, old coins and the like. When I was a kid I used to like playing with some of his less expensive finds and sometimes he would let me keep them. It was usually bits of old pottery, but he let me keep this too.'

The story was partly true and Suzanne was pleased how convincing it had sounded.

It had not settled Ed though.

'Where?' He persisted '*Where* did your uncle find it?'

'Oh, I don't know. Near his home I suppose. Cambridgeshire. He did not know what it was himself, but whatever it is, he mustn't have thought it was worth anything.'

Ed leapt on Suzanne's words. 'How can you be sure? Here, let me see.'

Reluctantly Suzanne retrieved the Brass from her pocket and handed it over to Ed.

'As I thought.' Ed said confidently while holding the Brass up in the late afternoon light.

'Medieval. It is most likely a pilgrimage badge or plaque. I have a friend in Dorchester - a valuer. If you like I can take it to him tomorrow and get it valued for you.' Ed paused, rotating the object round in the air. 'The condition isn't great, but it could still be worth something.' Ed stared back at Suzanne waiting for her consent, but Suzanne shook her head.

'It's okay. Thanks for the offer, but it has more sentimental value to me than anything else.'

'You mean you are not even slightly interested in its monetary value?' Ed persisted.

'Not really. I wouldn't sell it anyway. My uncle died last year so I keep it in his memory.' Suzanne felt bad about her last remark, using her late uncle George as an excuse. She silently prayed that he would understand her reasons for doing so. Luckily, the excuse seemed to have worked. Ed shrugged his shoulders he handed the object back to Suzanne.

'It's up to you. You know where I am if you change your mind. Oh, by the way, you will find more on medieval pilgrimage badges in my book.' Ed turned to his bookshelf and reached down a large hardback book entitled *Medieval Antiques* 'Keep it as long as you need it.' He said passing her the book. 'I must be getting on now Miss Brookes.' To Suzanne's surprise Ed held out his hand for a handshake. It all seemed very formal for what had gone before. When Suzanne took his hand it was icy cold but his grip was very firm and her fingers hurt following the gesture.

'And remember, if you change your mind about the valuation, or you want any more information, just call on me.'

* * *

Later on that evening in the comfort of Tilly Whim cottage, Suzanne would reflect on the look on Ed's face when he had noticed the Brass. She had seen that look before, in the eyes of a man she had witnessed drowning in the canal behind her house when she was a small child. The wide staring, yet non-seeing eyes of a man who was looking at death square in the face. Suzanne shivered as she dialed her parent's number.

CHAPTER 20

1325

Roger had waited three days before telling anyone what had happened at St. Alban's chapel. The reason was two-fold, firstly he had wanted to see if the irritation on his skin would return, and secondly he did not wish to share the details of the miracle with anyone until now. To speak of it would somehow make it less sacred. He had no choice now though, a number of people in the village had begun to gossip about the spring within St. Alban's chapel, wondering about its origins and meaning. Old wife Bet who was at least ninety four had said she remembered a spring of water appearing in the chapel when she was a child, and as sure as anything it was a portent of yet another failed harvest and harsh winter ahead. Fr. Eldrith on the other hand was trying to settle folks' minds. At Mass that morning he offered counsel to anyone who had superstitions or worries. As a result of this invitation, Roger had not followed his family when they filed out of the nave of St. John's but had instead had accompanied the priest into the south chapel. He knelt before the small altar, waiting for the priest to finish the prayer he was reciting. After a short while, Fr. Eldrith concluded and made the sign of the cross before turning to face the young man.

'Ah, so it is just yourself then Roger. Tell me, what is troubling you? Are you afraid of what others are saying about the spring at St. Alban's? '

Roger was anxious to dispel any thoughts that the priest may have about him fearing the holy spring. 'Father, I have no trouble with the spring at the chapel, it is truly marvelous.' He blurted.

The priest looked at him with curiosity. Without further hesitation, Roger explained exactly what he had experienced on the morning three days prior, how he had gone to the chapel to pray for Blanche's safe return and witnessed a small trickle of water appearing from the chapel floor, which in a matter of seconds, become a bubbling torrent that had soothed his raw skin. Not only that, but the irritation had not returned – he had been cured!

Fr. Eldrith had been quietly listening to the young man's account. His first thought was to settle any superstition with logic; but as he did not know what was happening himself, how could he offer an explanation to the young man? The fact that Roger mentioned Blanche was disturbing. Did he know more than he was letting on? Was the boy testing him?

'Could it be a miracle Father?'

'What?' The priest asked, his mind racing ahead. He was about to tell Roger not to jump to conclusions, but stopped himself just in time. The world *miracle* was lodged in his ears. The very mention of the word had set a tingle up his spine and now as Roger stared wide-eyed and waiting for his reply his thoughts were beginning to collect into a plan. A splendid plan, in fact he wondered why he hadn't thought of it before. 'A miracle you say? Well, that is quite possible. You were in a holy place, praying when it happened. The saints must have interceded for you. Tell me, who were you praying to?'

'I was praying to St. Aldhelm, I was worried about Blanche, that's why I went there in the first place, to pray for her.' Roger bit his lip, his eyes cast downwards. 'He has not returned her though.'

The priest thought for a moment. Roger did not have any anger in his voice, only remorse. His tone was not one of accusation, but of hopeless grief. He decided he was no threat.

'We have all being praying for Blanche's safe return. Perhaps she is safe and well, but now in the company of others.'

Roger suddenly looked up, tears were forming in his bright eyes. 'You mean with the angels in heaven?'

Fr. Eldrith's heart skipped a beat, he hadn't meant that at all. 'No, I mean that it is quite possible that she has run away, perhaps with travelers from the Fair.'

Roger shook his head. 'Blanche would not have done that. She would have told me if she was planning on running away.'

Fr. Eldrith put his hand on the young man's shoulder. 'Perhaps she couldn't take the risk of telling anyone. We all know that Lord Martravers is a fair yet firm man. Do you remember what became of Alfred Dyke and his family?'

Roger nodded glumly. Fr. Eldrith was referring to a hot-headed serf whose plans to escape had been thwarted by the Reeve of the manor. 'Yes, I remember. His family were turned out from their home in the middle of winter, all their possessions confiscated as punishment. That's why I don't think she would have tried to escape, the risks to her kin - her mother are too great. Besides, she wouldn't be any better off as a free woman in another town.'

The priest gestured for Roger to rise from his kneeler. 'Come. We do not know what was going on in that young woman's mind at the time. Try not to let it distract you from the wonderful healing you have received, you are clearly blessed! Tell me

Roger, does your condition usually come and go?' Fr. Eldrith asked, tactfully changing the subject.

Roger shook his head. 'Sometimes it is worse than others, but I always have some redness on my arms and legs, I have ever since I was a child.' Roger explained.

'Then this is what we must do; visit me in four days' time and tell me if your condition has returned. If it has not, it is possible that what has happened to you could be described as miraculous. I will of course have to consult with my elders on the matter but this is truly exciting and wondrous proposition.'

Roger gave a half smile in agreement. Sometimes the priest used words he did not fully understand. 'I should be getting back to my duties now Father.' Roger genuflected in the direction of the sanctuary and left the priest in the quiet stillness of the south chapel.

Fr. Eldrith's mind was racing. The seed of the idea that had formed in his mind only moments ago was already starting to germinate. With the presence of a miraculous healing spring at St. Alban's, his parish could become a great place; a place of pilgrimage and wealth. He would be the envy of other clerics in the area, if he played it correctly he could even become bishop! His hands shook slightly as he reached for his cloak and chastised himself for being too eager in his ambitions. He first had to check that the water was still there; when he had visited only yesterday, the spring had been dry.

As Fr. Eldrith left the enclosure of St. John's the nagging thought at the back of his mind returned. This presumed healing spring had appeared at the moment Blanche had disappeared, he knew the two events had to be connected in some way. Lord Martravers had already asked him to recant the story he had told the serving girl, Gwen, about witnessing Blanche leaving the village on the Priest's Way, but he had omitted the detail about her stealing the book. Fr. Eldrith had decided it might be useful to have Philippa on his side for now. There was no point in making enemies where there was no need. The priest squinted in the direction of the Chapel. Had Blanche gone for good? Would she return to break the silence and uncover the truth behind her disappearance? The thoughts continued to plague Fr. Eldrith's mind for the rest of that day.

CHAPTER 21

2009

'It's a fascinating story isn't it?' Suzanne concluded. Her mother on the other end of the line agreed.

'Wow, Suzanne. That's amazing. I had no idea that we are descended from landed gentry! I thought we were more likely to be from peasants working the land, or at best servants working for some grand family, not actually *related* to the grand family.'

'I know, I was surprised too but I still need to confirm this via the church records, but Ed next door seemed pretty certain. Did Gran ever mention anything at all?' Suzanne asked.

'She said nothing. I suspect she genuinely didn't know. If your neighbour has his story right, then there was quite a bit of shame attached to the rumours about Amos and the farmhouse fire and also to Eleanor, having a child outside of marriage I mean. It's likely it was hushed up and over the years it has been forgotten.'

Suzanne agreed. 'Well Eleanor was a mute so that is quite a plausible explanation!'

Suzanne's mother stifled a laugh at the irony of her daughter's comment before going on to change the subject.

'It sounds to me like you are feeling better since we last spoke, love. Your friend Melanie was right to suggest you take a well-earned break and get away from all the goings on at work.'

Suzanne paused before replying, she was wondering whether she should tell her mum about what had really been occupying her since her arrival in West Lytchett. Part of her yearned to tell her mother everything, to off-load the vivid dreams, her visits to the chapel, her experiences in the foreign world of the past, but she stopped herself. Telling her mother would only cause worry. Worse still, her mother could intervene and insist on Suzanne's immediate return home where her fragile state of mind could be investigated by the family doctor. Suzanne pictured her father standing at the front door of Tilly Whim, a stern but concerned look on his face. *No she should not say anything.*

'Yes, I do feel better for coming away. It was the right thing to do, I can't thank Melanie enough. Suzanne then went on to update her mother on the contract she had agreed with Pete Doyle, and how she felt more confident now she had some decent representation. She ended the conversation by promising to phone again once she had found more about connections between the Taylor and Martravers families. Climbing the stairs to her bedroom, Suzanne resolved to go to St. John's the following day to do what she had been meaning to do for that past few days, finally check the parish records.

CHAPTER 22

1325

The hayloft was gloomy, but it was light enough for Philippa to see that her lover's eyes were full of desire. She snuggled next to him, her nakedness pressing up against his firm body, her mouth searching his. They kissed for some time, after all they were in no rush; Thomas had informed his father, Lord Beaufort that he was off riding for the afternoon and was not to be expected back until supper. Philippa had feigned an illness, retiring to her chamber shortly after midday Mass. Gwen knew what was going on of course, she had been tasked with caring for the absent lady Philippa and making sure no one entered her chamber. This was something Gwen was uncomfortable with doing, but on each occasion prior, Philippa had always seen that she was rewarded for her efforts.

'It is a good time for you my love?' Thomas enquired while stroking her cheek with a loose strand of her hair.

Philippa knew exactly what Thomas was implying. The last time this had happened, there had been a scare, she had thought she was with child.

Philippa nodded and stared into Thomas' hazel eyes. 'It is a safer time now. I've made sure of that. Nothing will happen today, Old wife Bet told me that the stars are favourable.'

Thomas suddenly drew back, a look of horror on his face. 'You haven't told that old crone about us, surely?'

Philippa giggled 'Of course not! I went to consult her on another matter.' She paused, wondering if Thomas would enquire what the 'other matter' was. When he didn't, Philippa continued. 'I told her I was getting unwelcome advances and concerned that I would be ravaged by a certain gentleman!'

Thomas looked serious. 'Come on now stop playing the fool. What did you really tell her?'

'Exactly that! Except I led her to believe that it is one of my father's associates. Old wife Bet said that there would be no chance of getting with child if it did happen, which is what I needed to hear.'

Thomas still was not convinced. 'Philippa, I wish you would not tempt fate by discussing our love life with a gossiping old witch.'

Philippa put her arms around his neck and drew his mouth back to hers, kissing him firmly 'I love it when you scold me' she purred in his ear. 'She does not know about you. Besides, I have paid her well, so no matter.'

The worried look on Thomas's face had already faded and his hands were starting to wander to the small of Philippa's back, stroking her soft downy skin, pulling her towards him. She moved away briefly for a few seconds just to tease him, before returning to address their now urgent desires.

Sometime later, after dozing in his arms, Philippa felt it was right to explain to Thomas the other reason why she had been to see Old wife Bet.

'I thought she might sense something about what has become of Blanche Myddelton.' Philippa twiddled her hair around her finger. 'I'm going to see Fr. Eldrith first thing. I don't trust him, I think he is hiding something.'

Thomas looked surprised. 'What would he know about Blanche's disappearance?'

'Gwen told me he said he saw Blanche leaving on the Priest's Way, with my book.'

'So?' Thomas said indignantly.

'I don't believe she would intentionally steel anything belonging to me or my family. I think *he* is lying.'

'Perhaps what he told Gwen is the truth. Why would the priest be lying?'

'That is what I am trying to find out!' Philippa tossed her head back, resolutely. 'It was something that Gwen said. When she asked Fr. Eldrith about if he had seen Blanche, his first reply was that he hadn't seen her. It was only when Gwen mentioned the book that he said he had seen her.'

'Well, be careful! Don't go about accusing priests of things they haven't done. Besides, what is it that you don't trust about Fr. Eldrith?' A concerned look flashed across Thomas's handsome face.

'Feminine intuition' Philippa replied. 'Now I must leave. Gwen will be having kittens if I don't get back soon!' Philippa shook her undergarment to rid it of several strands of hay before pulling it over her head. She scaled down the crooked ladder as quickly as a cat and picked up her sideless gown which had fallen to the ground during the heat of the earlier passion. Thomas dressed quickly and followed her, although he wasn't as nimble down the ladder as she was.

'Wait!' He called out as Philippa's slender figure was already making its way towards the door of the hayloft. She turned back to face him, curious as to why he had suddenly become so twitchy.

‘You’ve forgotten this.’ Thomas waved his hand in the air, around his index and middle finger hung a silver and emerald necklace, a new gift to Philippa.

‘Of course!’ Philippa turned around and allowed Thomas to put the necklace around her long neck.

‘It matches your eyes, that is why I chose it for you.’ Thomas stopped. For a brief moment he looked as if he was about to say something else but had changed his mind. Instead Philippa bade him goodbye.

‘Farewell then my love, I will be thinking of you until our next meeting.’ Philippa bowed her head towards him before exiting the barn. When Thomas could no longer hear the rustle of her gown in the long grass, he too left the hiding place. He still felt uneasy about what Philippa had told him. He had wanted to tell her to be careful, not to ruffle feathers, but as sure as anything that would only make her more determined. Thomas chewed on his fingernail as he picked his way through the meadow. If their love affair became common knowledge then there would be trouble, especially if Lord Carringstone would no longer take Philippa as his bride. Thomas shivered at the thought of being on the receiving end of Harold Martraver’s wrath, and the fate in store for Philippa would be worse. The same feeling of unease lingered over Thomas all evening. He could not shake it.

CHAPTER 23

2009

The records were stored in a two-tone grey steel cabinet, the type one would find in an office. It was Monday morning and Suzanne had called on Margaret shortly after 9am, only to find that she was already at the village hall, assisting the vicar with the parish accounts. Judging by the piles of notes and coins, the garden party had clearly filled the coffers.

Before anything else, Suzanne had wanted to speak with Margaret privately, tell her about what had happened the day before, but with the vicar present she could only suggest a catch up over lunch.

Margaret produced some vinyl gloves from a cardboard box in the cabinet. 'You will need to wear these to examine the old books.' She explained.

Suzanne pulled the gloves on, they were on the large side but were adequate for what she needed to do. She had asked Margaret to look at records from around the mid 1800's to find Eleanor Taylor, and then work back in time from there. The warm glow she had felt earlier that morning was still there, the passionate dream she had been a part of was at the forefront of her mind so much so that she was concerned it somehow showed on her face.

Suzanne tried to remember the last time she had had a dream like that, or for that matter taken part in anything of that nature. Six, seven months ago? Had it been that long? It was *too* long that was for certain.

'So you are okay with those if I get back to the accounts?' Margaret was speaking to her again.

'Hmm? Yes, yes. I'll be fine thanks.' For dreaded moment Suzanne thought Margaret was going to ask her what was on her mind. The sharp blue eyes that watched as she carefully started to turn the yellowed pages of the Victorian book were somehow disconcerting and she was already finding it difficult to concentrate. After what seemed like an age, Margaret turned to leave.

'I'll be in Reverend McKay's office if you need to ask me anything.'

'Okay, thanks Margaret.' Suzanne listened as the clicking of Margaret's shoes against the stone floor faded into the middle distance.

Time passed by quickly. When Suzanne looked at her watch, she was surprised to see that she had spent well over two hours examining the parish records. In fact she was so absorbed in her research that she had failed to notice the church bells chiming eleven o'clock. Her floral notebook was opened beside her and on the back page she had sketched out was a rough family tree based on her newly found knowledge of baptisms, marriages and burials. It turned out that Ed was right, the Taylor family were related to the Martravers. Suzanne had discovered that in 1622, Mary Jane Martravers who appeared to be the only surviving heir of John Martravers, married Percival Taylor a jeweler from Bournemouth. Suzanne clicked her pen several times and stared ahead deep in thought. *She really was a descendant of Lady Philippa!* That was of course assuming Lady Philippa had actually existed in the first place. Suzanne had found no evidence of this from the records, but then they probably did not date back to Philippa's time. Suzanne narrowed her eyes in concentration, trying to recall details from her visions. Reaching for her notebook, she sketched the outfit she had seen Philippa wearing. A long red gown with no sleeves and the sides cut away to expose a white chemise underneath. Suzanne was still busy sketching when Margaret entered the room.

'Need a bit more time then?' She asked. She held a pair of secateurs and a bunch of pink chrysanthemums.

Suzanne rose from her chair, the sudden action making it scrape noisily against the floor. 'Actually I have just about finished. It's been fascinating, I've found out so much.'

Suzanne went on to explain how she had found the link between the Taylor and the Martravers family, and that made her a descendant of both.

'So you are descended from the great Martravers lot!' Margaret confirmed, beaming. 'You are a West Lytchett girl like myself. Tell you what, I'll finish off the church flowers and then we can head to the tea rooms for a spot of celebratory lunch if you fancy?'

'Yes that would be wonderful, we have a lot to catch up on.' Suzanne already had the lines rehearsed in her mind and was eager to share with Margaret what had happened the day before. Actually, there is something else you could help me with.' Suzanne started. 'The lady who I saw the other day with the walking group, Gracie I think is her name. Does she definitely live here in West Lytchett?'

Margaret lowered the secateurs and looked back in the direction of the church, a worried expression on her face. Closing the door of the office behind them Margaret turning sharply and looked directly at Suzanne, the piercing look had returned. 'Why do you want to know?' was Margaret's measured response.

Suzanne wasn't prepared for her question to be followed by another question. She was thinking back to the day of the walk and how strange it was that the woman had simply disappeared. She stuttered over her words a little. 'I'm just curious that's all, she seemed to disappear into thin air when I was talking to her the other day, and I haven't seen her around the village since.'

Margaret straightened and rubbed her lower back with both hands, she suddenly looked very old. Taking a deep breath she looked Suzanne directly in the eye. 'Gracie has been dead six years this autumn.'

CHAPTER 24

The greyhound was sleeping peacefully by Margaret's slipper clad feet when Suzanne returned from the bathroom. Following the revelation about the deceased Gracie, Suzanne had all at once become faint headed and queasy and as such Margaret had suggested she came back to her house for a while until she was feeling better. Suzanne hadn't actually been sick in Margaret's spotless bathroom, *thankfully.* But she had felt like her head and stomach had turned over on a roller coaster ride and had made a dash up the stairs as soon as the front door had been opened. Now perched on the end of a heavily patterned velvet sofa in the snug room, she was feeling better, well physically at least. She reached for the glass of water that Margaret had poured for her and took a sip. It had a mildew taste to it but she wasn't complaining.

Feeling more comfortable, Suzanne began to tell Margaret everything about the day before; how she had worked out what the Brass was, her ride up to St. Albans chapel and the blurring she'd experienced between past and present, just like the first time. She also felt it necessary to fill Margaret in on how she had come about the Brass in the first place, and how she had kept it all these years with nothing out of the ordinary happening. Margaret's reaction to the story had been amazingly calm and measured, a series of nods and 'hmms' as though she had somehow been expecting it. Suzanne noticed that on her lap, sat a couple of hardbound notebooks.

'My husband liked to keep diaries.' Margaret said wistfully, as though she had already forgotten what Suzanne had just told her. Jasper looked up at his mistress, seeming to detect the sadness in her voice. 'It is only since you have come here that I've had both the courage and conviction to read them.'

Suzanne felt nervous and curious at the same time. She took another gulp of water and noticed that her hands were trembling around the glass.

'But what have I got to do this with this?' Suzanne asked, carefully restoring the glass to a side table before it was spilled.

'Lance, like your good self, experienced visions of the past. It all started back in the mid 1960's. We had been married for almost five years and were desperate for a child. It wasn't happening for us though. All around us our friends were raising their children and we weren't getting any younger. To make matters worse my best friend Enid and her husband were blessed with three in one go!'

'Triplets!' Suzanne exclaimed.

'Yes triplets. Enid would often complain about how hard it was looking after three wailing babes at the same time. I helped out whenever I could of course, but I couldn't help but feel resentful. I would often think why did she have three babies all at once and yet I cannot even produce one.'

Suzanne could hear the hurt plainly in Margaret's voice. Hurt that was as strong now as it had been back then. Margaret sniffed a couple of times and looked out of the window, as though she was looking for a distraction. There was an awkward silence and Suzanne desperately wanted to comfort her but instinct told her to remain quiet and let the moment pass.

Margaret took a sharp intake of breath. 'I'm sorry. I don't know what that has to do with the story I'm about to tell you. Perhaps I'm just looking for answers.' Her voice trailed off once more. Turning the attention back to the notebooks on her lap, Margaret opened one and began to flick through the pages. 'Lance has left us with accounts of what happened to him in these, I think they may be of use to you – here.' She passed the diary to Suzanne. 'Read the entry dated 14th May 1973.'

Suzanne rested the diary on her knees. It wasn't heavy but she didn't want Margaret to notice that her hands were still shaking. She looked down at the handwriting in front of her, it was in black cartridge ink and flowed with a distinctive right slant. The first letter was illuminated, framed in purple and gold and beautifully decorated with leafy tendrils growing round a letter 'A'. She looked up at Margaret. 'It's beautiful. Was Lance an artist of some kind?'

Margaret smiled but shook her head. 'Not really. He taught English at a local high school, but he used to attend calligraphy evening classes. He got very good at it, but he never applied his skills anywhere except in his diaries. Now go on, read the entry' she prompted somewhat impatiently.

Suzanne looked down towards the elaborate text. Part of her wanted to close the diary and leave that instant. She wished she hadn't mentioned Gracie back at St. John's or for that matter even come to West Lytchett in the first place. She remembered her journey down to Dorset almost a week ago, racking up the miles and planning what she would do to occupy her time, perhaps a trip to Bournemouth for some high street shopping and lunch in a smart café. A part of her now longed for this version of events; for normality; even if it was to be overshadowed by problems at work. Instead Suzanne remained where she was, in the snug room of Encombe Cottage with the diary of a deceased stranger on her lap. There was nothing more she could do than read what Lance had written on that spring day in 1973.

14th May 1973– Dancing Ledge

As I stared out towards the grey limestone cliffs of Anvil Point and Winspit it occurred to me that everything is connected. The thought comforted me for a while, until the shadows of evening started to creep, lengthening across the wildflower meadows in this pretty wilderness. Earlier on today, with the St. Aldhelm Brass, I had gone to the chapel and saw her again. She was beautiful in her purity. Her cool hands were like balm to my sore limbs. It was true I loved her – although my love was unrequited. It ended the same as all the previous times. She is taken from me. I am getting closer though, when I spoke her name I was sure she had heard me, although my attempts to set her free were as usual, in vain. As I returned to this present time, I could hear my voice echoing round the chapel. Blanche! But before I became lucid, there was yet another name on my lips. A name so familiar, that it could be my very own. Roger Cheney. That is how I know that everything is connected.

Suzanne turned the page, eager to read on. Surprisingly there was no further writing on the following page, the account had come to an abrupt end. Instead was a pen and ink sketch that took up an entire page. The sketch was of a young woman, wavy hair cascading down her shoulders. Her fine delicate features were unmistakeable, the straight nose, high forehead and straight brows. Although Suzanne had only seen her once in her visions, she was certain she was looking at a portrait of Blanche. She looked up at Margaret who was waiting, pensively.

'It's her. It's the same girl I saw during my first visit to St. Alban's Chapel. Blanche. Your husband saw her too!'

Margaret sighed. 'Yes, he saw her alright. He saw too much of her, that was the problem.'

Suzanne's eyes narrowed. 'What do you mean?' A shiver went up her spine, the icy tingle reaching round to engulf her ribs.

'Let me explain.' Margaret cleared her throat as though she was about to make a speech. 'I said before that it all started back in the 1960's. Well, that was true as far as Lance's involvement went, but Gracie became a part of this long before Lance did, but at the time I did not realise it. Hold on a minute let me adjust the blind, the sun must be troubling you.'

Suzanne was so focused on what Margaret had to say that she hadn't really noticed that a sliver of bright sunlight had found its way through a gap in the venetian blinds and was making her squint. Margaret adjusted the cord and tilted the blinds in the opposite direction.

'Good, that's better. Now where was I? Oh yes Lance and Gracie. As you know Lance and I were trying for a family, but to no avail unfortunately. I'm not going to go into detail, but let's say that it put a huge strain on our relationship. I became irritable and I suppose difficult to live with, in fact *obsessive* is probably not too strong a word to describe how I became.' Margaret paused, playing with a ruby cluster ring on her right hand. 'As a result, for a brief period in our marriage I unwittingly pushed Lance away, and that is why I suspected he went to *her.*'

Suzanne suddenly felt awkward. It felt wrong for her to be hearing all this, a story so deeply personal coming from someone she hardly knew. However she remained silent and let Margaret continue, sensing that it must somehow be therapeutic for her to finally share the story.

'He was secretive was Lance. In the early days I thought it was because he was hiding something from me, but I later learned that he was trying to keep me out of danger. I will never forget the look on his face when I found the St. Aldhelm Brass in his bottom draw, hidden among his socks of all things. I was snooping of course, trying to find a reason why my husband seemed so distracted, why he kept disappearing for hours on end every weekend. It was that same day that I accused him of having an affair. Various people in the village had seen them together you see, Lance and Gracie, and all the evidence pointed towards it. I told him I was throwing him out, that I wanted a divorce.'

'What happened? Did he deny it?' Suzanne was suddenly curious, she did not think that Lance had sounded to the type to have an affair. Still, she thought, he was a man with the frailties that men sometimes have, and it was possible from what Margaret was saying that he had been unfaithful.

Margaret laughed. It was a strange noise that sounded like a small animal caught in a trap. Suzanne noticed that Margaret's eyes were fixated on a photo frame within a glass display cabinet, next to the fireplace. The photo was of a much younger Margaret wearing a puffy veil and fitted gown with lace sleeves. Stood by her side was a suited fair haired man, a little skinny perhaps, but with a kind face. Lance. Margaret spoke again.

'He was extremely calm. That is how he reacted to everything though. My Lance could always keep a cool head in most situations. Despite his calmness though, I could tell he was deeply worried, I could read it in his face. He told me to get in the car as we were going for a drive. He assured me he would explain everything when we arrived at the destination, and as you've probably guessed, the destination was St. Alban's chapel. Once we were inside, he told me about the dreams and the visions he had been experiencing. They were clearly frightening him. He explained that he came to the chapel as he often felt compelled to, that the young girl from the past was drawing him back, asking him to help her. I listened to his story but was not convinced at first, after all, it is a little fantastical isn't it?'

Suzanne agreed. 'Yes I'm not sure how I would react if my other half told me that story. Well, before I came here I would have had problems believing it, but not now.'

'Indeed. You would believe it now because of what has happened to you over the past few days. Nothing supernatural had happened to me before, I was a very practical minded person when I was younger, plus, I could not disregard what other people in the village had told me. I had witnesses to say they had seen him with Gracie on more than one occasion. You can't keep secrets for long in a small village like this one.' Margaret said tapping the side of her nose, a knowing look on her face.

'Of course, but I still don't know exactly where Gracie fits with this? Was she..' Suzanne hesitated and Margaret completed her sentence.

'Lance's lover? If you would have asked me at the time, I would have sworn to it, but now looking back I don't think it was that simple. Lance and Gracie were old school companions; both attended the village primary school with just a couple of years between them. They had a history that went back a long way, so when a distraught Gracie had knocked on our door one rainy November evening, when I happened to be out visiting my mother, Lance could scarcely refuse her plea for help. You see it was Gracie that owned the Brass, she was the one that started all this. Being the gentleman that he was, Lance took the burden of responsibility away from her and ended up bearing the suffering himself.'

'So that is how he came about the Brass, Lance took ownership because Gracie was having visions that were frightening her?' Suzanne confirmed.

Margaret nodded with a look of remorse on her face.

'After the empty threat I made about divorcing him, he made sure he saw less of Gracie, but he still continued to go to the chapel.'

Meanwhile, Suzanne's mind was racing. She wanted to know exactly what the St. Aldhelm Brass was, where had it come from originally and why had it ended up in the village pond. There was something that was troubling her too, something that didn't quite fit with what she had found out so far.

'So Lance would take the St. Aldhelm Brass to the chapel to purposely witness visions of the past?'

Margaret sighed. 'He did. And this went on for years according to Lance's diaries.'

Suzanne's mouth felt dry. She took another gulp of water which was no longer cold, but at room temperature. 'It's just I'm a little confused. I have also seen these visions while I have been asleep, they are like dreams but a lot more real.' Suzanne thought for a moment. 'In fact, I have had these dreams most nights since I've been here.'

Margaret frowned, she looked uncertain, and not sure of the point that Suzanne was trying to make. Suzanne continued; 'What I'm saying is, is that I don't seem to need the St. Aldhelm Brass or be present at the chapel to see these visions, I see them anyway, in my sleep. So what is their significance exactly?'

Margaret looked perplexed. 'I don't know myself. Lance never fully explained it to me. All I know is that the Brass has a connection to the chapel, and when the Brass went missing Lance was never the same again. The dreams haunted him, night after night, and without the Brass he said he was unable to do anything, he could not help her, Blanche I mean.

Suzanne thought for a moment, trying to make sense of what Margaret had just told her. It was true that there were only two occasions in which she had been able to act *within* the visions, that she was part of them more than just a mere observer. On both of those occasions she had been at the chapel beforehand.

'How did Lance lose the Brass?' Suzanne asked eventually. 'Could he have accidentally have dropped it in the village pond?' A flash of a memory came back to Suzanne, of the Brass sticking out of her juvenile hand. *The Brass had found her, not the other way round.*

'Maybe he did. I really don't know the truth of what happened, all that I remember is him turning the house upside down in a frenzied manner, which was most out of character for Lance as you can imagine. He never did find it though.' Margaret paused, she seemed uncertain of whether to finish the story.

'He had a breakdown of some kind then?' Suzanne asked gently.

Margaret nodded. 'Yes. In the end it was too much for me to bear you understand? He had to be looked after, properly I mean.'

Suzanne knew that Margaret was referring a metal health institution of some description. She noticed a look of guilt flicker across Margaret's face.

'What happened to Gracie?' Suzanne asked trying to change the focus of the conversation.

'Not long after I accused them of having an affair, Gracie moved away from the village. She went to live with her sister in London. I think she knew she had to get away, put distance between herself and Lance and this village. She only moved back here ten years ago, following retirement. I think she wanted to make peace with the past. I also think she was surprised to find me here still living in the same house, but without Lance of course.'

Margaret poured herself a small measure of brandy from a crystal decanter that was on the table beside her before offering Suzanne a glass.

Suzanne declined politely. She felt muddled enough without the influence of alcohol and she needed to get a least one thing straight in her mind. 'This St. Aldhelm Brass, I'm guessing it the same object as the Brass that I own?'

'This is what we need to check. Have you got it with you? I will know instantly if it is the same'. Margaret looked at her expectantly.

Suzanne leaned forward to grab the embroidered cloth shoulder bag from the floor. As she scooped it up disappointment struck her as she suddenly remembered. Dropping the bag back on the floor she looked across at Margaret. 'It's in my jacket pocket, back at the cottage.'

Margaret looked concerned. 'You must keep it with you Suzanne. If it is the St Aldhelm Brass it's important that something like that doesn't fall into the wrong hands. Perhaps you should get back now and make sure it is safe. I could come with you?'

'Yes of course, it will be fine though.' Suzanne felt strangely defensive at being cosseted by the older woman. 'I know it's definitely in my jacket pocket.'

'Just make sure that you keep it safe, won't you?' Margaret said as she sipped the drink.'

Suzanne nodded and managed a smile. Part of her had been shocked and frightened by the story she had just heard, yet another part wanted to take control, to put an end to the curse. She felt she had been singled out for the task, especially now she knew of her genetic links to the Martraver's family.

'I will. From now on and until I can work out how I can finally help Blanche, I won't let it out of my sight.'

Margaret put her drink on the table. 'That's very brave of you Suzanne, but I think you should reconsider your options, before you become too involved. If I were you, I would be getting ready to leave here as soon as possible and try and put the whole thing out of your mind if you can. When are you due to head home?'

Suzanne felt strangely resolute. 'I was only planning on staying a week, so that would mean Wednesday, but Melanie told me that the cottage doesn't have any bookings until Saturday, so I guess I can stay longer if I wanted to. Besides, the whole point of my holiday here was to escape from the problems I'm facing at work, I can't keep running away from things like a child. I need to stay, and do what needs to be done.'

There was a pause as Margaret drew in a breath through her teeth. 'Well, it sounds to me like you have made up your mind and I will support you in that decision, but I just hope you realise how dangerous this whole affair is. Be sure to stay in touch with those who care about you, for you will need their support - ultimately.'

Suzanne shivered at the gravity of Margaret's words. 'Can I have that drink you offered me earlier?'

CHAPTER 25

The cellar was dank and smelt of mould. A single light bulb was still swinging from the low ceiling where Ed had brushed past it a moment ago, its light just about sufficient to see the debris that he had accumulated over the years. He heaved a wooden crate away from the wall, noticing that a black sticky substance had leaked from it at some point. The crate contained a set of vintage sherry, collecting it had been a hobby of his at one time. He examined each of the eight bottles in the crate conscientiously and found no obvious leakage. No matter about the sherry though, he must press on, he didn't have long.

Where the crate had been resting was the entry point, he could see that the stones in this part of the wall were loose, but they hadn't been disturbed since the last time he had ventured down there.

Starting at the top, he tugged at the heavy limestone blocks, one by one, making a mental note of where each one had been positioned and laying them out on the floor behind him. Cautiously, he examined stones at the top of the hole, to ensure they were stable. Satisfied, Ed crouched down and on all fours crawled through the small gap into the neighbouring cellar. His eyes had adjusted to the darkness now, and the single light bulb was just enough to make out the short flight of stairs leading up to the kitchen of Tilly Whim cottage.

Pulling the door handle down Ed hoped that the cellar door would be open. It clicked reassuringly and there was no resisting pressure as he slowly pushed the door. The sight that greeted him was homely and bright, such a stark contrast to the underworld from which he had just emerged. He paused a few seconds to listen; the only sounds he could hear was the song of birds in the hedgerow and the distant hum of a farm vehicle. Ed scanned the room; no obvious sign of it in here, he would have to explore the house and hope that Suzanne did not return while he was there.

As it happened, it didn't take long to find it. After searching a navy shoulder bag that had been left on the sofa, his next port of call was the jacket he had seen her wearing the day before. Thankfully, Suzanne had left it hanging in the porch, the sleeve betraying its whereabouts from the sitting room.

Ed could feel his pulse quicken as he unhooked the jacket from the coat stand - he was certain he could see the outline of the Brass concealed within the left hand pocket. His bony fingers trembled slightly as he tussled with the zip. Cocking his head to one side he placed his good ear towards the direction of the front door. He was sure he could hear footsteps traversing up the path. He was so close, the last thing he needed was for Suzanne to come home, especially if he was empty handed. At last, the lining of the pocket came free and a wave of excitement and joy washed over him as he drew the prized object from within. Ed smiled to himself and without further ado, made off in the direction of the cellar. After all these years, the Brass was in his possession once more.

CHAPTER 26

1325

Gwen was sitting in a corner of the servant's hall embroidering her best veil. The pink lily she was busily crafting was nearly complete. She held it up and examined her work against the light of a nearby window and was pleased, all it needed was just a touch of deep pink on the inside of the petals. Her attention suddenly shifted to the long table in the centre of the room. Missing his late morning meal to prepare Lord Martraver's horses for the hunt, fourteen year old Edwy, the stable boy was now hungrily tucking into the leftovers. Gwen watched as he gobbled down hunks of brown bread and cheese and slurped weak beer from his mug. The noise of his eating and drinking was so loud that it was putting Gwen off her needlework.

'Slow down Edwy! I can hardly hear myself think'.

Edwy looked up and scowled in Gwen's direction. 'Yes ma'am' he said in a cheeky tone before defiantly taking another bite of bread and chewing it, noisily.

Gwen pulled a face at him and directed her attention back towards her veil. She had only just re-threaded her needle with a bright cochineal thread when the door of the hall burst open. Both Gwen and Edwy stopped what they were doing and hastily rose to their feet. It was Lady Philippa. She swept into the room, her long gown flowing out behind her. Gwen could immediately see that she was in a foul mood.

'Gwen you shall come to my chamber at once. I have to speak to you as a matter of great importance.'

Philippa eyed Edwy with a look that told him that he would incur her wrath if he dared to ask what was going on.

'Of course my lady. Right away.' Gwen turned and dropped the veil and loose thread on her chair. As she followed her lady out of the servant's quarters and upstairs to the Solar, she wondered why Lady Philippa was so angry.

The bed chamber was warm. A fire was roaring in the grate, something which was not seen commonly in July at Martravers Manor, but the creeping sea mist that had settled earlier that morning had made it necessary.

Philippa ensured that the door was firmly closed behind Gwen, she then grabbed her by the shoulders and stared angrily. Gwen cowered, Philippa was a full head taller than her, and the look on the noblewoman's face was one of rage.

'What did you tell the priest about Thomas and I?' Philippa's voice was no more than a whisper but it was sharp and full of resentment.

Gwen was both confused and frightened, Philippa's long fingers felt like they were burrowing through the flesh on her arms. 'Nothing! I don't know what you mean my lady. Please stop, you are hurting me.' Gwen pleaded.

Philippa released her grip a little but it was still strong enough to keep Gwen in place.

'Nothing? You haven't mentioned anything?'

'No my lady, I am your most loyal and faithful servant. I wouldn't breath a word......'

Philippa interrupted 'How is it that Fr. Eldrith knows about Thomas and I? You are the only person Gwen, I haven't told anyone else.'

'I don't know my lady, perhaps someone has seen you and Thomas together?' Gwen stammered.

Philippa, who was still clutching her maid by the shoulders was not convinced. 'Maybe I would have thought the same, it is possible that we could have been spotted together in the meadow or other places, people gossip about that.'

Gwen nodded in enthusiastic agreement, hopeful that her mistress was now seeing reason. Her hopes were soon to be dashed.

'What isn't quite possible however' Philippa continued, 'Is for anyone to know about the scare I had last month.'

The maid looked both confused and anguished 'Scare?' she uttered.

'Yes, Gwen. You remember? When I thought I was with child? How on earth did Fr. Eldrith come to know about that detail?'

Gwen thought for a moment trying to make sense of what Philippa was telling her. She clearly remembered that Philippa had shared her concerns a number of weeks ago, while she was dressing her. Gwen had worried for her mistress for a whole fortnight, and Philippa, who although seemed her vibrant self in public, had clearly been consumed with worry on the inside. One evening as Gwen had helped a tearful Philippa get dressed for bed, the pair had discussed how she might break the news to Lord and Lady Martravers. Fortunately their concerns were allayed the following morning when the tell-tale staining on her bed linen at last had appeared.

'I've no idea my lady. Are you sure you did not tell anyone else, for I swear on my mother's life that the priest did not hear this from my lips.'

Philippa stared long and hard at Gwen before releasing her from her grip. Gwen could see that she had won the battle in convincing her.

'Thomas'. Philippa whispered. 'He is the only other person who knows. But why would he tell Fr. Eldrith?' Philippa paused, playing scenarios in her mind. Up until now she had been convinced that Gwen had disobeyed her, but now she wasn't so sure.

'Confession?' Gwen suggested.

'Hmmm.' Philippa considered the suggestion, she had been thinking along similar lines. 'If Thomas wanted to confess our deeds why didn't he go to his own priest, Fr. Francis? Why come here and blurt it to Fr. Eldrith?'

Gwen straightened her pinafore and smoothed her crumpled sleeves. 'We can't be sure. Perhaps you should ask him yourself my lady. That way, you can understand his motives rather than speculate.'

'Yes, Gwen. You are right. I'm sorry for shouting at you like that. It's just I am so angry!'

Gwen cocked her head inquisitively. There seemed more to the story and she was curious to find out what it was. 'Is there something else you wanted to ask me my lady?' she asked.

Philippa had turned away and was brusquely walking towards the window. Gwen noticed that outside the sea mist had started to lift. Philippa spoke again. 'No, I've nothing further to ask of you, but to warn you. You must be careful of Fr. Eldrith, he cannot be trusted.'

Gwen swallowed 'I will. Out of respect for you I will no longer go to him for confession.'

Philippa nodded in approval. She sat down on the window seat and inspected her fingernails. 'That's not all of it I'm afraid. Would you believe that wicked priest has the audacity to blackmail me! That is what makes me so angry. I went to him this morning, after early Mass. I had been thinking about what you told me Gwen, about Fr. Eldrith seeing Blanche leaving on the Priest's Way with the book and it doesn't make sense. I think he is lying. Anyway, when I enquired about what he had seen and began to challenge it, he told me he knew about Thomas and I, our shameful sin, how I nearly got with child outside of marriage and what a scandal it would be if this news was to become public knowledge! The cheek of it Gwen!'

Gwen was stunned. She had never heard of a priest breaking the sanctity of confession before. She immediately thought of the many little sins she had confessed to him over the years, and wondered if he could be trusted. Her mind went back to what Philippa had said. This was all about Blanche again. It baffled Gwen why Lady Philippa so concerned about the serf girl, and the fact that she was now out of the equation was comforting. Gwen had to admit to herself that a streak of jealous uncertainty ran through her whenever her Lady mentioned Blanche. The friendship and bond between Philippa and Blanche had been strong, Philippa could have easily displaced Gwen in favour of Blanche, it had probably only been a matter of time.... Gwen's thoughts were interrupted by Philippa, she was now pacing round the solar facing her moral dilemma.

'So now I have no choice. I cannot afford to bring shame on myself and my family.'

'You are giving up on looking for Blanche?' Gwen enquired, her voice sounded hopeful, too hopeful and she feared her mistress picked up her tone. Philippa quickly spun round.

'No! I am not giving up on looking for Blanche, but I have to stay clear of suggesting Fr. Eldrith had any involvement, that is all I am saying. Go now, attend to your duties, and of course what has been said between these four walls remains with you and I only. As for Thomas, I will deal with him when he returns from his trip to Glastonbury.'

Gwen curtsied and left her lady's bed chamber. She was glad to be in the cool of the corridor, the stress of the situation coupled with the heat from the fire had brought her out in a sweat. As she scuttled along with her head bowed in case any of the family should see her, she felt relieved to be out of suspicion. Alas for poor Thomas! Given her mistresses quick temper, she would not want to be in his shoes in one week's time.

CHAPTER 27

2009

Suzanne! Suzanne are you still tired? I've brought you something to eat and drink.' Margaret set a wooden tray down on a table a couple of feet away from the sofa. Suzanne rubbed her eyes and pushed herself up into a sitting position. Looking around she could see she was still in the snug room. The last thing she recalled was Margaret covering her with a red tartan blanket before she drifted off. The dream was still fresh in her mind, she had been in a house this time, again Lady Philippa was present, but she had seen everything from another perspective. It had been that of the servant girl, the same who had accompanied Philippa at the Fair.

'What time is it?' Suzanne squinted at the clock in the corner of the room but it was too far away for her to read in the dimness of light provided by a single table lamp.

'Quarter past nine.' Margaret said gently. 'You've been asleep for a good couple of hours.'

Suzanne immediately sprung up 'Quarter past nine! I don't understand. I wasn't feeling tired until...'

Margaret finished her sentence for her, pointing to the table.

'..until you had a drop of brandy.'

'What?' Suzanne had almost forgotten she had requested the strong drink hours before, and noticing the empty glass in front of her she slowly reclined back into her seat. 'I remember now, my eyes became heavier and heavier, I could not keep them open - but how can one drink send me off to sleep so quickly? It's not normal!'

Margaret pursed her lips hesitantly. 'I suppose what I should be saying to you is not to worry, you must be suffering from stress and exhaustion. That would be the reassuring answer, but...'

'But?' Suzanne interrupted eager to hear what Margaret had to say.

‘But I have to be honest with you. This is exactly what happened to Lance. As time went by he increasingly became distant, he would often fall asleep in the middle of the day without warning. It was like he was being drawn in by the other world, it took over his life.’

Suzanne sighed and rubbed her eyes wearily. ‘I had the most vivid dream again.’ She reached for the mug of tea and took a sip of tea before continuing. ‘I was back in their time again. Lady Philippa was talking to her servant about going to see Fr. Eldrith and him blackmailing her because of Blanche, and Philippa thought she had been pregnant but it was just a false alarm and..’

Margaret raised her hands in a gesture that indicated to Suzanne she should slow down.

‘Sorry’ Suzanne said. It’s just I can remember all the details so clearly, I wanted to tell you before I forget!’

Margaret turned away briefly to switch on the wall lights and she started to search in a drawer in the dresser. Returning to the sofa, she handed Suzanne a small jotter and pen. ‘Here, bullet-point the main events and people from your dream. Lance used to find doing this helped him a great deal.’

Suzanne took the jotter and in between spoonfuls of tomato soup, wrote a summary of her dream. ‘There. I think that’s everything.’ She handed it to Margaret who read it back quietly to herself and then was silent until Suzanne had finished eating. ‘I think you should go back to your cottage now’ she said eventually.

Suzanne stopped and dabbed her mouth with a paper napkin. ‘Of course. I’m sorry, I should have left hours ago and here I am taking up your time.’

‘Oh I didn’t mean anything like that you silly girl! No, what I mean is you need to get back and find the Brass make sure it is safe and with you at all times. I can come with you if you like, double check it is what Lance lost all those years ago.’

‘Yes, of course!’ Suzanne affirmed and watched Margaret for moment as she turned to put her late husband’s diary away in a drawer in the dresser. Suzanne caught a brief glimpse of a number of other notebooks in the drawer and wondered if they too, were Lance’s diaries. Prickles suddenly crept over her skin as she thought about what they might contain, what other words had Lance etched that Margaret hadn’t shared with her today. Given Lance’s state of mind towards the end, she wasn’t sure that she wanted to know.

It was shortly after 10pm when Suzanne and Margaret arrived at Tilly Whim cottage. After flicking on several lights to make the place feel more welcoming, Suzanne went straight to her jacket to retrieve the Brass. As she unzipped one pocket and then the other, she could feel a frown creep across her face.

‘What is it?’ Margaret enquired.

‘I’m sure I left it in my jacket pocket. I’ve not taken it out since...’ Suzanne paused.

‘Since?’

‘Since yesterday when I was round at Ed’s.’ Suzanne replied. The events of the day had taken over her and she had completely forgotten to mention her discussion with Ed.

Margaret sighed. ‘Do you think you left it there?’

‘No! I mean, it did almost slip out of my pocket but I noticed and made sure it was safely zipped away.’

‘Right. Is there anywhere else it could be? Think now. What about your handbag on the sofa, could it be in there?’ Margaret went to retrieve the handbag. ‘Here, please check.’

Suzanne was taken aback by Margaret’s sudden assertiveness and urgency. ‘Of course’ she replied, taking her almost empty shoulder bag and commencing the search. As the seconds went by, a small feeling of panic started to rise within her. She could feel Margaret’s eyes on her, expectantly.

‘I’ll check my jacket again.’ Suzanne announced, trying to keep a tone of lightness in her voice. After fifteen minutes of searching her clothes, pockets and various other places around the cottage, Suzanne flopped into a chair. ‘I don’t understand. I’m sure I had it when I got back from Ed’s.’

Margaret raised an eyebrow inquisitively.

‘I had been returning those books that I had borrowed from him.’ Suzanne explained. ‘While I was round there he happened to see the Brass fall from my pocket. He suggested that I should get it valued as it is likely to be medieval. In his opinion, he thinks it is a pilgrimage badge, like those that appear in his antiquities book.’ Suzanne grabbed the book on Medieval Antiques from the coffee table and handed it to Margaret. ‘I have to say, there is nothing in there that looks remotely like the Brass’

Margaret frowned as she examined the black and white photographs which showed examples of medieval pilgrimage badges. ‘I agree’ she said after a while. ‘My memories of the Brass are nothing like these. It has a habit of disappearing, does the Brass.’ Margaret said wistfully, as if fate had already decided there was nothing to be done about it.

‘But how can it have just disappeared? I’m sure had it when I came home last night. and I haven’t left the house with it since and the door was locked when we got back.’

Margaret reached out and put her hand on Suzanne’s. Her face was lined with worry but the words she spoke were soft and reassuring.

‘Try not to worry about it tonight. I’ve got to leave now, Jasp doesn’t like it when he is in the house on his own after dark, he frets, the poor thing. You go to bed and get some more rest. Perhaps you will find it in the morning, you know how memories can come to you in the middle of the night? It could be that you did take it from your pocket and put it somewhere else but you just don't remember.'

Suzanne nodded glumly. She showed Margaret out of the front door, promising to contact her in the morning. Closing the door behind her, she felt quite alone. It was 11pm and she found she was not in the least bit tired. She padded into the kitchen and filled the kettle, a strong coffee would help her to think more clearly. As she spooned the granules into the stoneware mug she reflected on Margaret's advice. It was true that there was a lot going on in her head at present but surely, she would have remembered taking the Brass from her jacket? She stirred some milk into the mug and watched as the coffee granules swirled round, before disappearing. The flashing light of her mobile phone caught her eye and Suzanne was surprised to discover that Pete Doyle had been trying to contact her for most of the day. She was about reply to his voicemail message, but remembering the time she thought better of it. She would set her alarm early and ring him back first thing.

Flopping down on the sofa a sudden flash of inspiration came to her. Margaret's words rattled in her mind; *memories can come to you in the middle of the night.* Precisely! And what had happened just a few nights ago? Had she not woken up while she was sleep-walking, clutching the Brass? It was quite possible that she had done a similar thing again last night only this time she had no recollection of it. With a newly found enthusiasm Suzanne abandoned her coffee and commenced a more thorough search of the cottage.

CHAPTER 28

25th December 1325

A light frost had settled on the village overnight, the type that would easily melt away within just a few hours of watery pale morning sunshine. Fr. Eldrith's leather shoes made a soft crunching sound on the grass as he briskly made his way through St. John's churchyard. The priest rubbed his hands together to keep warm, and as he walked, pondered the summer's events in his mind once more. He had been cautious at first and had not approached the Bishop until he was certain that the miracles were indeed genuine, the last thing he wanted was to appear foolish in front of the elders. When Bishop Reynolds finally agreed to visit West Lytchett back in September, he had not been disappointed. In fact much to Fr. Eldrith's delight he had been eager to declare the site as an official place of healing and pilgrimage.

The countless stories the Bishop had heard from the lips of those who had been cured might have been enough to convince him, but better than that, the Bishop himself had benefited from the curative waters that sprung from the floor of the chapel. Fr. Eldrith recalled Bishop Reynolds had been suffering following the journey from Salisbury along the pot-holed tracks and the elderly cleric had been unable to straighten his spine for fear of intense pain. The Bishop's written account that Fr. Eldrith had arranged to be copied onto velum was a great testimony to the powers of the well;

I entered the chapel bent double. True, I was bowed in reverence to Our Lord and St. Aldhelm in his holy chapel, but my spine had been jolted from the journey and was painful to straighten. The waters were pure and cold. I washed my hands and face and when I put my hands to my back I found that I could straighten fully. I left the chapel standing tall, and leaping like a spring lamb for the joys of this wonderful miracle.

Fr. Eldrith smiled to himself. How lucky that his parish should become such an important place of pilgrimage. The revenues that the chapel was being to generate were substantial and the pilgrims were notable. Rumour had it that the King himself was planning a visit in the spring. Certainly if that were true then the profile of St.Alban's chapel would be raised even more. It could even out-do the Holy House at Walsingham, or St. Thomas's shrine at Canterbury! Fr. Eldrith clasped his hands together in excitement and he increased his pace. Around him the village was starting to wake, the common folk, most of which were looking quite thin were clearly looking forward to the feasting season that lay ahead of them. A scrawny man with a pointed nose nodded reverently in the direction of the priest as he passed him on the lane. Fr. Eldrith recognised him as Gerard Myddelton, Blanche's step-father. The man was always in confession for one reason or another, the last time had only been yesterday, requesting absolution for the particularly abhorrent sin of adultery. Fr. Eldrith had given forgiveness on the basis that he took proper care of his long suffering wife Elisabeth during the season of festivities and beyond. Blanche's mother Elisabeth had suffered a dullness of spirit for a number of years but this had only got worse when her daughter disappeared.

Fr. Eldrith felt a pang of guilt. He tried to convince himself that Blanche's disappearance was not his doing. It was an accident, and what followed he could not explain. But it was true, the events that had led up to the spring appearing from the floor of the chapel had been troubling Fr. Eldrith since they had occurred, the thoughts troubled him by day, and there was no escape at night as his dreams were constantly plagued by images of the girl with blood pooling in her open eyes, lying on chapel floor. Whether he had meant to or not, he had caused her death. Another matter of conscience that Fr. Eldrith battled with was his theory that Blanche was a practitioner of the dark arts, for now having considered all things, this explanation did not add up. The priest had heard of other curative springs, like St. Winifride's Well in North Wales that had sprung up on the spot were St. Winifride was decapitated by an angry prince. A *saint* not a witch. Was it possible? His thoughts were interrupted by the sound of an owl screeching as it returned to its nest with prey in its talons

Fr. Eldrith cleared his throat; the cold air was getting to his lungs. He needed to put those thoughts aside now. No one knew what was on his mind, no one had borne witness to what happened at the chapel that day and it was true that no one had seen hide nor hair of Blanche Myddelton since her disappearance, and this suited him well.

The priest strode down the path that led to the gates of the Manor with purpose. He had been invited to perform a private family Mass in the Martravers' chapel followed by a midday feast. It was an offer that Fr. Eldrith had willingly accepted. Lord Martravers was clearly grateful to his priest for bringing notoriety to West Lytchett, he himself had benefited both financially and socially, and with a potential royal visit this was clearly just the beginning. Fr. Eldrith understood the politics, that it was a case of one-upmanship against other nobles in the locality, in particular his arch rival Lord Beaufort. Fancy, Lady Philippa cavorting with Beaufort's son, she must have known it would have to end. It had of course been a worry that Lady Philippa had clearly suspected his involvement in Blanche's disappearance, something which he'd had to nip in the bud before it caused a problem. Fortunately, the spirited young noblewoman had not spoken of it since he had mentioned her foolish indiscretions with the Beaufort heir. Fr. Eldrith's thoughts were interrupted as the lodge keeper shouted down to him from his first floor window.

'Good day to you Father. Wait a moment while I let you through.' The lodgekeeper, dressed only in his chemise disappeared from the window and it was a few minutes before he unbolted the gate of the lodge house, now wearing more modest clothing.

'Sorry Father, the time had escaped me. Especially with the dawn coming so late.' Fr. Eldrith nodded and passed through the lodge and onto the short path that led up to the grand studded front door of the Manor. The priest was greeted by Lord Martraver's man servant William, who immediately welcomed him into the entrance hall of the manor; it was a dark oak cladded space that housed two benches and a fire spitting and cracking in the corner. On one side of the room hung the Martraver's standard; a red and gold shield with two lions passant and a sliver chalice. William offered to take Fr. Eldrith's cloak.

'If you would care to take a seat Father, I will inform my Lord of your arrival.'

Fr. Eldrith handed over his cloak and eased himself down on to the bench nearest the fire just as soon as William disappeared off through a doorway. He held his hands out to warm them in front of the fire and noticed that the swollen joints that normally plagued him at this time of year were no more – surely it was the work of St. Aldhelm's curative spring water.

The fire violently spat a fountain of orange embers towards his feet and he quickly drew them back under the bench. Fr. Eldrith pictured in his mind's eye the library on the first floor, a gap where St. Aldhelm's ancient tome had resided. Fr. Eldrith shuffled down the bench to put some distance between himself and the scorching heat. The book; this was where this had all began. The priest couldn't help but raise a smile. He had set off in search of notoriety and wealth and now he was on the path to finding both. The lost treasure had indeed been uncovered, not as ancient gold as he had originally thought, but something far better. He just had to make sure Lady Philippa kept quiet.

CHAPTER 29

In Philippa's opinion, the Mass had been said with considerable haste. Of course she believed that this was Fr. Eldrith's intention; to hurry through the religious celebrations so the feasting could begin. She peered at him down the line of the banqueting table. He was on this occasion the guest of honour, seated on the right hand of her father and his voice could be heard above all others, booming and arrogant.

Once more Philippa could feel the anger rising within her, she had managed to avoid attending the priest's services since the summer, instead opting for Mass at St. James's in Langdon. After much cajoling, Thomas had eventually owned up. He had sought absolution from Fr. Eldrith simply because he could not face confessing the deeds of their love to his own village priest. Following his admittance they had argued, and much to Philippa's dismay it had been Thomas that had suggested they no longer meet. Philippa's hand aimlessly wandered to her necklace. She no longer wore the emeralds that Thomas had given her, instead the delicate droplets of rubies that she twisted round her fingers had been gifted to her that same morning by the nobleman who sat beside her. Philippa reached for her cup and took a large gulp of wine, the warmth of the alcohol surged through her body and only fueled her resentment for the priest.

'You like the jewels I have given to you my dearest?' Lord Robert Carringstone whispered in her ear. 'You shall have more of them when you become my bride.'

Philippa smiled weakly at the portly middle-aged man on her left. She had tried to convince her father that she should wait a few more years before marriage in the hope that Lord Robert would get tired of waiting, but the single minded, stubborn Harold Martravers was not having any of it. A union between the Martravers and Carringstones would strengthen the power base they held in south Wessex, ensuring financial security for both sides. Philippa and her future heirs would indeed be well kept.

Robert's eyes narrowed with concern. 'You seem distracted my dear. Perhaps you will summon your lady in waiting once the feast is over and we can take a walk in the gardens?'

Robert's leg pressed intrusively against Philippa's. All at once she realised how much she missed Thomas. How the last few months had been painful without his companionship and love. Maybe she should try to speak to him? He was not yet married, perhaps there could be another chance? Without warning, Philippa pushed back her chair and rose from the table. The chatter round the table quietened to a hum, but the minstrels continued their playing.

'I wasn't meaning now!' Robert hissed as he tried to pull Philippa back to her seat. Harold Martravers leaned forward to see what was going on. Ignoring Philippa, he looked towards Robert for an explanation.

Reading his expression, Robert explained. 'Your daughter is looking a little pallid, I suggested that a walk in the grounds might be of help.'

Harold waved his hands in approval. 'You have my blessing. The feast is nearly finished. When you have finished walking with my daughter we can discuss the marriage plans. Come to the library when you are ready.'

Robert nodded and linked Philippa's arm in his and steered her past the heavy oak servant's screen and beyond towards the main door of the manor. In the privacy of this space Robert pulled her close and kissed her on the mouth eagerly.

Philippa recoiled in horror. 'My lord, kindly take your hands off me now!' she hissed. Robert could see that fire burned both in her eyes and her belly. The girl's reaction acted only to make him more amorous. He held her firm and tried to kiss her again.

Philippa turned her face away and closed her eyes. Tears of frustration and bitterness welled for a few seconds before brimming over and running down her cheeks like tiny glass beads. At last, Robert released her from his cumbersome grip.

'Come, I can see you are down in spirit. We shall take the air before the darkness sets in'. He suggested. Seeing her opportunity, Philippa ducked under Lord Robert's powerful arms and lunged towards the door. Lifting her gown a little so she would not trip, she ran down the path towards the lodge house and rapped on the door. Looking back over her shoulder she could see that Robert was stood outside, his arms folded across his chest in defiance.

'Let me through!' Philippa demanded as the lodgekeeper opened the door. He was clearly enjoying the drama judging by the bemused look on his face.

'As you wish Lady Philippa' The lodgekeeper fumbled with the keys on his belt. As Philippa stepped into the lodge house she heard Robert's voice ringing out behind her.

'I will not chase you Philippa.' Robert called. 'You may make a fool of me today, but not when we are married. I will see to that!'

Philippa did not reply to Robert's threat. Scampering from the other side of the lodge house she took a left, following the tree lined path which led to Kingston, the ancestral home of the Beauforts. The light blue of the early evening Christmas sky already had a smattering of pale stars and the half moon was starting to rise in the east. *She had to be at Kingston before it got dark*! Her breath appeared like white clouds in the frosty air as her feet pounded rhythmically against the frozen earth. She turned to look over her shoulder one more time, from here she could still make out the pointed gables of Martravers Manor and smoke rising from the chimney of the Hall. The comforts of home now seemed far away as thin branches from the skeletal trees whipped against her arms and face. For a moment Philippa's courage almost left her; but a voice in her head dared her to press on further into the unwelcoming depths of Inglebrook Wood.

* * *

The light was fading quickly from the library as the three men settled at the small table under the slender Oriel window. Summoning his man servant, Harold Martravers ordered for more candles to be lit and a fresh jug of wine to be brought up to them promptly.

Fr. Eldrith felt decidedly lightheaded. He could not remember the last time he had consumed so much good wine. Still, this was something he would need to get used to if he was to be circulating with the nobility. Directly across the table sat Robert Carringstone, Fr. Eldrith noticed that the nobleman's belt was unfastened slightly to accommodate his overfed stomach. He seemed subdued, perhaps due to indigestion, but more likely it was because of his quarrel with Lady Philippa. She was passionate, opinionated, outspoken in her views and very beautiful – a dangerous combination the priest reflected. Harold who was clearly still annoyed and embarrassed by his daughter's behaviour was doing his level best to put matters right with his future son-in-law.

'It is pre-nuptial nerves, Robert. Philippa has no experience of men, you must forgive her for acting like this. I have sent five servants on horseback out to bring her home, she cannot have got far.' Harold nervously smoothed his neatly trimmed grey beard as he spoke.

'You are right' Robert replied, his mood suddenly lifting. The explanation seemed to rest easily with him. Little did he know of Philippa's liaisons with Thomas Beaufort, Fr. Eldrith thought. Still, that was easily forgotten, provided Philippa kept her half of the bargain and didn't ask any further questions about her missing book.

'And that is in keeping with you and your practices Father?' Harold was asking.

'Hmm? I'm sorry?' Fr. Eldrith, who had been lost in his thoughts hadn't been aware that Harold was speaking to him.

'I was saying to Robert, that it is only right that he and Philippa should be married in St. Mary's, Kingston , given that she will be the future Lady Carringstone of that parish.'

Fr. Eldrith nodded in agreement. 'Rightly so. That is the tradition'

'Although, I was wondering if you would officiate at the ceremony?' Harold and Robert briefly exchanged looks. 'It's a slightly delicate situation you see, Robert tells me that the priest at St. Mary's is no longer of sound mind and will more than likely cause an embarrassment.'

Fr. Eldrith now understood why he had been invited to the library, and also why perhaps, he had been invited to the intimate family feast in the first place. He thought carefully before giving his answer.

'It is true that Fr. Gilbert is no longer of sound mind. Up until quite recently he was lucid enough to celebrate Mass and hear confession, but from what the townsfolk are saying he has got much worse lately, although he will not acknowledge this himself.' Fr. Eldrith took a sip of the strong wine from his pewter cup. 'It may be difficult to get him to step aside obligingly, but I will see what I can do.'

Harold beemed in the priest's direction. 'Good, all shall be well if you officiate. The date has not yet been agreed, but it shall be soon. Robert and I were thinking shortly after Christmastide, but before the beginning of Lent.'

'That should be fine.' Fr. Eldrith agreed. 'I will arrange a meeting with Fr. Gilbert at St. Mary's as soon as I can. In fact, I shall see him tomorrow at the feast of St. Stephen and will mention it then.'

Harold and Robert both looked pleased with the suggestion. 'Do have some more wine before you leave Father. It will warm you against the chill when you walk back to your church.' Harold pushed the carafe towards the priest.

'Thank you for your most courteous hospitality, but I really must be leaving. Fr. Eldrith pushed back his chair and stood up slowly. At first he feared that his legs would not take any weight and he swayed a couple of times before correcting his balance. Fortunately, the two noblemen who had been discussing the finer details of the wedding did not seem to notice. Instead they said their goodbyes to the priest, promising to talk further following St. Stephen's feast.

The shelves and walls of the library felt to be floating as Fr. Eldrith made his way towards the door. He desperately needed some fresh air to clear his head. It was strange, he reflected, that even in his inebriated state, the rows of shelves containing numbers of books were most impressive. There was so much wealth contained in just one room of this great house, he thought.

The half-moon was now high in the clear sky, its silver light shining through the second oriel window, picking out shadows and making odd shapes between the bookshelves. It was then that he noticed it. The moon light had picked it out, illuminating the ancient frontispiece. Fr. Eldrith strained his ears for although out of his sight, Harold and Robert could still be heard on the far side of the library, their voices muffled and low. As quietly as he could, Fr. Eldrith removed the book from its resting place. *It could not be!* His fingers glided over the indentation in the leather cover where the Brass image of St. Aldhelm had once been inlaid. A quick examination of the first few pages confirmed what he had initially thought; the book that had disappeared with Blanche Myddelton had somehow returned to the Martraver's library.

CHAPTER 30

2009

It was ten to midnight when Suzanne finally gave up her search. Reaching for the coffee she had made almost an hour earlier she considered resurrecting it in the microwave before changing her mind and tipping it down the sink. The caffeine at this time of night probably was not such a good idea anyway. Suzanne rinsed the mug and filled it with cold water before sitting down at the kitchen table.

Suzanne had searched every room in Tilly Whim cottage for the Brass, and it was nowhere to be found. She had even gone out into the back yard with her a torch and searched the shed, flower urns and troughs; all to no avail. The only place left to search was the cellar, but in considering the prospect she had made excuses to herself. She could not locate the light switch and the batteries in her torch were fading.

But now as she sat at the kitchen table; she noticed something. On the wall round the corner from the cellar door, Suzanne's eyes rested on the elusive light switch. She slowly rose from her chair, not believing that she had missed it on her first inspection and with stern resolve, flicked the switch down. She poked her head round the corner of the tongue and groove door and could see from a narrow gap under the cellar door that what was behind was illuminated. Suzanne stood for a few seconds, trying to decide whether to postpone her search of the cellar until the morning, but the persistent nagging voice would not let her rest. She knew herself that she would only sleep once the Brass had been found.

The change in temperature was noticeable as Suzanne began her descent down the narrow stone steps. The roof height was very low, and once she reached the bottom she found she had to stoop so as not to catch her head. Scanning the small space, Suzanne could see that Melanie did not make use of it for anything other than storing a few items of furniture. There were some wooden chairs resting against one wall, and next to them was a dusty pine dressing table with the top draw missing. Nothing about the space seemed remotely familiar; if she had slept walked down here last night she did not remember anything of it.

As she treaded with care in the direction of the dressing table, something scuttled by her feet. Suzanne shrieked; her cry resulted in a small echo which bounced off the rough limestone walls. Hopping from one foot to the other in an attempt to rid herself of whatever creature had encroached her space, her eyes were drawn to the far side of the cellar. The dark brown creature was running alongside the wall, its whiskers twitching; the thin bootlace tail trailing in the dust. She shivered. *It was just a mouse.* Taking a few deep breaths, Suzanne tried to calm her nerves. She turned to look in the direction she had come from and seeing the foot of the staircase reassured her that she was not far from means of escape. In fact, that is just what she wanted to do right now. Did it matter about searching for the Brass at this hour? The continuous crouching was making her shoulders and neck ache, surely it could wait till the morning. Suzanne was heading in the direction of the steps when she heard a voice.

'When the Brass went missing Lance was never the same again.'

Suzanne stopped in her tracks. 'Margaret is that you?' She stopped at the bottom of the steps and listened. She was sure she had heard Margaret's voice but how was that possible? As far as she knew, Margaret didn't have a key to the cottage and besides, she would be at home now, most likely fast asleep.

'Lance was never the same again'

This time Suzanne didn't physically hear the voice, it was merely replayed in her mind. Shaking her head she decided it was quite simply a projection, her own thoughts playing tricks with her. But isn't that how it started with Lance? The thought bothered her. If she could rule out the cellar, she could have another look around the cottage in the morning before her discussion with Pete, and then if there was still no joy, ask Ed next door. Eyeing the dressing table, she decided to take a quick look in each of the drawers before wrapping up the search for the night.

The cupboard doors within the pine dresser had warped slightly, and as soon as Suzanne tried the one on the left, it slid forward to reveal its contents; a black leather bound notebook.

Slowly she removed the book from the drawer and was about to turn the cover when she heard another noise. This time it sounded like the shuffling of feet. Suzanne frowned and listened again. She really wasn't imagining it this time, she could hear real noises; the scraping of metal against the stone floor, heavy breathing. Someone was in the cellar with her.

Daring not to look towards the opposite corner of cellar, Suzanne dropped the notebook and made a dash towards the steps and began her ascent towards the relative safety of the kitchen. She could feel the eyes of someone boring into her as she tried to escape and in her panic she misjudged the whereabouts of the fourth step, her right foot striking rather than clearing it. Stumbling forward Suzanne put her hands out to protect herself from the imminent fall, but it was too late. Her forehead struck the cold and decidedly sharp ridge of a top step. For a few minutes she remained conscious, the pain was beginning to register along with the horror of what was happening to her.

I have to stay awake.

A nauseating fizzing feeling at the top of her nose culminating in a surge of blood from both nostrils made her panic even more. From half way up the steps she could see the homely décor of the kitchen; it was so close yet so far away. Suzanne scrambled up the remaining few steps, the effort was making her wheeze and the torrent of blood was relentless. Collapsing at the top of the steps in a bloody mess she could feel both her strength and consciousness fading, the blackness beyond her current state seemed both foreboding yet inviting.

Edward Suthermount, who had been watching the events unfold through the gap in the cellar wall listened carefully; there was no noise from the other side. He had to get to her before the unthinkable happened. Hurriedly he began to remove the limestone blocks as he had done earlier on that day, laying them out in order as best as he could on the cellar floor behind him. When he reached Suzanne he shuddered at the sight that met his eyes; she was unconscious, perhaps dead even. Her face and hands were covered in blood and he could see the beginnings of a large bruise starting to form across her forehead. Ed knelt down and felt for a pulse. It was there. She was just concussed. Gathering his strength he heaved Suzanne onto her side into the recovery position. For a few seconds she lay there motionless and for a brief moment Ed considered calling for an ambulance, but then how would he explain how he had found her? They would take her into hospital, her relatives would be contacted, and she would probably never return again. His lifetime's chance would be lost. No, he could not let that happen. She was a strong young woman, she would pull through. As if to endorse Ed's decision, his thoughts were interrupted by the sound of choking followed by a rattling cough. He leaned over and put a rolled up tea towel down under Suzanne's face, her dark hair framing it in a way that was so familiar. A direct descendent of the Martravers, how uncanny! He would never have guessed it would happen this way. As Suzanne slowly opened her eyes and tried to make sense of her surroundings, Ed knew that there could be no messing about. He had to take his chance quickly.

* * *

From her reclining position across the back seats, Suzanne watched as street lights passed by the back passenger window of Ed's estate car. The thumping in her head had resumed and the motion of the car's tyres jolting over pot-holed terrain was making her feel worse. After a few minutes, she remembered what had happened; the black notebook, falling on the cellar steps, and then regaining consciousness for a moment or two to find Ed tending to her injuries. Thank God he had found her. As soon as she was able, Ed had helped her to her feet, put a blanket round her shoulders and slowly escorted her to his car, and now she was on her way somewhere – *hospital?* Suzanne realised she hadn't seen a street light now for quite a while. With nothing to be seen out of the window apart from the perpetual blackness of the night's sky, it was difficult to judge the speed at which they were travelling.

Suzanne cleared her throat a couple of times and winced as she could still taste the metallic of blood in her mouth. She noticed Ed flinch at her sudden noise.

'Are we near the hospital?' Suzanne managed. Her voice was croaky, barely recognisable as her own.

'Not too far now.' Ed replied. He had been silent during the journey, focused on driving the estate car down the narrow, unlit Dorset lanes. A moment or two later, the car turned a sharp left and came to an abrupt and bumpy halt. Suzanne struggled to sit up, trying to make sense of her surroundings.

Ed unfastened his seat belt and turned to face her. 'Stay there, I'm getting out now to help.'

Suzanne reluctantly slumped back into her seat. She still could not see anything out of the car window, nor could she hear any traffic. If Ed had taken her to the local A & E department then there would be street lights, the sound of ambulances and other vehicles. As her faculties started to return Suzanne felt a wave of panic wash over her. The rush of adrenalin gave her the energy she needed to haul herself into a sitting position and look out of the window.

Blackness. There was nothing to be seen; as she had suspected, there was no hospital building, they were in the countryside. Ed opened one of the back passenger doors. The smell of dew from the grass was strangely overpowering and in the distance, the roar of the waves could be heard crashing up against the shore before making their retreat. It was only when she tried to swing her legs over the side of the car seat that she noticed her ankles. They had been bound together with what looked like shackles. A feeling of sickness started to rise from Suzanne's stomach.

'Where are we? You said you were taking me to the hospital.' Suzanne was desperately trying to hide the fear in her voice but the wobble betrayed her.

Ed leaned in towards her. 'I never said I was taking you to a hospital. You just assumed I was.'

Suzanne was speechless for a moment. She had expected Ed to make up an excuse, try to pacify her in some way but his reply was cold and menacing. She had to try and stay calm, work out where he had taken her and then try and get help.

Reluctantly, Suzanne struggled out of the car with Ed assisting. She desperately wanted to push him away but feared that might only inflame the situation. What did he want with her? Was he some kind of sick rapist or murderer? *Stay calm. Don't lose it Suzanne.*

Almost as soon as she straightened and looked ahead, Suzanne recognised where she was. The door to the nine hundred year old chapel was swinging open in the breeze, as though to invite her in. She stared with her mouth open, unable to articulate what was going through her mind; shock, confusion – even a strange feeling of relief. There had to be a reason why Ed has brought her here, she just had to find out what he wanted and play along with it, and that would be the safest way.

As if reading her thoughts, Ed spoke softly 'You want to know why I have brought you here?' His voice was low and quiet in the night air. The clouds had parted slightly to give way to an almost full moon. The silvery light illuminated the stonework of the chapel and reflected off Ed's thin framed glasses.

'Yes I would like to know!' Suzanne feigned a slight irritation in her voice. 'I need medical treatment, you have to take me to hospital!'

'Come with me.' Ed beckoned her forward with his head, towards the open door.

'Rest assured, you won't be needing a hospital after this.'

Suzanne shuddered. What did he mean by the last comment? Before ducking her head to enter the chapel, Suzanne scanned the silvery fields that surrounded her. In the distance she could make out a light, possibly a security light on a house but it seemed a long way off. There was no way that her cries for help would be heard. Grabbing her wrists, Ed led her forward, into the darkness of the chapel. Their intrusion set a couple of gulls that had been resting there into a flap; Ed shooed them out through the door and tutted in irritation.

'That is why the sign is there. Tourists are always leaving the door open and then the birds get in and make a dreadful mess.'

The mundane statement from Ed seemed very much out of context in the wake of her kidnapping. She considered it was the type of comment a psychopath might make. Suzanne trembled at the thought.

Ed took a cigarette lighter from his pocket and set about lighting a number of candles, placing them in each of the four corners 'Don't worry, you are quite safe. I'm surprised you don't remember the mystical powers of healing that are contained within these four walls?'

Suzanne remained silent. It was now clear to her that Ed knew of the chapel's powers, though what he expected to happen, she wasn't sure.

With the small space now illuminated with soft candlelight, Ed tilted Suzanne's chin upwards so he could see her face. For a terrible moment she was worried that he might kiss her; the beginnings of what could end up being a lurid assault. She shivered against the touch of his cold hand but remembering her vulnerability, she allowed her head to rise. *Don't anger him.*

She was relieved when Ed set about examining the bruise on her forehead, pressing down hard checking for a fracture. Suzanne winced in pain.

'Interesting how parallels occur.' He muttered, as if to himself.

'What do you mean by that?' Suzanne asked. She wished Ed would stop talking in riddles. He was playing psychological games, trying to scare her.

'You don't remember do you?'

'Remember what? Please you are frightening me, if you won't take me to hospital, just drive me back to the cottage and I promise I won't mention any of this to anyone. I will pack my bags in the morning and head home, you will never see or hear from me again.'

Suzanne's pleading fell on deaf ears. Ed took a deep breath and shook his head. He was pacing back and forth in the small space front of the altar. Suzanne now wondered if he was regretting the abduction, the suggestion of letting her go with no further consequences she hoped, would appeal to him. All at once he stopped pacing the floor. A strange look set upon his face.

'You don't remember that you have been here before? In a previous life I mean?'

Suzanne's first reaction was to deny all knowledge of what had been happening to her since she had arrived in West Lytchett; but she pulled herself up short. Something told her that the longer she denied it, the longer she would remain in Ed's captivity. *Play along, see what he wants.*

The shackles that bound her ankles were beginning to cut into her flesh, she shuffled her feet a little in the hope that movement would somehow lessen their grip. It didn't. At last she replied, her voice deliberately soft and quiet.

'I do remember. Of course I do. I have seen so many visions of her since I came here, both in my dreams and on one occasions, while I was here, in this chapel.' Suzanne could feel the tears starting to well in her eyes, the fear and stress of the situation was getting too much. 'Please Ed, I don't know why you have brought me here. Surely we can talk further about this back at the cottage?'

Ignoring her plea, Ed pressed for more detail 'Who Suzanne? Who is it you have seen in your visions?'

Suzanne sniffed a couple of times and brushed away a tear from her cheek. 'We discussed her family when I was round at your cottage the other evening. My ancestor, Lady Philippa Martravers. I have been witnessing scenes from her life and times ever since I arrived in the village.' She paused for a moment to gauge Ed's reaction to her tearful state. Nothing about his expression indicated that he felt any empathy towards her. She shivered as his cold eyes met hers, urging her to continue.

'Of course, as soon as I found out I am descended from her line it made a bit more sense.'

Ed nodded slowly. 'So you find yourself believing in reincarnation then?' The cigarette lighter came out again, this time he went to the altar and lit a tall cream candle. Suzanne watched as beads of wax dripped down from the freshly lit wick and splashed on the stone altar plinth below. She wondered about the significance of this extra candle, whether a ritual was about to be performed or if Ed simply wanted more light in the building.

'No, actually I don't believe in it.' She replied, trying to sound as calm as she could. 'What the experience of the last few days has led me to believe in, however, is that we are somehow connected to our ancestors. We can witness what they have been through, poignant moments in their life, but I don't believe that we *are* them. Myself and Philippa Martravers for example, we are completely different personalities.'

Ed went quiet for a moment. He seemed deeply immersed in his own thoughts. Pocketing the cigarette lighter, he walked over towards the central stone column and laid his hands on the age old masonry.

'The reason why I have brought you here Suzanne is to ask a favour.' She noticed his voice had changed, it was somehow brighter, more optimistic. Perhaps at last, she was going to find out why Ed had taken her captive. 'First though, I need to explain.' Ed eased himself down onto the end of a pew. 'I suppose my story starts here, in this very chapel almost seven hundred years ago.'

Trying to ignore the pain from her injuries and the abrasive metal shackles that cut into her ankles, Suzanne listened as Ed described the precisely the scene she herself had witnessed on visiting St. Albans for the first time. Suzanne remained silent as Ed continued.

'I was seventeen years old when it happened, and myself, like others in this village were never the same again. Night after night I was haunted by the dreams. As a young man I thought that if I left West Lytchett, it would all stop, but I was wrong. In fact going away to University in Edinburgh at the other end of the country seemed to intensify the experiences. I simply could not escape mentally or physically.'

'Forgive me if what I am about to say seems crass, but what was it that was so bad about the dreams? What effect did they have on you?' Although part of her did not want to hear it, Suzanne felt she had to know the truth – especially if the same fate was awaiting her.

Ed inhaled deeply. Suzanne noticed that his hands were quivering slightly against the chill of the chapel's stone. He looked vulnerable and weary at the same time. Whatever had happened here, it had been enough to drive an intelligent man to this, a nervous wreck, *and another to raving madness.* All at once she felt a strange feeling of pity for Ed. If she could get to the root of problem, talk him round this could all end safely.

'It was the intense feeling of remorse, each time I awoke. You know the feeling you have had when you awake from a nightmare when a loved one has died?'

'Yes' came Suzanne's timid reply.

'Well imagine having that same feeling of melancholy, not just a few minutes after waking, but for the rest of the day, every day. That is what started to happen to me as a teenager. In desperation, I sought the help of several psychologists, all of which told me that what I was experiencing was more or less normal; I had lost my father the year before you see and they attributed it to anxiety and grief. Although I wanted to believe what they told me, deep down I knew there was more to it than that. It wasn't until I met Mr McCann that I became fully aware of what was going on.'

Although it was cool in the chapel, Suzanne could feel tiny beads of perspiration trickling down her lower back and between her breasts. She hadn't realised until now how much effort she was putting in to staying alert. Under any other circumstances she would be lying listless in her bed – she was running on pure adrenalin. 'Who was Mr McCann?' Suzanne asked, a forced inquisitiveness to her voice. If she could convince Ed that she was a trustworthy listening ear who was sympathetic to his plight, there was a chance he might remove or at least loosen the shackles around her ankles.

'I met him a year after graduating from Edinburgh. I had taken a teaching job in Bristol and so I moved back down south.

Ed answered without so much as even looking in her direction. He seemed completely absorbed in the story, almost unaware of what was going on around him.

'A few of us were drinking in a pub in Glastonbury when I got chatting to him at the bar. There are some interesting characters in Glastonbury, wiccas, mystics, druids and this chap was one of them but you wouldn't have thought so by looking at him. He offered to do a reading for me and being half drunk I accepted.'

Suzanne tried to imagine this much younger version of Ed, socialising with friends enjoying a drink or two. She found it almost impossible to equate this to the burdened old man who now held her captive. Time is cruel, she thought to herself.

Ed continued. 'We sat in a quiet corner of the pub and he began his reading. I will never forget what he said to me as he looked up from his cards. He said he could see an aura directly above me, but it was unlike most he had seen. This one was different. I pressed him to tell me what my aura looked like but he was reluctant at first. It was only after I began to tell him about my constant nightmares that he told me, no, *showed me.'*

'Showed you? How did he do that?'

Ed reached into his jacket pocket. Suzanne felt that she did not want to see what Ed was about to show her, tiny hairs on her arms had risen defensively. *Stay calm, stay strong and you will get out of this*! The voice in her head told her.

The piece of paper that looked like it had been torn from a lined jotter pad was ancient in itself, especially against the flickering candlelight. It took her a few seconds to for her mind to register the image on the paper. It had been crudely sketched using what looked like blue ballpoint pen, but the likeness was there. Immortalised on the ragged yellowing paper stared small devious eyes from their shaded hollows, a straight pointed nose and a tight-lipped mouth that was contorted into a grimace. It was a poignant and haunting image. Instinctively, Suzanne shuffled back a few steps.

'Seen him before?' Ed asked, his voice resounding off the four walls. The candle nearest to Suzanne flickered violently as if some unseen force had tried to snub it out. She nodded slowly, still taking tiny backward steps. As her foot made contact with one of the pews and lowered herself onto it. The words from Lance's diary entry echoed in her mind; *everything is connected.*

'Where have you seen him?' came Ed again 'I assume it was here, at St. Albans?' Ed didn't wait for her reply, instead he carefully folded the paper back into a small ragged square and tucked it away in his jacket pocket. 'Mr McCann gave me some sound advice that night in Glastonbury.' He was pacing again now, back in his own world. 'He told me that I should try and find out what the spirit wants from me, as he feared it would only rest if its wishes were fulfilled. I heeded his advice and the following month moved back to my parent's house, in West Lytchett. I felt sure that the secret rested here and as I had already found out, running away from the village would not stop the dreams and hauntings.'

'I take it you didn't manage to satisfy this spirit then?' Suzanne enquired. She was beginning to feel weak and dizzy and the last thing she wanted was to lose consciousness again. Ed picked up on the agitation in her voice and turned sharply to face her. He had waited all his life for this moment, he was not going to tell half the tale.

Sucking air through his front teeth, Ed started to explain. 'It wasn't until the 1970's that my first chance arrived. By this time of course I had worked out the gist of the story, unscrambled the meaning of events that unfolded all those centuries ago. If I hadn't have thrown myself into research and writing a string of books who knows what might have happened. Perhaps I would have lost my mind.'

Perhaps you did lose your mind. Suzanne thought to herself. 'Writing must have proved a suitable distraction for you.' Suzanne managed.

'Thankfully yes, and it turned out that I was quite good at it, able to make a comfortable living. Anyway, most of that is beside the point. When I heard the rumour and gossip about Lance and Gracie at first I took no notice. I thought it was just idle chit chat for the housewives of the village to indulge in, but that was until Lance came to see me very early one morning. He turned up at my front door looking a real state, his hair was tangled, his clothes torn and soiled. I was just finishing my book on the history of local villages – the one you borrowed and was keen not to be distracted, but reluctantly, I let him in. At first Lance wouldn't tell me what happened, all he said was that he had heard I was a good source of knowledge on local history, and what could I tell him about the chapel out on the headland. But it wasn't long before I got the truth out of him, and then more importantly, this.'

Ed held the Brass up for her to see, a half satisfied smile crossed his lips. It looked different from when she had seen it the day before. The Brass was now bright and shiny, the fine lines etched on to its surface were now clearly legible. As she had thought previously, it portrayed a human figure, the full face now visible, even from a few feet away.

Already knowing the answer to the question she was about to pose Suzanne decided to ask it anyway. A confirmation would mean it was likely Ed had deliberately taken the Brass from her too. 'You stole it from him, didn't you?' she said softly, trying not to sound accusatory.

Her captor cocked his head as though listening to something in the distance. 'Hmm, perhaps 'stole' is too strong a word. Let's just say I borrowed it for a while. Besides I don't think you were entirely truthful when you said your uncle found the Brass in Cambridge. You found it here didn't you, when you came here as a child?'

Suzanne looked at floor. 'Yes, I found it in the village pond.'

'Ah ha! So that is where it ended up. I had my suspicions about Gracie you know. I returned home one day back in the early 1980's to hear the back door closing. I ran into the kitchen only to see what looked like her scarf disappearing over the back wall. A couple of days later when I went to retrieve the Brass from its secret place, it was gone. So you see, I was wronged too!'

There was something in tone of Ed's reply that angered Suzanne. She thought of the suffering caused to Lance and Margaret in the wake of the Brass going missing, and of course Lance's ultimate fate of insanity and death.

'How could you do that to them!' Suzanne said angrily 'Lance was driven mad because you had taken the Brass from him. It ruined his life, and Margaret's too.'

Ed held up his hands in a mock defensive way. 'I know, I know. Perhaps I did keep hold of it for too long, but when the Brass went missing under my watch, I assumed that Lance had somehow got it back. You have to realise Suzanne that there was a good reason why I took the Brass in the first place, I was waiting you see.'

'Waiting? What for?'

'For you to turn up.'

Suzanne shook her head in disbelief. She found the tiny hairs on her arms prickling again at Ed's revelation. She did not like the way Ed was keeping her in suspense. It reminded her too much of his writing style which made his books such page-turners. For a moment she wondered if Ed had played all this out in his mind countless times before. The thought made her shudder.

'Okay. You were waiting for me. I'm here now. What do you want.' Suzanne asked, feigning bravery.

The corners of Ed's thin lips twitched into a smile 'Indeed! But I think you must know what I need you to do. We shall go through the Portal, and together we can set right what the wrong doings of the past.'

Suzanne felt a fresh wave of panic. How could this mad man expect her to do anything in her current state? A nauseous feeling washed over her and she feared she may faint.

'First, we must tend to your injuries. Remember when I said you didn't need the services of the hospital? Come.' He beckoned with his long crooked finger.

Mustering her remaining energy, Suzanne took as big -a-steps as the shackles would allow, and shuffled to where Ed was standing. He took her right hand and placed it against cold stone of the chapel's central column, and in her left placed the Brass. Muttering a few words in what sounded like Latin he turned his back towards her. Before Suzanne could gather what was happening she felt the strange sensation under her feet. Instinctively she tried to jump away but it wasn't long before the surge of water that was coming from a fissure in the ground was splashing around her swollen cut ankles. The relief was instant, the shackles sprang open and fell away. *Now is your chance!* Suzanne turned her head to judge the distance from the column to the door. She could make it if Ed remained turned away.

'Take some of the water and put it to the wound on your forehead.' Ed encouraged. Suzanne stooped down, she was still clutching the Brass but caught some of the water in her other hand. She poured a little onto her head, it felt good. With each application of the water, the pain was gradually fading until it was nothing more than a background headache. *Just a couple more applications and then she would make a run for it.* She was about to scoop water for the fourth time when Ed leaned forward and snatched the Brass from her hand.

'That's enough!' Ed ordered. 'You are strong again, and now the time has come.' He grabbed her firmly by the wrists 'We shall go now. I have been waiting too long to put right my misdeeds all those years ago. Blanche should have lived to fulfil her destiny, and now with your help we can change that.'

Even as he spoke the last few words, Suzanne could feel herself slipping under. She was helpless to the spell of this enchanted place, the calm blackness was once more embracing, inviting her to succumb to its peaceful realm. Once Ed's voice had faded completely for a brief moment she felt safe, cushioned between the present and past, in a place free of the laws of the physical world. Suzanne relished this emptiness until it started to fill again, the whisper of voices belonging to the long dead guided her until she reached her destination.

CHAPTER 31

1325

Tears of anger and humiliation welled in Philippa's eyes as she ran down the frozen dirt path that led her back to Martravers Manor. The cold air she gasped felt raw in her throat but she didn't care. What did it matter now anyway? Thomas was probably warm in his bed, romancing with another. She had seen them through the window of the Great Hall at Kingston, dancing closely, stealing kisses when they thought no-one was looking. But *she* had been looking, she had seen all she needed to see.

'Damn him!' Philippa cried out into the cold Christmas night. She was about to take the path which led to the lodge house, when she thought better of it. *I cannot face my father tonight.* Instead, she did an about turn and headed towards the woods. If she entered the curtilage from that direction, she could get to the stables without being seen. 'Damn Thomas Beaufort! Damn the day we met as children, for I loved him even then!' she cursed breathlessly.

Through teary eyes, Philippa picked her way through the trees, wiping her face with the back of her hand. At first, she did not hear the still calm voice whispering her name as she drew close to the Mayflower tree, but as she suddenly became aware of a soft light around her, Philippa stopped and raised her head. A man was standing just a few feet ahead of her, holding a lantern in one hand.

Philippa froze. 'Who are you?'

The man opened out his arms in a warm greeting. 'A man of God and a messenger.' He answered calmly.

Philippa could not help but notice that his clothing seemed unusual. Draped around his shoulders was a clean white sheepskin and underneath was a woolen tunic which had been bound to his legs by a strange pair of leather boots. Something about his presence settled her, although she could not fathom what it was.

'Kind Sir, you must forgive me but it is late and I need to get back to my manor.' She raised a weak smile as she passed him by on the track.

'Lady Philippa, are you not interested in the message I have for you?'

The sound of her own name on the stranger's lips rang out so clearly into the night that she could only stop and turn to face him. 'How do you know me Sir?' She enquired.

'I know of you by a mutual friend.'

Philippa could not help but notice there was a hint of sadness in his voice.

'A friend who has sadly passed from this life into the next.' He continued.

Philippa's heart started to race. Somehow, she knew who he was talking about.

'You have come to bring me sad news of Blanche's death?'

The man nodded and sighed deeply. 'We tried everything to save her, but her injuries were bad. Too much of her life's blood had spilled away.'

'But what happened? How did she get the injuries in the first place?' Philippa was indignant, once more she could feel the tears welling in her eyes and brimming over her soft lashes. 'You must take me to her, her grave, I need to see it!'

The man set the lantern down on the ground and once more reached out his arms in an embrace. Without questioning, Philippa fell into them and sobbed loudly. The man touched her head as if in blessing. 'Philippa, Blanche has been buried many miles from here but she is at peace, you must be assured of this!' The man smiled in apologetic reassurance, his wispy grey beard twinkled in the moonlight like stardust.

'Was it the will of God that she died, or was she killed?' Philippa managed between sobs.

The man was silent for a moment. 'It was through the actions of another, although this person did not intend her death. Listen – that is not important now, what is important is the message I have for you.'

Philippa wiped her face and tried to gather herself. 'A message? She asked, puzzled.

The man nodded solemnly. 'Before Blanche took her last breath, she asked me to come and find you. She told me you are to remember the holy spring at the chapel on the headland. She had a vision that the people of this village will need its healing waters. Perhaps not this Christmastide, or the next, or next ten for that matter, but there will come a time where the people will need the precious water as a matter of life and death, and you, Philippa, should be custodian of it.'

Philippa felt both confused and awestruck by the prophecy. 'But, how can I be? Fr. Eldrith has control over the chapel and healing well.'

The man shook his head. 'You are soon to take up a position of great influence through marriage. Although I feel you do not wish the union to proceed, it is through this that you will be able to fulfil the prophecy and save a great many from your village.'

'You mean my marriage to Lord Carringstone? I cannot bear him to be my husband, oh please say that is not the way! I was planning to run away tonight, to find Thomas and elope with him. I had it in mind to marry my true love in secret, and then Father would have to honour our pledge to one another and...'

The man raised his hand in a gesture to calm Philippa. 'You need not fear Lord Carringstone. I predict the union will not last long. The man suffers with his lungs and has episodes of breathlessness, although he will not admit this weakness to anyone.'

Philippa swallowed hard. Who was this man who seemed to know so much? 'If you know all this, then can you tell me, will there be children by my marriage?' She asked, testing the stranger's ability to know the future.

The man shook his head. 'There will be no children. But remember your calling, your true children are the people of this village, they will turn to you at their moment of need and Blanche has bestowed every confidence in your abilities.' The man stooped to pick up his lantern. 'I must leave now, Lady Philippa. But I hope this meeting has left you in no doubt as how to proceed. *Behealdan.*' He whispered and pointed to the ground at his feet. 'I will leave you with a precious gift, it will help you at times of need. Farewell now and go back to your house and family.' The man clasped Philippa's hands tightly.

'Please, before you go, you must tell me your name!' Philippa pleaded in desperation. It was already too late. Where only a moment ago she had felt the warm and comforting grip of the stranger's hands around her own, now all she could feel was the bitterly cold frosty air. Philippa looked around in a state of disbelief; it seemed all that remained of the mysterious bearded man was the bare skeleton of the Mayflower tree. Philippa stared straight ahead, as if to make the man reappear by her own will. *Behealdan!* The old fashioned word echoed in her mind as her eyes came to rest upon the spot where the man had pointed. It was then she noticed something on the ground resting by the tree. Kneeling down to get a closer look, Philippa gasped. An icy breeze had raced through the woods and the sack-cloth wrapped package flapped open, leaving the moonlight to reflect upon the Brass image inlaid on the front of a book. As Philippa brought the book closer she could see a strange likeness between the inlaid Brass and the spectre she had just witnessed. It wasn't just the strange apparel, but visible in the lines on its face and delicate elongated fingers. Reading aloud from the front cover she spoke the title '*Ealdhelm*'. The name, spoken in Old English resounded off the naked trees as it once had long ago, until it was absorbed in the stillness of the fourteenth century night.

CHAPTER 32

In state of wonderment Philippa had carried on through the woods and was relieved when she reached the stable yard. Above her head a million stars glittered down from the pitch black sky. Trying hard not to wake the stable boys, Philippa pulled down the latch that held the barn doors together. She winced as they creaked on their hinges and stepped onto the straw-carpet, the pungent smell of the horses clung to the insides of her nostrils. This was a world away from her comfortable bed chamber, but she couldn't go back just yet. She needed time to think, to make sense of what had just happened. Philippa's eyes darted from left to right; she was desperately trying to make sense of the gloomy shapes that surrounded her. Once her eyes had adjusted, she quietly padded towards a vacant corner of the barn with the book tucked under her left arm and was just about to settle when she heard the rustle of straw under some other's feet, shortly followed by a whisper.

'Lady, what are you doing here at this hour? Are you all right?'

Philippa spun round in the direction of the voice. It was Roger. 'Hush Roger! I don't want to wake everyone.' Philippa whispered breathlessly.

'Everyone? There's only Edwy and myself here tonight, the others I fear are still at the Tavern and they are probably staying there for the night now.' Roger bit his lip, immediately realising he could be getting his peers into trouble.

Philippa craned her neck to see the sleeping Edwy. 'My brother's over there' Roger pointed to a dark heap in the far corner. 'He sleeps like a hedgehog in the winter time, he will not hear us.'

Roger took the blanket from his shoulders and spread it out on the straw. 'Here Lady, do have some rest and get your breath back before you return to the house.'

Philippa set herself down onto the warm blanket, grateful for Roger's kindness.

'I'm not returning to the house, not tonight anyway.'

Roger took a step back, shocked at the proposition. 'But my lady, with respect you cannot stay here. It is no place for you on such a cold night.' He hesitated before continuing. 'The search party are still out looking for you, and besides, I will have your father to answer to in the morning when he finds I have been harbouring you here.'

'Have no fear Roger. He will not find out I have been here. I will leave before dawn and make my return. But for now I am more certain than ever that I need some time to sit and think without everyone asking about my plight or scolding me for causing embarrassment.'

A shaft of frosty moonlight had filtered through a gap in the barn wall and illuminated Philippa's face. Roger could now see that her eyes were wide with fright.

'What has happened lady?' He asked softly.

'You wouldn't believe me if I told you. I'm not entirely sure I believe myself.'

Roger lowered his eyes and waited humbly for her to speak.

'I saw a ghost, out there in the woods.' Philippa shuddered, and Roger turned to look over his shoulder as Edwy stirred in his sleep. When the boy was settled again, Philippa drew in a breath and swallowed. 'It was the ghost of a man. A man who professes to know about Blanche.'

'Blanche?' Roger repeated her name. It had been so long since he had spoken it out loud, although she remained in his thoughts daily. 'What does he know of Blanche?'

Philippa lowered her eyes, she did not want to deliver the sad news to Roger. She knew he had been fond of Blanche.

'Please lady, do not tell me the worst. I will not hear it or believe it!' Roger whispered earnestly. 'Blanche is still alive! She comes to me in my dreams, and I know she is well.'

Shaking her head, Philippa put a hand on the stable boy's shoulder. 'That is not what the ghost told me.' She paused to see if Roger was comprehending, or even believing what she was telling him. She could tell by his eyes that he was afraid. In the gloom of the barn his stark white face suddenly looked much younger than his years. 'The strange thing is, although he told me Blanche was dead, I'm sure I have seen her since her disappearance.'

Roger looked up, suddenly hopeful.

'You've *actually* seen her?'

'Yes. The first time I wasn't sure. It was at St. Peter's fair and I had been choosing some cloth with Gwen when all of a sudden I had a strange sensation, it was like the wind was blowing around my ears and my eyes became blurred. I blinked a couple of times and then she was there standing right in front of me!'

Roger's eyes were wide with fright. 'Did she speak to you?'

Philippa thought for a moment, trying to cast her mind back to the summer. 'She was trying to speak, her mouth was opening but no words came from it. Not that I could hear anyway. I didn't think too much of it as it was a warm day and I fancied the heat had confused my thoughts, but when I saw her a second time around the feast of Michaelmas standing outside the door of St. Alban's chapel, I was sure my eyes weren't playing tricks.'

Roger smiled 'You see, I told you she is fine! The ghost you saw is wrong. She has to be alive.'

Philippa put a finger to her lips in an attempt to hush Roger. She did not want Edwy waking. 'What I am starting to realise is that what I saw wasn't actually Blanche, but an apparition. I fear, Roger, that she is indeed dead, as the ghost, *Ealdhelm* told me.

Roger looked confused. 'Ealdhelm - *Aldhelm*? Are you certain, Lady?'

'I believe this man-ghost could have been St. Aldhelm himself yes, and like Blanche, Aldhelm disappeared before my very eyes! If that is not a spectre then I don't know what is.' Philippa paused for a moment, and then said sympathetically

'You were close to Blanche weren't you?'

Roger raised a sad smile. 'We were friends, nothing else. She was special. She made me flower balms for my sore skin. I know that my cure is her doing.'

Philippa frowned. 'The cure you received up at St. Alban's chapel? But that was the work of the Saint himself, it is now widely acknowledged, and you being the first to receive a cure makes you specially blessed.'

'I know that's what the church says.' Roger said sulkily. 'But I know what happened there that morning. I was praying for Blanche's wellbeing when the waters first appeared. She must have been there, listening to me.'

Philippa nodded. Under any other circumstances she would have dismissed Roger's account as fanciful, wishful thinking, but after what she had seen tonight she had reason to believe the stable boy.

'At least Aldhelm told me her body is now resting peacefully.'

Roger moved a piece of straw around in the dust with his foot. 'So she is dead. If only I could find out who was responsible, I would break their bones!'

Philippa contemplated telling Roger about Fr. Eldrith and her suspicions, but she held back. It would only serve to infuriate the boy, and right now what they both needed was some rest.

Wrapping the cloak around her body, she settled down on to the blanket that Roger had spread out for her.

'We will make sure all is put to right, mark my words. But now, we need to rest. Thank you for showing me such kindness, and I trust we can keep the conversation between ourselves?'

'Yes of course lady, I am your servant, I will not utter a word.' Roger confirmed.

'Good. Now go back to sleep and rest assured that I will be gone from here very early in the morning, certainly before my father can rest any blame on your shoulders.'

Roger's expression lifted and he bowed his head towards Philippa before settling back down onto his pallet. 'Good night my lady, and Happy Christmas.'

* * *

Conscious that she had to be up before dawn, Philippa lay awake for many hours before eventually drifting into a fitful sleep. Feeling tired and emotionally wrought, she left the barn just as the promise of morning could be seen over in the eastern sky. As she headed towards the grand entrance of the manor, nerves leapt in her stomach. She was not looking forward to explaining her disappearance to her father. Knowing him as she did Philippa, predicted she was in for a severe berating and most likely removal of some freedoms she enjoyed. Taking a deep breath, she rapped on the door of the manor.

CHAPTER 33

2009

The transition this time was seamless; as if waking from a long sleep to the sound of an alarm, Suzanne opened her eyes to find the thin bespectacled man leaning over her, his face lined with agitation. For a few seconds she could not understand who he was or what he was saying to her, but then all too quickly the horror of her predicament returned. She had only just left the impending wrath of Harold Martravers to be greeted by that of another angry man. She became aware that Ed was speaking to her again.

'What happened, where and when were you?'

Suzanne bolted up from her position on the chapel floor. Her sudden movement caught Ed off guard and he quickly moved to snap the ankle shackles back in place.

She noticed that Ed looked pleased with himself, he had the expression of boy who had captured a small animal, taunting it for his own enjoyment.

'You will stay here Suzanne, there is no point in trying to escape. Now then, as you are clearly not going anywhere for the time being, you can tell me what just happened.' His satisfied grin was replaced by a look of curiosity.

'I saw her again.'

'Who, who did you see? Tell me what happened. Tell me everything.' Ed barked impatiently.

'Philippa Martravers. It was night time, Christmas. She was making her way through the woods when she saw the ghost of a man.' Suzanne rubbed her ankles, the shackles were beginning to cut into her flesh again, making new wounds where the previous ones had just healed.

'Go on' Ed urged. 'What happened?'

Suzanne did not reply straight away. She felt the same protective instinct that her ancestor had all those years before, the message that ghost-man had given to Philippa was sacrosanct and had to remain so. She had been privileged to witness it.

‘Philippa was engaged to be married and was not happy with her suitor, the ghost-man was comforting her, telling her everything would be okay.’

‘I see, I see.’ Ed nodded to himself. ‘This sounds about right. Can you recall what the man looked like? Was he carrying anything – a book perhaps?’

Suzanne thought for a moment. She felt she could share some of the details with Ed, but not everything.

‘Yes, his clothing was odd, even for the medieval period. I thought he was dressed like a farm worker of some kind – a shepherd maybe.’

‘And did he have anything in his possession?’

Suzanne tried to picture the image in her mind once more. ‘A lantern, that was all.’

‘Just the lantern then, no book? In that case he must have already returned it to the Martraver’s library by the time Philippa saw her.’ Ed looked deep in thought.

Suzanne shrugged glumly. She wondered what time it was, and exactly how long Ed intended to keep her captive in the uncomfortable shackles. She looked at her wristwatch only to see its face was smashed, it read ten past midnight, the time when she had fallen in the cellar.

‘Don’t worry about the present time Suzanne, for you will find the sometimes it stands still, other times it is quicker. Either way there is nothing you can do about it. You may be surprised to know how long you were out for then, when you journeyed into the old world and back again?’

Suzanne didn’t answer. Although she guessed that she had been ‘out’ for at least two or three hours.

‘Four minutes.’ Ed eyed her for her reaction. ‘Although I have to say it seemed like a long time for me, especially as I was hoping to be accompanying you on your journey. Anyway, you are back now and we must try again.’

Suzanne sighed. ‘Try again?’ She said, exasperated. ‘I’ve done what you have asked, I’ve tried my best. How do you know that this will work? Perhaps the Portal only works for one person at a time?’

Ed gave her a stern look. ‘As I told you we shall not be leaving here until I have completed what needs to be done. Now get up from the floor and come this way.’

Suzanne struggled to get up. Her head was swimming with visions, thoughts and ideas. What was happening was too much to take in, the abduction, the miraculous healing of her wounds. She found herself craving the mundane. Melanie had suggested that she needed a week away to put things into perspective, but this was madness. Suzanne suddenly found that she didn’t care about the ‘crisis’ she faced at work, at least that was a real world problem that existed in the 21st century, a time she understood and belonged to. That could all be sorted out, even if she did end up losing her job. What was happening now though was a whole different game, she was being asked to change the course of history by a manipulative madman. There was no guarantee that even if she could give him what he wanted, he would stop there. All of a sudden she felt the need for answers, surely she had a right to know why the events that took place 700 years ago were so important to him?

'I will try again.' Suzanne offered. 'But I think this can only work if I understand what you are trying to achieve from this. At least explain to me *why* you need my help. You say you want to correct your own misdeeds, yet you want *me* to play a part in this? Perhaps if I understand my role in your plan, then I can play it better?'

Ed stared into the middle distance for a moment, a flickering candle made odd shapes in shadow on the chapel wall behind where he was standing. Suzanne could tell he was calculating, weighing up the benefits of telling her more. After a short while he spoke.

'Okay. I suppose you might have a point, I shall explain, but first I have a question for you. Do you know what my last project in this life was, Suzanne?'

'Project?' What was he going on about now and why was he talking in the past tense? Suzanne felt dizzy and confused. Fear had all but left her now, all she wanted to do was simply drop to the floor of the chapel and close her eyes.

'Yes, my last literary project. It's a book about Blanche. *Or St. Blanche* to use her deserved title. I was going to send it to the publishers by the end of this year by way of repentance. You see I realise now in this life time what she was. She was no witch as I thought back then, quite the contrary - she was actually a saint! That was the reason for the healing waters appearing upon her death and the reason why I have been suffering of her wrath for centuries. I took her life away from her you see, I caused her to stumble and she had a terrible blow to the head.'

Suzanne thought it odd that someone who was supposed to be a saint could inflict such punishment, but she didn't want to challenge Ed. He had all but confirmed his belief that he was a re-incarnation of Fr. Eldrith, and now, he looked as though he was capable of doing something dangerous, pacing again, like a frenzied wild animal.

'You have no idea what it is like Suzanne. You come here for a few days and you think you know the story, but you are wrong. Do you know what it feels like to die and to be reborn again, to live over and over carrying the same burden of guilt and grief each time? To believe there is no escape from this cycle of torment? First a misguided priest, then a farmer, now an author.'

'Farmer?' Suzanne queried, her eyes wide in surprise.

'Yes. Remember that book I lent you about the farmhouse fire?'

Suzanne swallowed, the lump in her throat the size of an apple as she realised who Ed was talking about.

'Amos Taylor?'

Ed nodded, staring directly at her, and then without warning changed the subject. 'You are a history scholar Suzanne. Tell me, did you study the cult of saints and pilgrimages to holy wells as part of your course?'

Suzanne searched her memory. She still needed to play along, keep him level until someone realised she was missing. 'Yes. The one that sticks in my mind is the story of St.Winifride, in Holywell.'

'Very good.' Ed smiled. Can you recall what happened in that story?'

'Suzanne wracked her tired brain once more 'Wasn't she slayed by her suitor – beheaded by him?'

'Exactly, and where her head fell, a gush of healing water rose.' Ed suddenly laughed to himself. 'It seems so obvious now, but at the time it suited me to deny the true identity of Blanche, and I have paid for it ever since. Now I have a chance to make amends, at long last.'

'Forgive me for asking this, but I'm still not sure exactly what you want me to do? I mean I don't think I'm capable of changing what happened to Blanche. When I go back through the Portal, I only witness past events, no one can see or hear me.'

Ed stared at her for a moment. 'It takes practice, but I believe if we can get back to the right point in time, that afternoon in late June 1325, then it will come naturally to you.'

Suzanne cast her mind back to the first time she had travelled through the Portal. Perhaps Ed was right, she had been able to open the chapel door, prompting Blanche to attempt her escape. There was also the occasion where she *had* been seen by Philippa, at St Peter's fair and she had been desperately trying to tell Philippa about the plight of Blanche. As she had mulled over with Margaret, this seemed like the true purpose of the Portal, the people connected with it would experience dreams and visions of what had been, but it was only at the chapel that you could influence and play a part in these past events. How was she to save Blanche though? Surely it was up to Fr. Eldrith not to take her captive in the first place? Perhaps that is what would happen, she would just be a conduit, to get Ed back to the point in time when Blanche had mysteriously disappeared. Having made as much sense as she could out of the situation, Suzanne nodded in consent. 'I'll agree to try one more time, then you must let me go.'

Ed's eyes narrowed. Surprisingly to Suzanne, words of agreement formed on his lips. 'All right, I agree. If it doesn't work this time then you are free to leave.'

The assurance should have made her feel better but it didn't. Ed did not strike her as the kind of man that could be bargained with. What had happened when she refused to let him have the Brass for supposed valuation? He had simply taken it.

Suzanne made her slow approach to the centre of the chapel, and as she did so, out of nowhere an icy wind blew the door open and instantly brought the temperature down by a few degrees. Ed smiled. 'This is it. The past is reaching out to us.' He announced, a terrible smile crossed his face. Trembling, Suzanne proceeded to touch the stone. Ed hovered over her, his gnarled fingers resting to cover her own. Only seconds seem to pass before she was once more feeling the rush of time and space around her.

CHAPTER 34

Christmastide, January 1326

The midwinter's daybreak came late and the skies around Martravers Manor were still gloomy as Philippa ventured out into the cold and damp morning. Frozen specks of rain settled on her cheeks and she wrapped her thick lambswool cloak around her for protection. Edwy had been instructed to prepare the horses for the morning ride, yet he and the horses were no-where to be seen.

Tutting to herself, Philippa contemplated waiting in the entrance hall until her mount was ready but something made her stop in her tracks. It was the sound of twigs snapping underfoot. Turning her back sharply on the door of her family home she stared in the direction of the noise and was surprised to see a tall hooded figure had emerged from the lodge house, some distance away. Philippa squinted, trying to pick out the features that were partially hidden by the hood.

What was Fr. Eldrith doing here at this hour? Her thoughts were quickly answered as he approached with stealth.

'Ah, Lady Philippa! A good morning to you on this eve of the Epiphany.'

Philippa scowled. The news that Fr. Eldrith would be conducting her marriage ceremony had angered her, although she had done her best to contain the displeasure given that she was already in a great deal of trouble for running away on that Christmas night.

'My Father is not here. He has been away for the past three nights on business at Winchester.'

The priest did not look discouraged. 'I don't think that will be too much of a problem given that it is you I am here to see.' He beamed falsely.

Philippa's heart suddenly leapt into her throat as she remembered something. Gwen would soon be here! Fr. Eldrith must not see the book. She was waiting for the correct moment, and this wasn't it. Thinking quickly, Philippa opened the heavy oak door and showed the priest in.

'William, could you bring some wine while I find a suitable place for Fr. Eldrith and myself to meet.' Turning to the priest Philippa said 'Excuse me, please take a seat while I see where my servant has got to'. Philippa turned and was just about to step over the door threshold when just at that moment Gwen appeared, hair ruffled, her cheeks crimson. 'I'm sorry I'm late my lady'. She blurted breathlessly clearly not seeing Fr. Eldrith in the entrance hall. Philippa tried to hush her maid.

'Gwen. Its all right. Let us go round to the stable yard. I fear there is something wrong with my mount, she does not seem herself of late.' Philippa tried to steer Gwen away from the door way.

'No, there is nothing wrong with your mount, she is saddled and ready. I asked Edwy to see to that. No the delay is on my part. When I got to the library I found it was locked, I need to get the keys from William. I'm sorry I should have got the book last night as you asked me, but I forgot to do it. I shall get it now for you and there will be no more delays I promise!'

Philippa detected movement behind her. 'If you don't mind me asking lady,' came Fr. Eldrith's voice, 'Which book is your servant speaking of?'

Philippa's heart sunk for she knew at that moment that the priest had heard too much. She had to come up with a plausible answer to throw him off her trail.

Turning her back on the surprised Gwen she explained; 'Our family prayer book. It is my wish to go to St. Albans chapel and spend some time alone in prayer and contemplation before the day of my wedding.'

The priest nodded approvingly. 'In that case, why don't we hold our little meeting in the library? I can offer you some suggestions on suitable meditations and prayers.'

Philippa stared, mouth agape. Although her expression was full of protest she could not find any reasonable excuse to deny him.

* * *

Even with its elegant large windows, the library was gloomy due to the lack of daylight. This suited Philippa well; the darker it was in the library, the less chance there was of the book being discovered. Gwen who was feeling decidedly guilty for blowing her lady's cover was flitting around lighting candles.

'That's enough Gwen.' Philippa instructed waving her hands in dismissal. The sheepish serving girl curtsied and left her lady and the priest alone in the library.

Philippa was the first to speak. 'What is it you came to see me about Father? As you know I am extremely busy at the moment with my wedding preparations.'

Although she tried to hide it, her voice betrayed the contempt she had for the man sitting opposite to her, and it did not go unnoticed.

'Of that I am well aware'. Fr. Eldrith said brusquely. 'The reason for my coming is two-fold; firstly to make sure you are spiritually ready for what you are about to undertake. I was here the night you disappeared and caused great shame and embarrassment to your father and Lord Robert. I trust there will be no repeat of such hasty actions before the day?'

Philippa could feel the anger rising in her body. The priest was chastising her like a misbehaving child. She sucked air in through her teeth in an attempt to calm her fury and quell words of ill-meaning before they formed on her lips. 'Of course I am ready. Since Christmas I have spent many hours in prayer and contemplation. I am truly sorry for what I did and you can rest assured that I will not be running away again.'

The priest sank back into his chair and sipped at the spiced wine that Gwen had poured. 'Good. That has settled that matter then.' Philippa noticed Fr. Eldrith's small crafty eyes were searching about the room, distracted. She said nothing and waited for him to speak.

'There is one other matter.' He said eventually. Leaning forward and lowering his voice to a whisper. 'Have you seen anything of the Myddelton girl since her disappearance?'

'No Father.' Philippa answered sounding genuinely surprised. 'I have not seen Blanche since last summer, just before St Peter's Fair. Why do you ask?'

The priest tapped on the side of his goblet with long crooked fingers, Philippa thought he looked nervous. 'I couldn't help but notice that the book she was carrying when she disappeared off along the Priest's Way has been returned to your library. I'm curious as to how it got back here, if she herself did not return it.'

Philippa's heart had started to race. The priest had not been in the library since she returned the book. How could he have seen it? 'You must be mistaken, Father. I have not seen the book myself, and if Blanche had returned it, surely I would have known?'

Fr. Eldrith rose to his feet. 'I am not mistaken, I can prove it to you. Come here.'

To Philippa's horror, the priest headed towards the shelf near the oriel window, but then she breathed a small sigh of relief when Fr. Eldrith did not stoop down to the lowest shelf and retrieve the book she had put there herself a week ago, but instead, reached across and pulled another volume down.

'There. See, it is the same book, only the inlaid Brass has vanished from the front. I remember seeing it with my own eyes, it was tucked under Blanche Myddelton's arm as she headed through the village towards the Priest's Way.'

Smiling to herself, she could see that he had made a simple mistake. Fr. Eldrith had not realised that Aldhelm had not only returned the first book, but left her a second copy that night she had run away.

'Ah. No, Blanche did not return the book herself.' She assured him. 'I remember now, back at the time of Michaelmas, one of the common folk from the village found it in the woods near the Mayflower tree. I was pleased to see it returned to our library, but sad that it was not Blanche herself that had returned it.'

Philippa's false words seem to settle the priest's mind. A look of relief was apparent on his thin lined face. 'It is indeed a great sadness that she has not returned.' Fr. Eldrith paused, swishing the last of his drink around the goblet. 'I must be leaving. I have the sick of the parish to attend to.'

Philippa rose from her seat, relieved that the meeting was drawing to a close. Gwen was waiting patiently to receive them on the other side of the library door.

'Gwen, show Fr. Eldrith out will you? He has a busy morning ahead of him.

Philippa and the priest exchanged a glance before he turned sharply on his heal and disappeared down the corridor, the sound of his flapping cloak growing increasingly distant as Philippa shut the library door behind her and sank to the floor in relief.

CHAPTER 35

2009

'That was better, an improvement, on the last time anyway.' Suzanne could hear Ed's voice resounding enthusiastically off the chapel's walls. Rubbing grit out of her eye, she pulled herself up onto a nearby pew. Suzanne wondered why it was that Ed seemed so bright and energetic while she felt like death itself? It was like he was draining the energy from her. Putting her head into her hands, she massaged her aching skull. Perhaps it was just extreme tiredness she was experiencing.

'Come, let us try again. We are getting closer.' Ed paced back and forth impatiently.

'You promised that would be enough, no more!'

'Yes I did say that but we are so close now, I can't give up not when we are so near! I was there Suzanne, talking with Philippa in the Martraver's Library, just as it happened nearly seven hundred years ago. I remember it all so clearly now!' Ed rubbed his hands together excitedly. The transformation in him was significant, he reminded Suzanne of a child at Christmas who had just been shown a pile of gifts. Reluctantly, Suzanne eased herself up from the pew.

'Just give me a minute, please.' Suzanne asked, her voice nothing more than a muffled whimper.

'That's it.' Ed said encouragingly. 'Just focus on that night, the night before the fair, here at this same chapel. Think about the book, how beautiful it was, the brightly coloured lettering and illustrations. Don't think about Philippa. Remember, it's Blanche that is important. We need to save Blanche!'

Suzanne closed her eyes. She found Ed's voice strangely hypnotic, almost soothing. Yes, she wanted to think about that night before the fair, she wanted to see

Blanche again, to try and help her. For at this moment, that now seemed the reality, not her 21st century life. She was no longer aware of her hand clutching the Brass as she touched the stone, and nor did she notice it disappearing from her grip as she fell. For a moment Suzanne thought that the Portal hadn't worked. She dreaded the sound of Ed's exasperated voice as she slowly opened her eyes, instead it came as a shock to see Fr. Eldrith leaning with his hands resting on the altar, a large book spread open in front of him. Candle light flickered as he looked directly at her.

'I was educated in Poiters. French is my first language, and Latin is the language I learned as a scholar. English is secondary to me but in this form it is almost illegible. How is it Blanche, that you are able to understand this text?'

The Portal had worked. Suzanne was back at the precise point where Ed had wanted her to be – the night when he had killed Blanche. Suzanne found herself breathing an odd sigh of relief, scanning her eyes round the small enclosed space looking for Blanche. To Suzanne's surprise, Blanche was nowhere to be seen. Her attention was drawn back to Fr. Eldrith, his fingers tapping impatiently upon the altar stone.

'Do not think about leaving until we have finished our conversation. It seems to me you know more about this book than you are letting on.' As he spoke he held the book out in front of him, examining its delicate binding. Suzanne's heart leapt when she saw what adorned the front cover, the tarnished Brass image of St. Aldhelm. It suddenly struck her why the book was important; it had nothing to do with what was written within it, it was simply a distraction, a false trail. *Where had Blanche got to?*

'Come now. Enough replaying what has been.' The priest was speaking again. 'Living out many lives throughout the centuries caused me nothing but torment. Both my soul and yours need to rest peacefully following this life. That is, after all, why I have brought you here Suzanne, or to use your present day name, *Blanche.*'

Suzanne swayed a little. Looking down she could see she was wearing a russet wool tunic fastened round her waist with a narrow belt. The fabric felt decidedly scratchy against her wrists. Her twenty-first century clothes and the restraints that Ed had bound her with had vanished. It was then she realised what was happening; she was no longer witnessing the past, she had become part of it. Suzanne swallowed nervously. 'How could this be?' She uttered in disbelief. 'I'm descended from the Martravers family, surely – my connection is with Philippa, how can I be Blanche?' Her voice sounded different, like it was someone else who was speaking. Fr. Eldrith grinned, the cunning smile continued to play on his lips as he replied. 'Because my dear girl, *you are* Blanche!'

'But *Philippa* is my ancestor.' Suzanne was aware of the hopeless protesting in her voice as she suddenly realised she had been purposely led down this path like a lamb to the slaughter, and now this terrible realisation struck her like a tonne weight. Of course Ed had known exactly what was going on, it had been convenient for him that her ancestral connection was with Philippa rather than Blanche.

The priest had stooped behind the altar stone, out of view. 'Co-incidences do happen you know' His voice floated across the chapel. 'I couldn't quite believe it myself. Centuries of searching and then one day, Blanche turns up as the girl next door! I knew who you were as soon as I saw you walking up the front path, but I had to be certain.'

'It was you who planted the scarecrow in Melanie's yard, to get me outside?'

Fr. Eldrith gave a small chuckle as though the matter was trivial. 'Oh yes, and as soon as I saw the fear in your eyes that confirmed it. That look is imprinted on my psyche. One thing you probably didn't find out from your family research is that Suzanne is directly descended from Philippa's older brother, Hugh, rather than Philippa herself, but nevertheless, it is still a fantastic co-incidence.'

It took a few seconds to digest the information. Suzanne wanted to ask what would happen next in this unpredictable turn of events, but she decided she had already given this man too much power, she had co-operated with his game for too long. Nervously she looked towards the chapel door; it was firmly closed. She could still make a run for it, if she could find Philippa or Roger, either one of them would help. Her thoughts of escaping were interrupted as the thin hooded shape straightened from behind the altar. In two alarmingly quick strides he had approached, grabbing both her arms and forcing them behind her back. Suzanne yelped in pain as she felt her wrists being bound tighter than was necessary.

'I thought you wanted to protect Blanche! Wasn't that your whole reason for this madness?' She blurted helplessly.

'Yes, and that is precisely what I am doing. Precious items need to be stored safely, where they can come to no harm.'

'What?' Suzanne cried. 'What do you mean by that?' It was then that the priest quickly tied a rough piece of sackcloth around her mouth, fastening it tightly at the back of her head. Bound and now gagged, she was being led towards the altar, her heart pounding wildly. As soon as she saw the open strong chest a feeling of horror came over her.

'Get inside.' Fr. Eldrith hissed. Suzanne did not move. 'Get in now or face the penalty for disobeying your protector. I am ill-practiced at removing tongues, but if it is necessary to keep you safe, then that is what I will do.'

Suzanne now noticed that the priest was waving a strange metal implement in one hand. A shiver went up her spine as she realised there was no other option. Reluctantly, she climbed in and couched low into the box.

'Keep your head down.' The priest warned and only seconds later, the lid was slammed down and darkness engulfed her. She could hear Fr. Eldrith's muffled voice as the straps were fastened and the lock was turned.

'Do not fret Blanche, you shall not be in there for long. You will soon see that what I am doing is for the best.' Suzanne heard more rattling as another couple of straps were fastened around her makeshift prison. 'Now I must be leaving. I am going to Martraver's manor, I have an urgent task for their Blacksmith.' He paused for effect. 'There is this troublesome Brass depiction of a saint that keeps popping up throughout the centuries. I'm going to see that it is destroyed once and for all.' There was a throaty laugh from the priest as his footsteps faded away. Suzanne could hear the door of the chapel slamming shut.

Suzanne was already feeling uncomfortable, the wooden boards under her knees were raised in places and pressing awkwardly into her shins, and blood had rushed into her head. She tried lifting her head a little to alleviate some of the pressure, and to allow her mind enough capacity to think. The only consolation was that Fr. Eldrith had told her she wouldn't be in there for long, but then again, what did that really mean? She assumed that once he returned from the manor, she would be let out, but what would happen to her afterwards? The priest had already made a threat about removing her tongue, whether or not this was a hollow threat intended to scare her into submission, she did not know, or wish to find out. One thing was for sure, he had the tools on hand.

In a fit of panic and desperation, Suzanne pulled her wrists in opposite directions. She winced in pain as the cord that bound them cut into her skin; it was no good, the knots were holding fast. As she defaulted to her curled position once more, she thought of what would soon be taking place at the Martravers blacksmith forge. The Brass, her means of escape back into the 21st century would be melted down, destroyed. She would be trapped in the fourteenth century for the rest of her miserable life.

As the minutes turned into an hour, the blood that had pooled in her brain was somehow causing her thoughts to become tangled and confused, for a moment she wasn't there in the darkness, instead the sensation of the warm sunshine graced her as she reclined on the grassy banks of the village pond. A much younger version of her parents were close by, concern etched on their faces as they examined her damaged hand. The memory of the pain came back then, along with the taste of salty tears as they streamed down into her open mouth. The Brass lay next to her on the grass. She kicked it with a small sandaled foot in defiance and it flipped over and over, the murky waters beckoning its return. Her father caught it just in time. 'We'd better keep it, Suzy. We need to show the doctors what was stuck in your hand.' Suzanne's mind wandered from one poignant moment to another. Now it was Christmastime and she was in the woods with Philippa once more. In her mind's eye she picking up the book that Aldhelm had left, the same Brass highlighted in the frosty moonlight. But and even in her confusion something jarred in her thoughts, she became aware that the two images of the saint were in fact slightly different.

The word played on Suzanne's mind and stuck uncomfortably. Christmas of 1325, but wasn't it only June 1325? If they had changed history, then Aldhelm would not be visiting Philippa to tell her about Blanche's death, Aldhelm would not be leaving a second book in the woods outside Martravers Manor. Realising the truth, Suzanne felt her heart sink once more. She could only hope that somehow, Aldhelm would intervene now, and change the chain of events that were about to unfold.

Slam! The chapel door had shut, waking Suzanne from her dream like state. This could be her chance, she had to take it. With all the energy she could muster, she let out a muffled cry. To her dismay, there was no immediate answer, only the sound of footsteps approaching; Fr. Eldrith had returned.

* * *

At Martraver's Manor Philippa stirred; a warm ray of afternoon sunlight had come to rest on her face, gently waking her from her slumber. At first she did not know what day or time it was so strong was the dream she'd just experienced. She lay on her bed for a few minutes trying to recollect as much as possible. It had been the winter time, frost was thick on the ground and the tree branches were tearing at her clothes as she breathlessly paced through the woods beyond the manor. Blanche had been there too, running a few steps in front of her. Philippa had turned around to see what it was they were running from and to her horror saw the face of grey snarling wolf only paces behind them. Its teeth were pointed and ready for attack, its hot breath turning to puffs of steam in the cold air. Blanche had turned around, her eyes were wide with fright. 'Don't worry, Blanche.' Philippa had reassured. Then without warning as often happened in dreams; Philippa had found herself transported to another place; this time she was alone, in the relative safety of her library. It was then that Philippa remembered what Gwen had told her earlier that day. Blanche had not returned the book she has lent to her, in fact nobody knew where she was. It must have played on her mind as she slept.

Philippa sat up and blinked a few times; she was about to summon Gwen for a beaker of wine but thought better of it. If dreams served as warnings, then this one had been clear. Blanche was in danger. Following her instincts, Philippa grabbed her cloak from the coffer and made her way down to the stable yard. Roger had already saddled her horse in preparation for her ride to Langdon; the outing with her mother would have to wait. She left a message with Roger, mounted her horse and galloped off in the direction of the village.

CHAPTER 36

2009

At first he did not know why he had awoken; all he knew was that he had a decidedly uneasy feeling. Greg reached out for his bedside lamp and groped at it until he found the switch. His eyes squinted against the fierce illumination it gave, eventually focusing in on the digital alarm clock. It read 2:15am. He fell back down against his pillows and tried to recall what he had been dreaming about. Closing his eyes momentarily, a vision came to him. It was of a mound of earth, and a series of pale faces appearing, staring down at him. One by one they had each took a handful from the mound and cast it downward towards him. Greg shuddered. He had been dreaming about his own burial. He had been grappling with the soil around him, spitting it from his mouth and more handfuls had been thrown down. He reached once more towards the bedside table, this time for the bottle of mineral water and gulped almost desperately. *Just a nightmare. Go back to sleep.*

Greg tried to reassure himself that everything was okay but after about an hour of tossing and turning in bed, he decided to get up. Retrieving his laptop from the small lounge of his flat, he slid back under the covers. Habitually, he opened his email account. It had been a couple of days since he had gone in to do the usual task of clearing the spam and advertisements and responding to the odd social media request. Scrolling down, his eyes fixed on a familiar name in the address field. P.Doyle.

'Pete'. Greg said out loud, his voice cutting through the silence, making him realise how alone he felt. Putting the feelings to one side for a moment, Greg clicked open the email from his old friend. It had been sent only a few hours earlier.

Hi Greg,

I thought I'd send you this via your personal email than your work's email for obvious reasons. Just to let you know that your friend and colleague Suzanne has officially instructed me to represent her at disciplinary hearings, and there is a forthcoming hearing a week on Wednesday. I've been trying to contact Suzanne all day to inform her about the date for the hearing but all I'm getting is her voicemail. I've sent her a couple of emails too. I will try again tomorrow morning, but I'm conscious that the clock is ticking and I need to speak with her a.s.a.p. If you hear from her in the meantime, or know of another way to contact her please could you advise accordingly?

Hope you are keeping well Greg. We must go for that fabled pint we never seem to have to time for these days. Perhaps after my meeting with Suzanne?

Keep in touch mate,

Pete.

Greg read the email a second time before closing it down. There was something about the situation that didn't seem right. Why would Suzanne have her phone switched off when she would be expecting contact from Pete? If she had lost it somewhere then wouldn't she have checked her email account? She was staying there alone at Melanie's holiday cottage, who would know if something had happened to her? Greg had already decided that if he could not make contact with Suzanne in the morning, he would speak to Melanie. It was with these thoughts swimming around his tired mind that Greg eventually fell into a black, dreamless sleep.

CHAPTER 37

1325

She did not know how long she had been in the chest, but it seemed like over hour, maybe two. The scent of dust and long felled oak clung to her nostrils, stifling every breath. Fr. Eldrith had briefly returned a while ago but had left again, promising food and drink on his return. Suzanne felt like a trapped animal, her legs had gone completely numb and she wondered if they would ever regain their feeling again. Why was he doing this? Surely if he wanted to make amends for Blanche's death then this wasn't the way to go about it? Her thoughts were interrupted by the sound of a key turning in the lock, she hadn't even heard her captor approaching. The priest lifted the heavy lid and began to untie her gag

'Here, I have brought you some bread and ale.'

Suzanne hadn't realised how hungry she was until Fr. Eldrith pushed some of the bread into her mouth. She chewed eagerly. 'My legs are completely numb.' She explained in between mouthfuls. To her relief, the priest untied her wrists and offered his arm to help her to stand. As Suzanne rose on her wobbly legs, she noticed that the light in the chapel had faded slightly, she guessed it must be later on in the afternoon. She gulped down the ale, it tasted nothing like modern day beer, it was watery and smelled of rotting grass but her body ached for it.

'I suppose you want to know what plans I have for you?' Fr. Eldrith said after she had finished the foul tasting drink.

'Plans?' Suzanne exclaimed, suddenly worried that the ale might have contained poison. 'I thought your plans simply involved keeping Blanche alive and safe, out of the way of your wrath, whether that be intended or unintended.' The emotion in her voice was raw. 'I hardly think that keeping me in this chest for hours on end helps your plight.'

'My dear girl. I made sure there were breathing holes in the chest. I have brought you food and drink. I did not put you in any danger, quite the contrary in fact. We have now gone past the time where you had your accident and disappeared so I believe all will be well now!'

Suzanne suddenly felt hopeful. Perhaps Fr. Eldrith or his 21st century incarnation, Ed had achieved their objectives. As soon as he let her out of his clutches she could find Philippa and hopefully the second book and get back to her own time. 'So you can let me go now right? We have changed the course of history and Blanche is safe. That is exactly what you wanted.'

'Go?' Fr. Eldrith frowned. 'But where is there to go? The St. Aldhelm Brass has been destroyed, the Portal is closed forever.'

'But' Suzanne protested and pulled herself up short. If there was a second book as she suspected, Fr. Eldrith was clearly not aware it existed. Thank God she had not mentioned it when Ed had quizzed her about what she had witnessed alongside Philippa in the woods at Christmastime.

She sighed deeply. All she could do is play along, the last thing she wanted was for Fr. Eldrith to find out about the possibility of a second book.

'Well, I know I cannot return to my own time for you have made that impossible. No I simply meant you can let me go to Blanche's family home in the village, I'm sure they will be missing her.'

The priest sniggered 'I don't doubt they will be missing you, no one to stew their pottage and mend their clothes.'

'But Blanche's...my mother is sick, I need to tend to her at her bedside.'

'Listen to me. Your destiny does not lie in a hovel looking after that crazy old woman.' He spoke through gritted teeth, he held her in his stare which was as cold as ice.

Suzanne felt a lump in her throat. Her emotions were a mixture of anger, upset and confusion. Reluctantly she asked the question; 'And what destiny is that?' She noticed Fr. Eldrith had positioned himself between her and the chapel door. Slowly, so as not to cause alarm, she stepped out from the strong chest.

Fr. Eldrith's expression lifted, his eyes focused on something far away. 'Your destiny to become a saint. To be revered and renowned throughout the ages! I thought I had already made that clear? I am glad you now feel safe to come out from your hiding place.' He nodded with his head towards the wooden chest. Suzanne felt sudden annoyance, was he mocking her or spinning the truth? She couldn't be certain.

'I think the time has come to see if you can make your miracle waters appear.'

Suzanne gaped, he was expecting her to conjure up the healing spring? Reading the look of disbelief, the priest beckoned.

'All you need to do is believe. Place your forehead against the column and pray.'

Suzanne shrugged and stepped forward. When she was in range she leaned her forehead against the cool of the stone. They waited in silence for a few moments. When nothing happened, Suzanne was the first to break it. 'Its not working. Perhaps I need to rest. If you let me go home now I will return tomorrow and try again.' She paused, trying to gauge the priest's reaction to her suggestion. 'Look its hardly as though I can tell anyone is it? If I say I'm from the 21st century they will have me burned as a witch!'

Fr. Eldrith looked deep in thought, as though he was turning over the possibilities in his mind. Eventually he spoke. 'No. I cannot risk anything happening to you. You shall remain here until your cell is ready.'

'Cell?' She could feel tiny hairs rising on her arms at the mention of the word.

'Yes, your anchoress's cell.' Fr. Eldrith said as matter of factly.

Suzanne knew what he was referring to. In the middle ages individuals who had received a religious calling would sometimes brick themselves up in the walls of churches and chapels and devote their lives to prayer and solitude.

'But.....you never said anything about that! This is not part of the deal. You said you simply wanted to clear your conscience, to have the blame taken away for Blanche's death, to put an end to your perpetual reincarnations and the torment you suffer.' Even as she spoke Suzanne realised the scary truth; this had all been part of Ed's plan. If he had simply wanted to remove himself from any blame for Blanche's disappearance then he would have wanted to go back to the time before he had even abducted her. No; Ed had realised that he could still benefit from her miracles. West Lytchett could remain the place of pilgrimage and wealth that Fr. Eldrith had so profited from in the fourteenth century, but this time without the charge of murder bearing down upon his conscience. She needed to try a different approach if she was to convince him otherwise.

'Don't you see that what you are doing is wrong? Do you think that you won't be punished for treating Blanche in this way, locking her up against her will? The same fate will await you that you've been trying to escape from. She will haunt you for eternity.'

'Silence!' Fr. Eldrith's voice boomed. 'I do not need to explain myself, but I can see that you are misguided, so for your benefit, I will.' Suzanne noticed that the priest had placed two large blocks of stone against the door of the chapel, presumably to slow down any escape attempt she might be planning. Slowly, he eased himself down on to one of them. 'King Edward came to visit the Holy well of West Lytchett during the spring of 1326. By that time St. Albans chapel had become a highly favoured pilgrimage destination, the stories of cures and healing were plentiful and so were the revenues generated by the pilgrims. I benefited greatly from this of course, I was able to wear the finest vestments and jewels, plans for a handsome new priest's house were being drawn up, and importantly I won the respect of the nobility. Being the custodian of this holy chapel meant that I had status and power, but sadly, that was not to last for very long.' Fr. Eldrith sat with his head cupped in his hands. When Suzanne asked him why, she noticed a wistful and faraway look on his face.

'I received a great honour from the King at the end of his visit. Such an impression had been made on him by the powers of the well that he invited me to become his personal confessor, to take residence at Court and hear his confessions.'

'You must have been extremely thrilled at the prospect.' Suzanne ventured.

'Yes, indeed. I could not have dreamed of such an opportunity landing my way before the miracles happened here, I was just a parochial priest, paid to listen to the confessions of peasants, half-wits and drunkards. Now I would hear the confessions of the most powerful man in the land – or so I thought'.

Suzanne thought back to her history lectures and the monarchs of fourteenth century England. If her memory served her correctly, the king in 1326 was Edward II. His reign would only have lasted another year, for in 1327 he was famously deposed by Mortimer and his wife Queen Isabella. 'Fall out of favour when Mortimer seized the throne?' Suzanne asked, quietly hoping that she had got the right period in history.

'What? Oh Mortimer, yes he was a power hungry trouble-maker if ever there was one. No, as it happened, I didn't even get chance to take up the King's offer.' Fr. Eldrith looked down at the floor. It was as if the pain of the memory still cut deep. After a short while he rose from the stone block. 'It was your fault! You made me do it, you drove me to it. You would not let me rest!'

Such was the outburst from the priest that it made Suzanne shrink back in fear.

'But it's not my fault! I may look like Blanche on the outside, but it's still me, Suzanne. You can't lay the blame on my shoulders.'

'After you did your disappearing act at the chapel, that wasn't the end of it was it.' Fr. Eldrith spat, completely ignoring her plea. 'You returned to me in my dreams. You did it to taunt me, to play mind games.'

'No! I don't think that's it.' Suzanne said, trying to keep the wobble from her voice.

'It wasn't an easy choice you know. Several times before I had stepped up to the rope and not followed through. But the nightmares got worse you see. It was only when I saw the angel of death staring me in the face that I knew it was not the way out. The sacrifice of my life was not enough! I had the blood of a Saint on my hands and I would continue to be haunted by you in the next life, and the one beyond that and so on.'

'You committed suicide?' Suzanne was taken aback. Up until now she had assumed that Fr. Eldrith had lived to a ripe old age, living out his life in relative comfort having greatly benefited from the guilty proceeds of the healing well. She hadn't for one minute thought that guilt had got the better of him.

'Yes. I'm ashamed to say I did.' Fr. Eldrith looked down at the floor, a mixture of both regret and defeat on his face. 'It made me wonder actually'. There was a brief pause. 'If you had seen me take my own life in your visions, but then I guessed probably not. Poor Roger, for it was he that discovered me dangling lifelessly from a beam in the Martraver's fodder barn. That's what eventually drove Lance mad of course.'

'Lance had witnessed events through Roger's eyes.' Suzanne simply confirmed to herself what she had first suspected when she had read Lance's diary entry. She looked up glumly as the candles flickered in a breeze which had gone undetected.

'Yes Lance was Roger as you are Blanche. We are all connected to the past, but what you have to realise is that we are not connected to the future, that of course can be changed.' There was a madness that flickered across his face as he spoke.

'And so can the past!' Suzanne interjected.

Fr. Eldrith shook his head. 'Not any more Blanche. This is for real now, no more changes, no more dabbling. No more visions. Don't you see that my plans are the best for everyone?' Fr. Eldrith snorted, suddenly up-beat again. 'I've certainly spent a lot of time thinking this through, you can't argue with that.'

Suzanne could see that no amount of pleading or logic on her part would convince him. She was better off saving her energy. Someone would eventually come by before Fr. Eldrith even had chance to brick her up in the cell, the chapel, was a place of public worship after all.

'You must spend time in prayer, Blanche.' The priest's voice was softer now, interrupting her troubled thoughts. 'You need to concentrate on making the healing waters appear again. Think about what a positive influence you can be on so many people. Come, I have brought you a kneeler. Let us pray together for divine intervention.'

CHAPTER 38

Back from her ride to the village and surrounding fields, Philippa allowed her legs to give in to the tiredness and slowly sunk to the floor of the library, her back resting against a small chest containing Psalters. She had needed a quiet place to collect her thoughts and the library at this time of day was perfect. Over two hours of searching and making enquiries after Blanche had proved fruitless.

The last sighting of her had been earlier on that morning; the sheepherder had seen Blanche crossing the track in the direction of the church, but no one had seen her since. Still, it was of course quite possible that she was fine and well, perhaps taking her time over running an errand to the next village. After all, the days were long at this time of year, there would be plenty of time for Blanche to return before darkness set in, and who could blame her taking her time? Escaping the thankless chores put upon her by that lazy step-brother and drunken step-father for a few hours would be an opportunity to be seized by any sane woman. Philippa smiled as she tried to imagine a more rebellious and adventurous side to her friend, but her smile faded as she could not picture it; Blanche was too dutiful, too steadfast and the dream about the wolf had been so real and threatening.

As she tilted her head back against the bookshelf and her stomach groaned, reminding her that she had not eaten since breakfast time. She would call for Gwen to bring her a supper in her room. Pulling herself to her feet, she became blinded for a few seconds by the sun making its descent in the west, its warm amber rays reaching through the dusty air like an embrace. Philippa stood there for a few seconds; enjoying the warmth on her body before turning to focus in on the bookshelf. *Something else had caught her eye.* Leaning closer, Philippa realised what had all but blinded her a few seconds earlier. Her mouth open in amazement, she reached for the book. The frontispiece glowed brightly, but it looked different to when she had last seen it. This wasn't the book she had lent to Blanche, but a very similar copy, she'd had no idea it existed until now.

'Just like my dream.' She whispered to herself as she gently removed the book from the shelf.

CHAPTER 39

2009

The old man stirred in his sleep, somewhere in the building a phone was ringing, its shrill tone stabbing at the silence like the devil's pitchfork. There was nothing unusual about it, for the phone calls came at any time of the day and night, but it wasn't the phone that had awoken him. Rubbing his eyes he felt for the bedside lamp switch and pressed it on. The room was as familiar as ever, blue checkerboard curtains which didn't meet in the middle, a faded watercolour print of a distant Scottish moorland scene hung on the wall opposite him. He strained his ears as he heard a female voice answer the phone. The clock read 5:40 am, whoever was calling clearly needed urgent help.

With his thin withered arms the old man carefully levered himself up in bed and adjusted the pillow behind his back for extra support. As he lay there, recovering from the effort of the movement, he reflected on recent times. There was no denying it, the lucid moments had been frequent if not regular occurrences over the past few days and although they would never last beyond a couple of hours each time, the main thing was that they were happening. A faint smile crept over his lips; the optimist within suggested something of a recovery, a cure from the fog which shrouded his mind all too frequently, while the pessimist told him that it was death that loomed, playing tricks on him in his final days. Whatever it was he thought pragmatically, it had disturbed him from an otherwise good night's sleep.

Reaching over to the table beside him, he poured himself a tumbler of water and frowned as bits of sediment swirled round. Just how long had the water been stagnating there? As he put the plastic tumbler back on the table he spotted something that wasn't a part of his usual surroundings. *An envelope.* His fragile heart crept up its pace as he carefully gripped the envelope between thumb and forefinger, his hands shaking slightly. The handwriting on the front was familiar; neat and unpretentious. As the old man peeled the long strip of tape that held the envelope closed, the flash back came as clear as day. Although he couldn't explain how or why, he knew there was another chance. Removing the letter he sniffed the paper and held it to his chest with affection. *Lavender.* Suddenly there were tears welling as the fond memories came back. That's why they didn't like him having visitors here. The upset, the aftermath, it was too much hard work for them. As he scanned the content of the letter, he realised his hunch was right. Wiping his face with the arm of his pyjama shirt, he folded the sweet smelling paper and put it under his pillow. He hoped, how he hoped he could keep strong in body and mind for what was about to take place. With a huge amount of effort, he swung his legs round to the side of the bed. His beloved wife would be here in a couple of hours, he had to look presentable. Feeling pleased that he had remembered where his comb and razor were located, he slowly washed, shaved away a day's stubble and for the first time in months chose some proper clothes from his meagre wardrobe – clothes for the outside world. As he dressed, he thought about the content of the letter. If he could be of use, then he would. He would do all he could to help. The sound of a nurse bustling past on the corridor outside alerted him to switch off his lamp until the noise faded into the distance. Retrieving the letter from under his pillow and tucking it into his shirt pocket, Lance Willows climbed back into his bed and quietly waited for Margaret to arrive.

CHAPTER 40

1325

As Roger approached St. Alban's he could just about make out two figures standing near the chapel, one he could see was Fr. Eldrith, the other a thick set man with a crop of hair the colour of rust – it was Len the mason's assistant. Roger stopped in his tracks, he had wanted to be alone in the chapel, to eat his supper of bread and cheese in peace and quiet away from both the manor and his family home in the village, but he could see that wasn't going to happen. He was about to turn on his heels when Len spotted him and shouted something. Reluctantly, Roger moved closer so he could hear what he was saying.

'St. Albans is closed.' Len repeated. Fr. Eldrith was standing next to the thick set labourer, hands on hips and peering down his nose in an authoritarian way. Roger noticed that behind the two men was a significant pile of rubble and stones stacked on the grass. 'Urgent repairs.' Len explained nodding in the direction of the rubble.

'If you have prayer petitions then go and make them at St. John's until the work is finished here.' Fr. Eldrith said while shooing Roger away with a bony hand.

Feeling self-conscious all of a sudden, Roger nodded. 'That's fine. I wanted to offer prayers for my youngest sister, but I can do that in the village. But what has happened to the chapel if you don't mind me asking?'

The two men exchanged glances and Len opened his mouth to speak but it was Fr. Eldrith who spoke first.

'Buttresses. There is a problem with one of buttresses and I've asked Len here to fix it.'

Roger frowned, he hadn't noticed a problem with any buttresses on the far side of the chapel, but then again how often had he actually walked right around the outside of it? Hardly ever. 'God willing it can be repaired soon and with ease.' Roger offered. With a nod of his head, he turned around and started to walk back towards the village. His supper break would almost be over anyway and he could eat his meal as he walked.

'One other thing Roger!' The priest called. Roger turned back around to face him. 'Could you inform those at the manor that St. Alban's will be closed until after the Fair? I would not wish a wasted journey upon the family. I did mention it to the Blacksmith earlier on, but I can see he did not do such a good job in circulating the message.' The priest gave a hollow smile before turning his attention back to Len and the pile of stones that lay beyond.

'Of course. I shall see to it as soon as I return Father.'

When he was sufficiently out of sight from the two men, Roger dug his hand into his nap-sack retrieving the small portion of cheese and hunk of bread. Dusting them off, he ate hungrily. He hadn't noticed how bad his arms were until now; the late heat of the day coupled with the constant tickling from the long grass was only serving to make the itch worse. His thoughts turned to Blanche and the soothing balm she routinely prepared for him which he kept safely hidden in his corner of the stables. Blanche. What a sweet caring girl, and pretty too in her own way. Roger had on many occasions wanted to tell her how special she was to him, of his plan to rescue her from the miserable life she endured at her step-father's house; he had come close, but somehow had never found the right words. There was something else though, another reason why he hadn't made his feelings known. There was a pureness about Blanche, and an intellect which far outshone anyone he had ever known. In essence she was above him, untouchable. In his heart of hearts Roger knew that was how it should remain, he would not risk her most valued friendship.

It came as welcome relief for Roger to escape the irritation of the tall grass and step back on the path that led to the village. His eyes narrowed a little as he thought back to earlier on that afternoon and Lady Philippa's impromptu horse ride, a hasty and fruitless effort to find the missing Blanche. Roger hadn't been too concerned, he had seen Blanche earlier on this same day and knew that she would sometimes have to walk some distance to collect the medicinal herbs needed to make her remedies and scents. Perhaps she had gone a bit further than usual and lost track of the time, more than likely she would be back at home by now. Squinting at the sun's position in the sky, Roger tried to determine if he had enough time to go through the village and check on Blanche's well-being. Gobbling down his last piece of bread he stepped up his pace. For his most valued friend, of course he had enough time.

Roger's late appearance in the stable yard did not go unnoticed by Roldan the blacksmith. His return was greeted by a booming voice across the yard, demanding a reason for the bad time keeping.

'Forgive me, I am not usually late.' Roger looked down at his torn shoes. He did not want to say where he had been. It was after all his business.

'Well, I had to make excuses for you didn't I my lad?'

Roger frowned as Roldan set down a pair of tongs glowing red hot from the fire.

'Lady Philippa has been looking for you, she said something about her horse being lame?'

Roger scratched his head. He was still hot and sweaty from his search of the village. A bead of sweat trickled down his forehead and spread along his eyebrow.

'Lame? The Filly seemed fine when she brought her back before.' Roger was perplexed. 'But I will go and check. Did she intend to ride again this evening? It seems a bit late now.'

'It is not up to us to question what they do in the big house is it?' Roldan sneered. 'Now if I were you I'd let Lady Philippa's servant Gwynne know that you are back so the Lady can discuss it with you in person.'

'Gwen, her servant's name is Gwen.'

'Gwynne, Gwen. All the same.' The blacksmith batted Roger away with a scarred hand. 'I've got another three horses to shoe before the fair tomorrow and I've already had enough delays for one day.

It was at that moment that Roger remembered what Fr. Eldrith had told him. 'The priest was here slowing you down?' He ventured, curious as to what Fr. Eldrith wanted with the Roldan.

'Ah? Yes he was here alright. Strange man, God forgive me for saying so. Wanted something melting down so he did. Most peculiar. Anyway I did as he asked.'

'And he mentioned about St. Albans, the building work going on there?'

'Oh by God's teeth, yes he did. I meant to pass the message on!' The blacksmith had straightened now, tools resting where they could not maim. 'I must get the message to them right away otherwise I'll be in trouble if one of our betters head up there to find it closed!'

Roger put his hand on the blacksmith's shoulder. 'Wait. I can do that. Am I not off to see Gwen this very minute?'

'Yes of course. If you could do that for me Roger then I can concentrate on getting these horses shod in time.'

CHAPTER 41

As she opened her eyes, the first thing Suzanne noticed was the grey roughly hewn stone blocks that surrounded her on all sides, accompanied by a prevailing scent of damp mortar. Wincing with effort, she hauled herself up from her crumpled position and was dismayed to realise that she now occupied what seemed to be small stone cell. The last thing she remembered was praying with Fr. Eldrith in the chapel and then being offered more of that wretched ale. But how did she end up in here? Furthermore why did she not remember anything of it?

Pulling herself up against the rough masonry her memory was jogged; Fr. Eldrith had been serious about her becoming an anchoress; this small enclosure was most likely her cell. As she tried to stand on her numb legs her foot nudged something over with a hollow clatter. Suzanne froze for a second before stooping to examine the source of the noise. Although she could not see clearly, Suzanne could tell from the shape that it was a wooden pail, probably intended as a makeshift lavatory. Deflated, she sank back to the floor. 'Help!' Her cry had come out of desperation, almost an involuntary reflex. She listened carefully; she thought she could hear footsteps approaching. 'Help me, please.' The last word came as a sob. Almost instantaneously light flooded into the cell. Suzanne squinted in its direction. In one wall above her there was a small square of light, slightly less than a square foot in size, but it was large enough to illuminate the small space around her. Grabbing the and setting it upside down she used it as a step to get as close as possible to the light source.

'What is it you need?' Came the voice. It wasn't one she recognised.

'Fr. Eldrith'? She began uncertainly.

'Fr. Eldrith has gone to St. John's to celebrate Mass. I am watching over you in the meantime.' The voice was softly spoken and calm.

'Who are you?' Suzanne asked. With Fr. Eldrith out of the way there was at least a glimmer of hope.

'My child I thought you would recognise my voice? Have I not known you since your baptism? It is I, Deacon Christopher.' There was a brief pause as he drew in a breath. 'I thought then that you were special. As the holy water was poured out on your head a pure white dove rapped on the east window of the church. Not just once, but several times! I took it as a sign.'

For a minute Suzanne did not know what to say, Deacon Christopher sounded kind, but was very much under the impression that Blanche had been singled out, blessed by God. She groaned at the prospect of having to stay in the cell for even a minute longer.

'Look, there has been a dreadful mistake.' She began, her voice desperate as she angled it towards the small aperture in the wall above her. 'I did not ask to be shut away in this cell, it was Fr. Eldrith's idea! He thinks I should become an anchoress, but this isn't what *I* want!'

There was a long silence that followed, it was so long that Suzanne began to fear that Deacon Christopher had gone away. When he eventually spoke again his voice was calm and measured.

'You must not fear it Blanche. We are all called by God to perform his duties here in this world. Some are called to lead, others to serve. Some, like yourself have been given the gift of miracles and they are the most special of all.'

Suzanne's heart sunk. Had he not heard what she had just told him? 'But I haven't performed any miracles!' As she said it she instantly regretted it. How could she be so certain? She did not know Blanche's life story, it could be peppered with miracles for all she knew.

'You are indeed meek and not in the least self-assured! I can think of a few holy brothers and sisters that could learn a lesson from you my child. Listen! Can you hear the evidence of what you have raised from you where you stand?'

Suzanne strained her ears; all she could hear was the distant wail of gulls. 'No' she replied, feeling bewildered.

'Ah, you must still be overcome. Fr. Eldrith warned that you might be. I can assure you that the waters you have commanded are pure and good and still bubbling from the ground in the chapel. Tell me, for I have not asked this of Fr. Eldrith, did you have a vision when you prayed with him today?'

So the miraculous spring had appeared after all. Suzanne crinkled her brow as she reflected on the events earlier that day. Of course, she remembered praying in the centre of the chapel, but she was praying for her escape rather than anything else. That was the last thing she could recall before finding herself stuck in this dingy space. Fr. Eldrith must have laced her drink with something so the whole drama could take place around her, without her being capable of protest. Suzanne could feel the anger and frustration rising within her, anger directed towards the manipulative priest, and frustration with the fact that no matter what she tried to do to help herself, the hole she was in just kept getting deeper.

She had to get Philippa to come to see her. The spirited yet practical Philippa was the only person with influence who could help her right now, and she held the key to her escape. Between them they could think of a way to escape the cell. Suzanne was sure that Fr. Eldrith would not oblige to her wishes, but the kindly Deacon Christopher might if she talked him round.

‘A vision? Perhaps there was a holy vision, but I do not remember. Maybe if I could be let out of my cell to pray again in the chapel?’

‘Let out of your cell? But it has only just been sealed’ Deacon Christopher began. ‘It is not a straight forward matter of opening a door, as I’m sure you are aware, it has been constructed around you as you wished.’

It was worth a try. Suzanne knew that in all likelihood the cell had no door, the only apertures were the hatch that she spoke through at the top, and a small drainage hole on the floor; most probably intended as a sewer.

‘Of course. I wasn’t thinking straight. Look, perhaps you could give a message to Lady Philippa of the Manor?’

The kindly priest thought for a moment. ‘What is the message?’

‘That she will be as good to come and see me, I have something rather important to tell her.’

‘I will see what I can do. Now do you want me to close the hatch or leave it open for you.’

Suzanne shuddered at the thought of being left alone in the darkness again. ‘Please! Leave it as it is.’

‘Very well. Fr. Eldrith will be returning shortly. Remember, keep praying; I am sure the vision will return to you in all its glory, you just need to have time to reflect.’

CHAPTER 42

Philippa was getting ready for supper when Gwen announced Roger's return. 'Tell him I will come down and meet him outside the stables.' Philippa had instructed. Abandoning her plans to wear a silken red gown, Philippa pulled on an old green gown that was awaiting repairs and clutching the book under her arm marched purposely out from her chamber. He plan was to show Roger, to see if he had noticed Blanche carrying a similar book when he saw her earlier on that day.

Roger looked worried when she met him in the stable yard. Dusk still hadn't fallen but the midges had already started to swarm. Wafting them away with one arm Philippa greeted him.

'Roger! I am glad you are back. I was looking for you earlier.' She noticed that the seriousness in the stable boy's face remained. 'Oh do not worry, you are not in trouble with me. I just wanted you to take a look at my horse. She was limping as I rode her back here this afternoon.'

'I know. Roldan told me. I have checked her, there are no breaks. I think maybe she just isn't used to all that exercise.' The boy's sullenness gave way to a cheeky grin.

'Oh be damned with you!' Philippa cursed light heartedly. 'I would give her more exercise if my father would let me out of his clutches more often.'

'If you allow me to say my lady, perhaps when you are married things will be different?' Roger ventured.

Philippa sighed. That depended on to whom she would be married. If her father got his way then Lord Carringstone would surely keep her under lock and key for the rest of her days. 'Perhaps' she said glumly. 'Anyway, no matter. If my horse is safe for riding then I thought perhaps I would go out again in the morning before the fair.'

'To search for Blanche again?' Roger asked, his eyes widened with worry. 'When I went to check on her not too long ago I found that she still isn't back with her family. Even her step-father is starting to get anxious.'

Philippa nodded. 'I think she might be in danger Roger. I thought this afternoon that I had checked most places, asked many people of her whereabouts but there is one person who I should have asked and he was not there when I checked.'

'Who is that?'

'Fr. Eldrith. He might know something. After all, the last person known to see Blanche was the sheepherder and he said that Blanche was heading towards St. John's.

Roger interrupted 'I have seen Fr.Eldrith only but a few hours ago. He was up at St. Alban's chapel supervising the building works.'

Philippa frowned. 'Building works?'

'Yes, he said there was a problem with one of the buttresses. The chapel is closed until after the fair.' He paused for a moment before adding 'And before that Roldan saw him too. The priest wanted something melting down in the forge'.

Philippa was curious. It seemed odd that the priest would close the chapel on the eve of a significant feast, and what was it he wanted melting down? What gave him the right to ask Roldan to do it? He was blacksmith to the manor, not the clergy.

'Is Roldan around? I must speak with him.' Philippa said indignantly.

The blacksmith was hammering noisily as Philippa and Roger approached the forge. He looked up sharply, seemingly irritated at yet another interruption. Seeing that a member of the house was in his presence his expression changed immediately.

'My lady.' Roldan exclaimed bowing his head. 'What brings you in here at this late hour?'

'Roger tells me that Fr. Eldrith was here today requiring your services?'

Roldan begrudgingly lifted the almost completed horseshoe from the anvil to a stone plinth. It would need heating again at this rate. Mopping the beads of perspiration from his brow with the back of his hand he stepped away from the heat of the furnace. 'Shall we?' He indicated towards a small door way to the left. 'It's dreadful hot in here, no place for you my lady.'

The room Roldan had ushered them into was no more than an oversized store cupboard. Iron bullion was stacked against one wall, while against another was a large coffer, its lid opened and with random bits of metal sticking out from it. Slamming down the lid, he offered Philippa a seat and then drew back the sash from the window, letting the fading evening light filter in.

'Fr. Eldrith was here earlier, that is true. He came to inform the manor about the closure of St. Alban's for a few days. I trust Roger has told you of this?' Roldan's black eyes shifted towards Roger then back to Philippa. Philippa smoothed the creases from her old dusty gown and set the book down beside her.

'Yes. Roger has told me thank you. I do think it is odd that he should be closing the chapel before St. Peter's fair, it is such a busy devotional time and many will be wishing to pray there. Besides, the chapel is on my father's land, he should at least have his agreement or have had the common courtesy to give notice.'

Roldan shrugged his hefty shoulders. 'I agree my lady, but it's not my job to ask questions of the clergy, I could only pass his message on to the household, so I could.' There was an exchange of glances between Roger and Roldan. Roger mischievously wanted to add that the blacksmith had not even gone as far as that but refrained from doing so.

'You are right Roldan'. Philippa agreed breathlessly. 'And I suppose when he asked you to use the forge for his own purposes you felt you could not deny him?'

A look of confusion washed across the blacksmith's podgy face for a brief moment before he realised what Philippa was referring to.

'Oh that. No it was a tiny job. He only wanted something melting down in the furnace.'

'And what was it he asked you to melt?' Philippa held Roldan with a fixed gaze. She could tell he was beginning to feel uncomfortable at the cross examination, and there was something else too. A look of panic and bewilderment had suddenly flashed across his usually stern face. He was pointing at something beside her.

'It was like th-that.' He stuttered. Philippa and Roger followed Roldan's pointing finger to the book that rested beside her on the coffer.

Philippa sprung up from her seat 'Do my ears deceive me? You allowed him to burn one of *our* books in the forge?'

Roldan looked at Roger and then back to Philippa. 'It belongs to the family? My lady I honestly did not know. What was the priest doing with it?'

'Lord only knows Roldan!' Philippa spat angrily. 'Surely, even you would know that questions should be asked before a book is thrown to the flame. The expense, the workmanship involved....'

'But...' Roldan interrupted. 'There wasn't a book. It was just that – the Brass image on the front. That is what he wanted destroyed, by the grace of God there is no way I would give a book to the fire, even if Fr. Eldrith asked me to!'

Philippa's eyes narrowed. Her mind was full of questions. Turning to Roger who had remained silent throughout, she leaned towards him, her voice a husky whisper. 'Roger, I need my horse preparing. We have questions to ask Fr. Eldrith, in particular how he has come upon property of the manor and the whereabouts of Blanche. Go at once!'

Roger nodded obediently and scuttled out of the forge. There would be no questioning of Philippa's instructions; she believed she was on to something. As he got to the stables Roger realised his hands were shaking. What of Blanche? Was she really in danger? He did not understand what was happening, but he prayed that they would not be too late.

As Philippa prepared to leave Roldan in an uneasy and guilty state, she heard him mutter. 'My lady, there was one other thing.'

She turned to face him again, strands of disheveled red hair clung to her flushed cheeks.

'The priest asked to keep the Brass in its melted down state, so I collected it into a small reservoir. He said he will come back to retrieve it when cooled. If you give me authority, I can trap him upon his return and your father can call on the Bishop to administer the appropriate justice!'

Philippa forced a smile. Roldan was only trying to be helpful, he wasn't to blame. 'Thank you Roldan. And do not worry about this misadventure for you were not to know. As for Fr. Eldrith returning here, I am hopeful that Roger and I will get to *him* first.' She turned on her heels and ran the short distance across the yard towards the stable block. Passing Gwen, she handed the book to her with the instruction that the servant girl safely return it to the library at once. Whatever the reason for Fr. Eldrith defacing the book she had lent to Blanche, she could not risk it happening to the second volume. Following her instruction, Roger led the horses from their stables; at this rate, they might still be in time to catch the end of the vigil Mass at St. John's.

* * *

Sitting on the up-turned pail in the dismal cell, Suzanne absently chewed on a ragged fingernail. She had been worrying not only about her captivity in the fourteenth century, but what was happening in her own time. How much time was passing by in the 21st century? Ed had told her it wasn't constant. Did she still have some physical presence there, or had she simply morphed into Blanche and disappeared altogether? One thing was for certain; if 21st century time was passing by then her family and friends would be starting to worry. What if her parents had tried to contact her to no avail? Also, Melanie would expect the cottage to be vacated in a couple of days' time. Even if she had physically vanished, all her things would still be there, the new inhabitants would certainly complain and the alarm would be raised. But how could anyone help her?

Running her hands through her hair which was slightly greasy to the touch, Suzanne tried to clear her mind and apply logic to her situation, in doing so she immediately thought of Margaret. She was the only link she had in the village; if she had disappeared then Margaret would guess what was happening. But did Margaret have the capability to actually *do* anything? She had never experienced the visions and dreams, nor had she said anything about accessing the Portal, plus if Margaret told her story to the police they would think she was a superstitious old woman, possibly slightly barmy too. Sighing in despair, Suzanne slumped back against the cool-damp of the stone, the mortar was still soft from the construction only a few hours earlier and it was now clear why she was being guarded – her chances of a successful escape were diminishing as the hours went by and mortar set firmly. She scraped at the mortar nonchalantly with a stubby fingernail, wishing she hadn't spent the last few minutes biting what could have been her only tools for escape. The fading light from the hatch at the top of the cell told her that the evening was fast drawing in and now she would have to face the likelihood of spending a night in the cramped cell. Suzanne knew her only hope of escape lay in Philippa's hands. Silently she prayed that Deacon Christopher would be true to his word and get a message to Philippa as quickly as he could.

CHAPTER 43

The stallion was a fine horse, but certainly an animal that was built for power rather than agility, as Roger was beginning to discover. Philippa was riding out ahead of him, her dapple-grey filly nimbly weaving through the trees with little effort, while Roger hung on some distance behind, conscious to keep his head down and away from the gnarled moss covered branches. The stable boy had respectfully suggested that Philippa give the dapple-grey a rest and take another horse, but after a trot around the stable yard, the young horse seemed as spritely as ever, and clearly, it was happy to run on this terrain. A twig snapped off against Roger's face and his hand instinctively went to touch his cheek. When he pulled it away, there was a trail of crimson on his fingers. They could have stuck to the paths; it would have taken longer, true, but this was the quickest route. Roger suspected that Philippa was enjoying the excitement of this chase; this was a young woman whose spirit yearned for adventure. He was sure that given the choice, she would prefer the exhilaration of the battlefield rather than music lessons and tapestry. How cruel that she was to be a woman, he thought.

Roger breathed a sigh of relief when the tower of St. John's came into view. Following Philippa's lead, he slowed his horse down to a gentle trot and dusted dried leaves and other woodland debris from his mantle. There simply hadn't been any time to talk before or on the journey, Philippa had wanted to set off urgently –her intention was to catch Fr.Eldrith as he finished saying Mass. As it happened, they weren't to be disappointed with their timing. While Roger set about tethering both horses to a nearby tree, the cloaked priest emerged from his door set within the south wall, his eyes scanning left to right as he turned the key in the lock. Philippa wasted no time in making her presence known;

'Fr. Eldrith! I need to speak with you.' She shouted across the narrow dusty track that separated the woods from churchyard. Roger thought he detected a look of panic cross the priest's face as he recognised who was addressing him, before he forced an awkward smile. The pair hastily crossed the track and soon they were within the confines of the churchyard. Roger crossed himself as he walked past an unmarked mound of earth where his grandparents laid. *Watch over us,* he thought in silent petition.

'Good evening Lady Philippa' the priest spoke politely, completely ignoring Roger's presence. 'How can I be of assistance?'

Philippa did not seem taken aback by the priest's overt deference. 'There are a number of things actually.' She replied, still a little breathless from the journey.

'Well then, shall we?' He nodded towards the door that he had just locked before turning his attention towards Roger. 'Does your servant need to be party to the discussion?' Roger felt Fr. Eldrith's mean eyes on him for a moment before they returned to Philippa.

'Yes he does' she answered assertively 'he had an important stake in this too.'

Once inside the church Fr. Eldrith ushered them into the south chapel, lighting only two candles in an attempt to banish the gloom that had settled within with four walls. Roger felt there was something different about the mood within the building, different to how it normally felt certainly; somehow brooding and watchful. He shivered as a cool breeze wafted through the gaps in a stained glass window that depicted the Tree of Jesse, and noticed that Philippa was shivering too.

'So then, what is it you have to say Lady Philippa?' Fr. Eldrith had invited them to sit on a small bench to the side of the altar. Smoothing her crumpled green gown Philippa did not waste any time in getting to the point.

'It has come to my attention that you have the property of the manor in your possession; a book from our library. I want to know exactly how you have come about this book and why you asked our blacksmith to deface it.'

The air was still and silent. Roger could tell that the priest was busy thinking, the old man's eyes flickered energetically. All at once he exhaled quietly, almost to himself.

'There is no point in hiding this from you my lady, for sooner or later you will find out and see it with your own eyes.'

The curiosity within Philippa was instantly roused. She would not realise it now, but she had taken the bait that the clever priest had laid.

'See what?' she asked, her eyes round with intrigue.

'Something marvelous has happened here in West Lytchett today, although I have not spoken a word of it to anyone yet. I suppose it is fitting that you, a lady of high status should hear it first, but I had planned to tell your father and mother in the first instance.' The priest cleared his throat as though he was about to make an important declaration of some kind. 'We have a miracle worker in our midst. Someone who our Lord has chosen to do his good deeds here on earth.'

Philippa frowned. It was a bold thing to say, and certainly out of character for the priest to be so unrestrained with his speech.

'Are you sure of this Father? Who is this person – am I well acquainted with him?

'Many questions Lady Philippa! But I understand. If my ears were greeted with such news I would not know which question to ask first. I think it sensible to explain exactly what I experienced earlier on today, at the chapel out on the headland.' Fr. Eldrith briefly glanced towards Roger and gave a look which told the boy he was not to interrupt what was about to be said.

'So let me start from the beginning. It was mid-afternoon, after I had finished giving the sacrament to the sick of the village when I arrived at St. Alban's chapel. The door was ajar, and the most beautiful sound of heavenly music was coming from within that dark and humble space. I trod carefully so I would not disturb the chorus, but when my eyes adjusted to the dimness there was but one solitary being, kneeling in prayer by the altar.'

'Yes, and who was it?' Philippa asked, irritated that the priest was keeping her in suspense.

Fr. Eldrith took a deep breath. 'Blanche Myddelton, you know, the peasant girl from the village.'

'Blanche? I was beginning to wonder when I would hear her name mentioned.'

'Oh?' The priest cocked his head inquisitively. Roger thought he detected a slight disturbance flicker over his eyes. Fr. Eldrith did not wait for Philippa's reply; instead he eagerly pressed on with his account. 'Blanche was kneeling in prayer at the front of the chapel, reciting complex Latin which surprised me as I did not think a girl so lowly would speak the language of the church. Slowly, I crept in and knelt at the back, listening to the words she spoke so eloquently. It was then I saw the most miraculous of things! Not far from where Blanche was knelt in prayer, a little surge of pure clear water had sprung up the ground.'

Roger was listening intently, trying to imagine the scene that the priest was painting. Blanche praying, speaking Latin. Yes, all of that he could imagine, her father had taught her the language as a young girl, and she was devout in the faith of the church, taking opportunity to pray in church or chapel at least once every day as long as he'd known her. What Roger could not imagine however, was the pompous priest acting so deferent towards a girl from the village. He put the thoughts to one side and continued to listen to what Fr. Eldrith had to say.

'She had not seen me there at the back of the chapel, yet she said to me *put your hands into the water Father.* Slowly I did as she had asked. The result was most wondrous, my fingers, usually crooked and sore at the joints were at once straightened and regained the flexibility of youth. I was amazed for I knew what had happened was nothing short of a miracle.'

Roger looked in Philippa's direction. The young noble woman seemed intrigued by the priest's story. She was not however, about to let the matter of defacing manorial property go so easily.

'That is truly an amazing account Fr. Eldrith, but you have failed so far to tell me what this has to do with the book from our library?'

'Yes, I was coming to that.' Fr. Eldrith smiled falsely. 'I spent quite some time thereafter talking to Blanche. She explained to me that she had witnessed a vision of St. Aldhelm, the patron saint of the chapel. In this vision, he had revealed to her the healing spring, and; her true vocation.'

Roger's ears pricked up. He had remained silent for long enough. 'True vocation?' The priest looked at him with slight distaste for a moment before turning back to Philippa.

'Blanche explained that St. Aldhelm had selected her to serve at the chapel, offering prayers and petitioning on behalf of pilgrims and the people of the village. He had told her a cell must be constructed as her dwelling place, built onto the outside of the chapel wall.'

Philippa's eyes narrowed. 'A cell? Like a hermit you mean?'

'Yes, exactly like that. This is where your book comes into the fore. She told me she had gained much knowledge and wisdom from that book, but there was something which troubled her deeply. The Brass depiction on the front, she said that in the vision, St. Aldhelm had told her it must be destroyed for it was an object that had been possessed by no-one other than the Devil himself. I took it upon myself to see to her request before she was sealed in her cell. The book itself which I'm sure is of great value, has come to no harm though, it is up at the chapel under lock and key, guarded by Deacon Christopher. I will see it gets back to your library promptly.'

Philippa shook her head in disbelief and looked towards Roger. For once she seemed stuck for words. The meagre candlelight flickered as she took in a deep breath and exhaled. 'Look, Fr. Eldrith. It was I who lent the book to Blanche. My father does not know about this and the least he knows then the better for me. If I can retrieve the book and put it back on the shelf without him noticing it was ever missing then I will overlook your hasty behaviour. As for Blanche, I am in awe at such a story, but it is not beyond belief. Knowing her as I do, I always thought there was more to Blanche than one would judge by her appearance and status, and I now understand why you have needed to close the chapel at such short notice.' Philippa paused for a moment. 'I should like to go to the chapel first thing tomorrow, before I set off to Wareham and speak with her in person.'

'Of course' Fr. Eldrith assured. 'I have to warn you though, she may be in denial about the episode. Such is common when people have experienced holy visions. I will rely on you, Lady Philippa as a superior to reassure Blanche that her chosen vocation is the right thing to do.' Roger noticed the strained smile had returned to the priest's lips. Blanche – an anchoress? It certainly seemed fitting given Blanche's religious convictions and her abilities to cure people with her herbal balms, but was she sure about her decision? Why would anyone want to spend the rest of their days enclosed in a cell? A wave of emotion came over him, he simply hadn't realised it until now, how much he loved her. She mustn't fritter her life away, she had so much to offer to the outside word. What was said about the parable of the lamp? That it must be put on display so all could benefit from it, not hidden away! As the thoughts crossed his mind he felt his fists clenching defensively. He had to find out for himself, Blanche could talk openly to him, they were of a similar station. Roger had made his decision. He would go, under the cover of night and see her.

CHAPTER 44

Suzanne awoke with a jolt. Something was on her face, smothering her nose. Panicking, her hands scrabbled at what was covering her head and it was then her fingers made contact with the course fabric that she instantly remembered. It was a woolen blanket that Deacon Christopher had given her to protect against the cool night air. At least someone was considering her welfare, things could have been a lot worse.

Pushing the blanket away, she realised something else. The cell was pitch black; even the small hatch at the top offered no light. Rubbing her eyes, a new and sinister thought came into her mind. She held her hand up in front of her face and stared at it. Nothing. *Am I blind?* Groping in the darkness for the pail, she stood upon it. Feeling the source of the draft with her hands she pulled herself up towards the hatch and peered out, trying her best to look upwards towards the night sky. There was instant relief when she spotted a collection of stars towards the horizon. *There's nothing wrong with my vision, it's the countryside 700 years ago. It's bound to be dark!* She scolded herself. She remained there for a while longer focusing on the distant, spinning stars and the not too distant crashing of the waves against the shore.

There was something particularly melancholy about the moment, it was a little like being a teenager again. Confined within her own bedroom, surrounded by the feeling of being totally alone. That no one else understood. A wistful smile crept around her lips, the thought of her childhood home, the semi-detached that was hundreds of years away from being built, her parents, grandparents, great-grandparents, not yet even born. What if Fr. Eldrith had been right - what if this was her destiny? She hadn't even stopped to consider the consequences of what this meant or that of going back to her own time. If she did manage to get back, there was the risk that she would be haunted by the dreams, like Lance, driven mad by constant visions and then to an early grave. She sighed loudly to herself and pondered which was the better option; imprisonment in the middle ages, or psychosis in the twenty first century? One thing she did know is that the first was a reality, the second, still only a possibility. As she was deep in thought, she noticed hedges in the distance had suddenly come into view. Suzanne watched as the silvery light crept nearer, the previously elusive moon was now illuminating the landscape in differing tones of grey. Suzanne wondered if anyone was keeping watch over her tonight, she could not see the balding head of Deacon Christopher, but if he was there, he would almost certainly be sheltering in the chapel at this hour.

Carefully, Suzanne stepped down off the pail and returning to her makeshift bed, she pulled the musky scented blanked up to her chin. Closing her eyes she desperately tried to clear her confused mind of thoughts and allow sleep to embrace her. After what seemed like an hour, she was still awake. It was no good, her brain was active; turning everything over like a tangle of clothes in a tumble dryer. It was then that she noticed a change in the air around her, movement. Vibrations. They were quiet at first but after a few moments the noise became louder, closer.

Thud-thud Thud-thud Thud-thud.

It was the galloping of a horse. Suzanne clambered up to her tiny window. She could hear the sound of hooves really clearly now, whoever it was, was nearby. Suddenly a wave of fear embraced her, prompted by some distant memory of a story about ghoulish headless horsemen. She closed her eyes and unwittingly held her breath. The galloping had stopped and the sound of footsteps on the grass could be heard. Suzanne wanted to get away from the window and retreat into the safety of the cell, but she found she was frozen to the spot.

'Blanche.'

The whisper was soft, almost tender. The tight grip of fear loosened and she opened her eyes. In the moonlight was the silhouette of a young man, he extended his hand to hers through the aperture. At once she recognised him from one of the dreams she'd had about Philippa.

'Roger?' She spoke his name uncertainly.

'Yes, it's me. Listen I know the hour is late but I had to come and see you, make sure you were all right after the miraculous goings-on! Tell me Blanche, is what they say about you true, that you have raised a holy spring there inside the chapel?'

'There is a spring, yes, but I'm not sure that it had anything to do with me!'

Roger turned his head away, as though he was listening to something.

'I thought I could hear running water as I approached! Trouble is, is that I couldn't go in the chapel because someone is in there.'

So either Fr. Eldrith or Deacon Christopher were indeed keeping watch over her. This was her chance, she probably only had a few moments to convince Roger of the truth. She gently squeezed his hand to draw his attention back. 'Roger you have to help me. Fr. Eldrith is suffering from delusions. He believes this is the life I should lead, as an anchoress, shut in this cell for the rest of my days, but this is much against *my* will.' Her voice was breathless with panic. Roger opened his mouth a few times to speak, but Suzanne hadn't finished. She may only have this chance to escape and she could not squander it. It was a long shot, but if St. Aldhelm had not wanted Blanche locked away against her will, perhaps he had already intervened. 'Listen Roger, what you need to do is clear, Lady Philippa may have a certain book in her possession, one with an inlaid Brass on the cover. Don't let Fr. Eldrith know of it, but you need to bring it here, bring it to me.'

Suzanne stopped talking, they had both heard it, the creak of the chapel door followed by slow pondering footsteps. Roger disappeared from the window for a brief moment before reappearing. 'It's Deacon Christopher!' He announced. 'We've disturbed his slumber!'

'What are you doing here in the middle of the night Master Cheney?' Deacon Christopher croaked in a state of confusion.

Suzanne could just about hear the discourse between Roger and Deacon Christopher, thankfully Roger had said nothing about her desires to escape the cell. Roger appeared back at the window, his eyes round and sparkling in the moonlight.

'Blanche, I am going now, but I shall return'. He paused for a moment, looking away shyly and Suzanne was reminded that this was a young boy she was dealing with, no more than fifteen or sixteen years old.

'Take heart because Lady Philippa is coming to see you tomorrow, and I will take her your message.'

Suzanne's mood was lifted by hearing Roger's words. She hoped to God he would remember to ask Philippa about the book - that was of critical importance. Roger's comely face was then replaced by that of Deacon Christopher.

'Are you comfortable in there Blanche? I can offer you another blanket to ward of the night's chill if you wish.'

'No thank you, I am warm enough.'

'Very well, I shall leave you to get some rest. Good night maid.' With that the Deacon padded over the grass and closed the chapel door behind him.

As she settled back down under the blanket, the matter she had been battling with her since her enclosure had partly resolved itself; how she would be able to access the Portal without leaving her cell. She now had an idea. All she needed to do was figure out a way of getting the extra help she needed, and importantly, make sure that Fr. Eldrith stayed away.

CHAPTER 45

It was well after dawn when Gwen reluctantly knocked on the door to Lady Philippa's chamber.

'Knock harder Gwen, that's never going to wake her.' Roger urged.

'I'm not sure what all the urgency is about Roger.' Gwen snapped. 'I'm sure Lady Philippa isn't going to thank either of us for this rude awakening on Fair day!'

Roger curled his fingers into a fist and was about to rap at the door himself, when to his surprise a jaded voice came from the other side.

'Gwen? What is the hour - have I slept late?'

Gwen turned to Roger. 'You stay here out of sight. My lady does not wish to be ogled by a stable boy first thing.'

Roger opened his mouth to protest but Gwen was quicker. 'I will first see that she is dressed and willing to speak with you. Wait here.'

Roger stood still and quietly in the corridor. He was not supposed to be in the house. He strained his ears, trying to pick out sounds of other members of the household rousing, but thankfully, all was still. After what seemed like an age, Philippa eventually appeared in the doorway. Her face was a fresh as morning daisy and there was a glint of excitement in her eyes.

'Pardon the awakening My lady' Roger averted his eyes respectfully. 'But I have an urgent message from Roldan, the blacksmith.'

'Then we shall go and see him at once.' Philippa replied.

Hovering in the background was Gwen. 'I do not know why he hasn't come himself my lady.' She offered. 'Unless of course Roger has been granted a new position, messenger as well as stable-hand!'

Turning to face the maid, Philippa addressed her curtly. 'Gwen, I would be pleased if you stay in my chamber. Fresh linen is needed for my bed.'

Jilted, Gwen stopped in her tracks. Her face suddenly flushed. Nodding obediently, she turned and disappeared back into her lady's chamber.

Philippa smiled. 'She is a good maid, but a little prying at times! Don't worry, she will not sulk for long, I've promised her some free time and spends at the fair. Come, let us get out from these walls and see what Roldan has to tell us.'

The blacksmith was busily hammering holes into his last horseshoe when Philippa and Roger arrived outside the forge. The hammering was so loud that he did not even notice he had company.

'Roldan!' Roger's voice was raised against the backdrop of clanging metal. Roldan stopped hammering and looked up sharply.

'My good lady.' Roldan straightened his burly back. 'The job is almost done I can assure you. With the help of young Roger here, the horses will be in fine fettle for your ride out to Wareham later.'

'Thank you Roldan, but I am not here to check on your work. Since when have you left horses unshod before? I do not question your ability to meet the timescales as challenging as they may be, especially when it is my father that is giving the orders!' She smiled at him revealing a shared understanding of her father's unreasonable requests. 'No, there is another matter you wanted to broach with me is there not?'

'Yes there is my lady, but it is nothing so important that you should have come in person. No, I wanted to tell you that the priest, Fr. Eldrith was here first thing. He had come to collect the cooled brass bullion; you know, the metal that formed the figurine on the front of your book. I told him that I would not hand it over, with it being property of this great house. Anyhow, Roger tells me that you had addressed him yesterday about it, and he plans to return the book. Pray tell me that I did the right thing by not meeting his earnest demand?'

Philippa had taken a step sideways and was peering behind Roldan's lathe. She had spotted the small cube of Brass that sat on a smoothed stone. 'Of course you did the right thing Roldan. The priest has no business with that nugget of metal, no matter how small. I will see that you are rewarded for your diligence.'

Roldan puffed out his chest proudly.

'Oh it was nothing my lady, just doing my duty to protect the household's property. Here's your Brass, or what's left of it. Mind you, Fr. Eldrith was quite persistent in his petitions and I was most pleased when the badgering stopped and he left me alone!' The blacksmith paused to wipe his moist brow with the back of his hand. 'He's probably chewing the ear of your father right now, rather him than me I dare say.'

Philippa took the misshapen metal from Roldan's stocky hand and looked him in the eye. 'What did you say?'

'Oh, I'm sorry my lady, that wasn't meant disrespectfully towards your father, no I was merely saying...'

'No, no I meant what did you say about the priest being with my father?'

Roldan's black eyes moved from Philippa to Roger and then back to Philippa again. 'Well, that is where he said he was going next, a meeting with Harold Martravers. I'm sorry is there something wrong?' The blacksmith was stuttering.

Philippa's mind was racing. 'Possibly.' Turning to Roger she spoke quietly. 'I have to go into the house to check on something.' Her eyes flashed 'If you prepare a couple of horses for our ride up to St. Albans I shall meet you in the stable yard before the hour is finished. Roldan, tell me one thing, when Fr. Eldrith was here earlier, you did not mention the presence of a second book, the one I had with me yesterday?'

Roldan's eyes flickered then cast downwards. He opened his mouth but no words came.

Philippa sighed. 'So he *does* know that it exists? Please tell me the truth Roldan.'

Roldan nodded hesitantly. 'Yes, he said he had been up to the library but he did not find it. He asked me if I knew anything, but I swear lady, I didn't not tell him anything.'

'Well, that at least is something.' Philippa forced a weak smile, but as she did she noticed that Roldan looked decidedly uneasy. 'Is there anything else you want to say Roldan?'

Roldan shuffled on his sturdy leather boots. 'No lady, that is all.'

'Good. Thank you Roldan, and if you see any more of Fr. Eldrith then I need you to tell me at once.'

'Of course lady.'

Philippa strode purposely out of the stable yard with Roger following a couple of paces behind. When they were out of Roldan's earshot Roger spoke up.

'Lady Philippa, before you go in I have to tell you something.' Roger swallowed. He was not sure how Lady Philippa would react to the news. 'Last night I took a horse from the stables and rode up to St. Albans.'

Philippa stopped in her tracks.

'I'm sorry I should have asked permission first before taking a horse, but I had to see Blanche, make sure she was fine and well given what Fr. Eldrith had told us. I could not wait until this morning. She asked me if you will come and see her, and she said something about that old book from your library, the one you were talking about just a moment ago, the same one you had yesterday in the blacksmith's forge.'

To his surprise Philippa laughed. 'Roger, brave Roger! I am glad that you followed your heart. And no, I will not scold you for taking a horse without permission, given the circumstances.' Roger watched Philippa's expression change to host the weighty seriousness suddenly full of concern for her friend. 'And how is Blanche after the miraculous goings on? I am eager to see her, but first let me fetch the book from the library, it obviously has some important value not only to Blanche but to Fr. Eldrith and I need to keep a close guard on it.

CHAPTER 46

2009

Greg aimed the TV remote at the screen and flicked it off. He glanced nervously at his watch; it was just after 3pm. He stared for a moment as the second hand ticked round the dial wondering if Suzanne's parents had received the answerphone message that he had left. It had been Melanie's suggestion that Greg look through Suzanne's personal file details of next of kin, but when he phoned the family home in the well-to-do suburb of Great Chorley some forty miles away, no one had answered. It seemed that Suzanne's last known contact had been a telephone conversation with Pete Doyle on Friday, now it was Wednesday. Greg had been into the office that morning, but unable to concentrate had left shortly after midday feigning a migraine. This was not the Suzanne he though he knew, reliable, empathetic and conscientious. He could not help but think that the only explanation was that something bad had happened.

When he'd reported his concerns to Melanie, she had at first shrugged off any suggestion that something was wrong. It was only when she tried Suzanne's phone herself throughout the morning that she reluctantly agreed to share Greg's worries. In an attempt to trace Suzanne, Melanie had tried phoning Ed Suthermount, the eccentric chap who lived in the cottage next to Tilly Whim, but his phone was ringing out. After Greg's suggestion Melanie had also telephoned the village pub to ask of recent sightings of a slim brunette in her early thirties. The landlady had told her she had seen a young woman fitting the description having a drink with a lady named Margaret Willows, but that had also had been on Friday. The landlady had promised to ask Margaret if she knew of Suzanne's whereabouts and get back in contact, but so far they had heard nothing.

Greg slid his fingers through his dark hair; the time had come to take further action. His stomach was knotted with nervous energy as he picked up his phone from the coffee table and dialed Melanie's number.

CHAPTER 47

1325

The morning had turned grey and heavy. The air was filled with tiny droplets of rain which clung to Roger's sandy hair, making it appear much darker than it really was. Philippa who had appeared not to notice the inclement weather was seething with rage. She dismounted her horse, handed the bridle to Roger for tethering and stomped up to the door of St. Alban's chapel. Before Roger had finished securing the horses, she had flung it open. All this action was much to the surprise of the startled weary-eyed Deacon Christopher who had barely roused himself from a tangle of blankets on the floor.

'Where is he?' Philippa demanded. The Deacon looked confused with sleep.

'Who are you asking for?' He managed through dry lips.

'Fr. Eldrith of course!' Philippa's voice was raised, almost frenzied. Deacon Christopher suddenly came awake, hauling himself up from the floor he brushed the creases from his tunic in a bid to look presentable.

'Please keep your voice down my lady. Remember you are in a holy place. Fr. Eldrith has been and gone this morning. He should be well on his way to Wareham by now. What is it you need? Can I be of service?'

Philippa wrung her hands in frustration. 'No! No you cannot. It is Fr. Eldrith who I have need to speak with and I....' Roger, who had been standing in the open doorway, watching the scene unfold suddenly spoke up.

'Yes, Deacon Christopher perhaps you can be of service' He interrupted. 'We have come to see how Blanche is faring.'

Philippa and Deacon Christopher turned in surprise at Roger's forthright statement. Never before had he challenged or contradicted someone of noble birth, but he felt that Philippa needed reminding of why they had come to the chapel in the first place.

'Yes, Roger is right. Please let us see Blanche.' Philippa's voiced had softened slightly.

Deacon Christopher eyed the pair warily before leading them towards the door of the chapel. 'Very well. I dare say all these visitors won't be doing her spiritual health any good. I would kindly ask my lady that you consider the girl's need for solitude and reflection. She needs time to come to terms with the miraculous happenings and adjust to her new vocation. Contact with the outside world will only hinder that at present.'

'Very good Deacon Christopher.' Philippa had finally composed herself. 'Pray tell me before we leave the confines of this chapel, where the holy spring is? I can neither see nor hear any water.'

'The spring comes and goes my lady. Today it is not here, but yesterday its waters could be seen bubbling up from the ground in the centre there.' Deacon Christopher was pointing towards the central column.

Philippa nodded somewhat skeptically. 'And Blanche can conjure these waters of her own free will?'

'It would seem so. Now remember what I have said, only a few moments with Blanche. I shall remain here in prayer. Let me know when you are departing.' Deacon Christopher nodded and showed them out through the door.

The rain had become even more persistent as Roger and Philippa made their way round to the north-east side of chapel, where the makeshift cell had been constructed. Roger took off his mantel and offered it to Philippa.

'Here my lady, please wear this to keep the rain off you.' He draped the mantel over Philippa's shoulders as she drew level with the tiny window.

'Blanche' Philippa whispered uncertainly. 'Are you in there?' The cell was very dark, but Philippa could just make out a tangle of dark brown hair and a pair of bright eyes staring up towards the light.

'Is she well?' Roger asked. He could not hide the concern or impatience from his voice. He moved to stand behind Philippa, so he could catch a glimpse of Blanche himself.

The girl was now peering out through the aperture. On seeing her visitors a look of relief and joy swept across her wide set eyes.

'My lady Philippa!' The girl smiled warmly. 'I am so glad to see you.'

'And I too. Tell me Blanche, how is it that you are confined in this cell? Are the stories the clergy have told us true, that you have performed a miracle?'

'No, my lady. At least I'm not sure, for the truth is that I cannot remember how the waters first appeared in the chapel.'

Philippa peered hard at Blanche, as if trying to establish the truth from the girl's face. 'So it is not your wish to be shut up in there, away from your kin and friends in the village?'

Roger winced, it was possible that the Deacon Christopher could hear what Philippa was saying, she was talking too loud. He noticed the pleading and desperate look in Blanche's eyes.

'That's right. Please lady Philippa I need your help in getting me out of here, but we must speak quietly Deacon Christopher listens on the other side of this wall.'

Philippa leaned closer to the girl. 'I will help, of course I will. My father has the authority over the land that this chapel stands on, I can get him to order your release!'

To Roger's surprise, Blanche did not seem overjoyed at Philippa's solution.

'The clergymen are very convincing my lady, they may have already told your father what happened here and when your father sees the waters, and experiences their powers, he may *want* to believe them.'

Philippa looked away for a moment, Roger guessed she was playing out the scenarios in her mind. 'What is it you need me to do Blanche? Arrange some men to break these walls under my authority?'

'It may not be necessary to *break* the walls my lady.'

Philippa looked confused. 'How then are you to get out?'

Blanche smiled, her eyes suddenly became alive again. Roger felt his heart skip a beat. How he wanted to be with this girl, to marry her and make her happy. His thoughts were interrupted by Blanche's urgent voice.

'The book you lent me, it has special powers, powers to transport people a great distance without them moving physically.'

Philippa looked excited all of a sudden but the excitement was tempered by a skeptical frown. 'It does? Is that is why Fr. Eldrith wanted the book.'

'Yes! But that is what I wanted to ask of you my lady, in your family library I am sure you will find another book, a copy of the one you lent me. If you can..'

Philippa cut her short 'Blanche, I'm afraid Fr. Eldrith has that book too. He came to the manor early this morning and took it without me knowing.'

Blanche looked panicky.

'But how does he know of the second book?' Tears welled in her blue-green eyes, making their colour almost luminous.

'Come come now!' Deacon Christopher had appeared behind them. 'The girl is upset, she needs to be left alone. Fr. Eldrith will be most displeased if he finds out I've been allowing visitors to disturb her solitude.'

'Fr. Eldrith has a lot to answer for!' Philippa snapped. Deacon Christopher turned away, his placid nature refusing him to become embroiled in a quarrel.

'Your horses await you, and I bid you a good day.' He said waving an arm in the direction of the restless tethered steeds.

‘Very well Deacon. We will leave now as you wish. But tell Fr. Eldrith this, he has no business to confine Blanche in that cell, at least not until he has my father’s word on the matter.’

Amidst the raised voices, Roger looked back towards the cell. Blanche was staring out, her small face forlorn, helpless. He desperately wanted to run back, to kiss her and tell her that all was not lost but instead he raised his hand and mouthed a good bye. There hadn’t been enough time to talk, he should have interrupted Philippa and mentioned the melted down-Brass ingot, but then perhaps it was best that it was not spoken of, matters spoken privately had a way of getting to Fr. Eldrith’s ears. Reluctantly he turned his attention to the horses, and helping Lady Philippa on to her mount, silently vowed to himself that the next time they came here, they would set Blanche free.

CHAPTER 48

Harold Martravers looked towards the window of his private solar. The rain had finally stopped, he would ride out soon to Wareham where Richard of Cambridge would be waiting for him. Harold rubbed his eyes, he had had an uneasy night's sleep. The past two years had been a challenging time for his estate, a combination of crop failures and payment of debts to Richard had put his wealth into a state of jeopardy. He reached for his goblet of wine and drained the last drop. Still, it wasn't all bad, the marriage arrangements he had made for his daughter should provide some security, it was fortunate that Lord Robert owned most of the fertile eastern counties, even in a bad year those lands could yield far more than his could when the conditions were good. Certainly, an alliance with Robert Carringstone would set the Martravers in good stead. There was just the matter of Philippa's dowry. Setting his goblet down Harold strained his ears, there was rustling coming from beyond the door.

'William? Is that you?'

There was a brief silence which was broken by a soft feminine voice.

'Father, it is I, Philippa. May I enter?'

Setting aside his writing equipment and papers, Harold rose to his feet. Feeling a little dizzy, he steadied himself against his desk. 'Of course.'

Philippa was in the room before he could gather himself. She looked so much like her mother when she had been younger. A beauty, but not the retiring type, like Maude. No, she was headstrong. Like himself in that way, so many people commented. Harold hadn't realised it until now but a smile played on his lips.

'Father what is it? You look a little dazed. Are you well?'

'Yes, save for the sleeping trouble I am well enough. Now what have you come to tell me? Make haste, I am leaving for Wareham soon, there are important business matters to take care of.'

'Yes I know.' Philippa bit her lip and looked down at the floor, and Harold wondered how much she knew about the problems with the estate, not that it was her business to know of course. 'I am here to ask you a favour.' Philippa paused and looked her father in the eye before averting them respectfully downwards. 'Fr. Eldrith is holding a girl from the village captive up at St. Alban's chapel. He is making all kinds of false claims that she has performed miracles and wishes to be enclosed in a cell. Do you realise he has even constructed a..........'

'Philippa.' Harold interrupted. 'I know about this. The Myddelton girl, yes Fr. Eldrith came to tell me about this first thing. He told me about a miraculous spring of water appearing up at the chapel at the command of this girl. I have to say it sounds far-fetched but our priest is more qualified than me to judge.'

'But Fr. Eldrith cannot be trusted! He has stolen two ancient books from our library. He is lying about Blanche too. She does not wish to be enclosed in the cell. Please, you must instruct Fr. Eldrith to let her go.'

Harold frowned; Philippa was clearly upset.

'My dear daughter, you have got this wrong. Fr. Eldrith has not stolen any book of ours, no, I gave him my permission to borrow one of the volumes for a short while. He is studying the lives of the ancient saints, he is a very learned man.'

'No, he had deceived us! Fr. Eldrith has two of our books, the one you talk of, and also a copy- he has even defaced it, removing the Brass from the cover and melting it down, Lord only knows why!'

'But Philippa, there is only one book of this kind in the library. There aren't two copies. You are mistaken my love. Now go and get ready for the fair, the other women folk have been dressing and preparing all morning, I'm surprised you have not been doing the same.'

A wave a frustration and anger flashed in Philippa's eyes.

'If you don't believe me about the book, then please believe me about Blanche. He has no right to keep her prisoner in this way.'

'Why are you so concerned about this simple girl Philippa? Shouldn't we wait and see if Fr. Eldrith's claims are true? It will soon prove folly if the miraculous water cannot be conjured again. Don't you see, if the priest is right there are good prospects for West Lytchett . Pilgrims; noble visitors; notoriety.' Harold preened his beard thoughtfully. The girl is safe, she is being fed and watered, Fr. Eldrith assured me of that. Now stop concerning yourself with these matters of men and go and dress for the fair.'

'But!' Philippa's eyes were pleading, but Harold's resolve was firm. He'd had to take this approach with her since she was no more than a small child. She knew his authority was not to be challenged.

As Philippa left his solar, defeated; Harold collected his papers into a tidy bundle. He wondered about what his daughter had said. *Two books, two volumes written by St. Aldhelm? Was that possible?* As he left his solar he summoned William.

'Yes Lord?' William lurked out of a gloomy doorway, as though he had been waiting for his lord's summons.

'William, see that the stable hands have saddled my horse. I shall ride to Wareham promptly.'

'Very good my lord.' William nodded in deference. 'I have asked the kitchen to prepare a knapsack for your journey.'

Harold forced a smile, 'Thank you William.' With that Harold put the uneasy conversation with his daughter aside and concentrated instead on how he would placate Richard of Cambridge and try and buy some time in terms of the debts he owed.

CHAPTER 49

2009

Her hands were shaking as she stood at the door of St. Alban's chapel. The voices from within were muffled, but clearly distressed. A shiver went up her spine and radiated out over her shoulder blades. *Come on Margaret,* She silently chided herself. *Pull yourself together now.* Shakily, she reached towards the latch and then reluctantly leaned her weight against the door. It creaked open nosily and Margaret winced. Up until now she had kept her eyes firmly fixed on the floor, too afraid to look up. When she finally summoned the courage to raise her eyes a mixture of relief and shock met her, for with the exception of a young gull padding round the pews, the chapel was completely empty. Leaving the chapel, Margaret strode purposely towards the silver hatchback and opened the front passenger door to help her frail husband climb out.

'It's all clear, no one is around.' She whispered, the covert nature of their mission leading her to talk in hushed tones.

Lance nodded but said nothing. He had a look of dread about him, like he was walking towards the hang man's gallows rather than a place of worship, Still, Margaret completely understood why. Before she opened chapel door the second time, she turned to face Lance, tears welling in her pale eyes.

'Come back to me Lance, please come back to me this time.'

Lance smiled sadly before embracing his wife with thin weak arms.

'It needs to be finished.' Was all he said before stoically pushing the chapel door.

CHAPTER 50

1325

It was mid-afternoon before Roger was able to take his leave from the stables. Most of the Martravers family, including Philippa had left for Wareham and there was little to do except run errands for the kitchen staff who were busy preparing the evening's feast. Edwy, who was lying propped against a hay bale squinted as his brother stepped over him and began to untether the old plough horse, Toby from his stall.

'What's the matter with you today brother? Shouldn't you be having a break from the 'orses given it is fair day?'

Roger stopped and looked Edwy in the eye. 'I thought I might take a trip down to Wareham myself and see what all the fuss is about!'

'You are?' Edwy sat up suddenly alert. 'Well, I will come with you if you do not mind my company.' He turned his eyes to the sun which was already lowering in the south-western sky. 'Say, do you think we can make it there and back in time?'

Roger's heart sunk. He would not have guessed that Edwy would be bothered to accompany him. He was trying to think of something to say when Hawise, the new kitchen maid appeared at the servants entrance at the back of the manor. Instinctively Roger stepped inside the stall out of her view.

'Are you quite comfortable Master Edwy?' Hawise mocked. 'We could do with some help in here.' The maid wiped her brow with her forearm. Edwy opened and closed his mouth a few times and looked in Roger's direction.

'Go and help her Edwy' Roger whispered. 'You are right, it's too late for the fair. I'm going to the village for there is something I need to do, but I will come back and help you and the kitchen maids soon.'

Edwy rubbed his face and reluctantly pushed himself up off the ground. 'All right, all right. I'm coming.' Edwy bawled in Hawise's direction. He looked back at Roger. 'Well you'd better come and help us Rog, no sneakin off to see that saintly sweetheart of yours.'

Roger's heart quickened, he was about to ask Edwy exactly *who* he thought his sweetheart was, but thought better of it. Instead he directed his attention to Toby. Skillfully attaching the yoke to the horse's harnesses, he waited until Edwy and Hawise were out of view and led the shaggy-shod horse across the stable yard and out towards the headland.

* * *

Suzanne knelt in her small cell. Her legs were stiff and she was suffering from cramp. The news that Fr. Eldrith had taken the second book had hit her hard. Up until that point she at least felt some hope, but now she was almost certain that the priest would destroy the second Brass too, leaving her well and truly stranded in the past. Suzanne thought back to when she was doing her history degree, and how she had often imagined how amazing it would be to travel through time, to observe what the past was really like. Being an imaginary observer, and taking part were two very different things, there was no justice here, the rights of ordinary folk stood for nothing. Disheartened, she slumped down to the ground, her nose felt tickly and she bit her lip to stop the tears from falling.

Closing her eyes, she leaned her head back against the stone of the cell wall. The base of her skull ached badly and the pounding she now felt as her head made contact with the stone was getting worse. At least she had Philippa and Roger fighting her corner, but just how convincing could Father Eldrith be? Philippa's father, Lord Martravers hadn't exactly rushed to send anyone out to verify the priest's claims; it was fair day, everyone was busy enjoying themselves – Philippa and possibly Roger too. No one really cared that a simple village girl was being kept against her will. It was hopeless, in a time of superstitions and poor justice she would be held at the whim of Fr. Eldrith for as long as he saw fit. Suzanne's nose tickled again and this time she let out a sob, it sounded detached from her, like it was Blanche who was crying, and not really herself. Slowly she was losing her grip, Suzanne did not exist, at the moment she mattered even less than Blanche.

CHAPTER 51

Roger's eyes narrowed as he approached the chapel on the headland. He thought he saw two figures disappearing from sight towards the front of the building. He groaned to himself, he had assumed the priest and his deacon would have been making merry at the fair, allowing him time to do what he needed to do. Roger considered he could perhaps overpower Deacon Christopher, but there was no way he could manage this if there was a second man present. Roger pulled on Toby's harness gently and the horse obediently quickened his pace. If he could get to Blanche round the other side of chapel, he could do most of the work before they even knew he was there. He led the horse through the tall grass, his shaggy feet occasionally catching in the undergrowth, Roger paused to listen; he was out of site from chapel door now and he could hear talking; it was Fr. Eldrith and the Deacon. As quietly as he could he took down the coil of chains attached to Toby's saddle and whispered at the cell window.

'Blanche, its Roger.' He heard scrambling before a bramble of hair and pair of blue-green eyes appeared at the window.

'Quietly now!' Roger warned. 'I've come to get you out, but Fr. Eldrith is here now so I must do it with stealth.'

'What? How are you going to...?'

Roger cut her short. 'Look, I am going to pass you a heavy piece from an old yoke. What I want you to do is wedge it across the window and hold it there till I give you the signal, then curl up small and cover your head against the roof thatch that may come down.'

The girl nodded; she squinted in the direction of the plough horse and Roger sensed that she had worked out his plan.

Using all his strength, Roger heaved the worn piece of oak which he had skillfully attached to the chains, and placing it end forward, fed it through the aperture of the cell.

'Its very heavy' He breathed. 'I hope you can hold it up.'

Inside the cell the small boned girl struggled under the weight of the dusty piece of oak, her arms quivered as she gathered all her strength in preparation to turn the wood onto its side. She waited patiently and hopefully for Roger's signal.

'What brings you here again, boy?'

Roger jumped, the priest had crept up so silently that he was caught completely unawares. Nevertheless, he was ready with an answer.

'Father, my conscience would not let me rest with Blanche trapped inside this cell. Seeing as no one was fighting her corner I have taken it upon myself to set her free. Move aside now while the horse does his work.' His voice cracked a little, betraying his nervousness. The priest, to Roger's dismay, started to chuckle.

'Roger my son. You take upon a great burden, to fight as you believe, the *good* fight. But have you not considered what you are fighting against? Come! I think there is something you should see before you break the walls of that cell.' Fr. Eldrith turned on his heels making off towards the chapel door. Roger reluctantly lowered the chains which he had started to connect to Toby's harness, confused by Father Eldrith's response.

'Roger, don't listen to him! He will try and talk you round.' The girl's pale face was pleading at the tiny window as she rested the heavy yoke against the wall of her cell.

'I won't be talked round, Blanche, I'm no fool. Let me see what the priest wants to show me if it is that important to him and then I will get you out of there, with my bare hands if need be!'

'Promise me Roger?' The girl's hand was extending through the window. Reaching up Roger clasped it with both his hands.

'I promise.'

Roger secured Toby's reins to a nearby tree and went to join the the priest and deacon on the other side of the chapel door. At first Roger feared that he would be lynched, but he quickly realised that they were deliberately obscuring something from his view.

'I'm glad you have taken the opportunity to see with your own eyes the miracle in our midst.' Fr. Eldrith spoke quietly, almost whispering. Roger could hear it now his ears had adjusted from the sound of the strengthening winds across the headland. The delicate trickle of running water. Fr. Eldrith and Deacon Christopher stepped aside in an almost stage managed fashion. The build-up, Roger considered to be a significant anti-climax.

'That is why we have kept Blanche a prisoner? A meagre spring? I bet it won't deliver enough to even fill my pail!'

Fr. Eldrith's eyes narrowed, Roger could tell he was doing his utmost to remain controlled. 'I would suggest that you would not criticise this most pure water, not at least until you have witnessed its powers.' The priest swallowed before speaking once more. He was looking more closely at Roger now. 'Is that a sore I see on your forearm?'

Roger was suddenly reminded of the irritation to his arms. Both of them were sore at the moment, but his left was particularly bad. 'Yyyes. I've had the condition since I was a child.' He stuttered, feeling self-conscious.

'Go and wash in the spring. The water will soothe you.'

Slowly, Roger stepped forward to the little spring, its water gently splashing onto his tattered shoes. Aware of the clergy men's eyes on him he made the sign of the cross and crouched, putting his hands into the unusually warm water. Dabbing a little of the water on to both his forearms he waited a moment before backing away from the spring. It was mystical, certainly, but was this all part of Fr. Eldrith's unfathomable charade?

'Recite the Lord's Prayer my son'. Fr. Eldrith's voice was hushed and reverent. Doing as he was told, Roger recited the prayer in Latin, as he did often at Mass. It wasn't until he concluded that he noticed the change to his arms. His skin was no longer chapped and blistering; it was smooth, virtually flawless.

Roger was astonished. 'My arms! They are better!'

'Of course.' Fr. Eldrith nodded with a smile. 'Now will you believe in the holy power of this spring?'

'How can I *not* believe in it now I have witnessed this for myself?' Roger examined his arms again. It was incredible, a true miracle.

'Perhaps you will see my wisdom in incarcerating your friend Blanche.'

Roger's eyes narrowed. 'No Fr. Eldrith. I do not yet see what Blanche has to do with this.' His voice beguiled an air of uncertainty.

'My son, it is Blanche who has the powers over this spring. She can summon it at her will. She herself acknowledges this.'

Roger stepped away from the priest. For the first time he had noticed that Deacon Christopher was behind him, blocking his exit. There was something all of a sudden unpleasant about the atmosphere in the chapel and he couldn't put his finger on what it was. His gut feeling was to run, run as far away as he could or at least back to the relative safety of the manor. But he couldn't leave Blanche. His instincts told him she needed his help right now. He *wouldn't* leave without her.

'How would I know that Blanche has these powers unless I see them with my own eyes.' Roger swallowed hard. Challenging the priest was never easy and now he felt especially vulnerable. *No one knows I'm here.* The thought echoed round his brain.

'*Because*' Fr. Eldrith spoke through gritted teeth. '*Because I am telling you, you have to trust me.*'

'Perhaps we might ask Blanche to make the waters stronger.' Deacon Christopher suggested. 'Show young Roger here that our claims are genuine and how we are acting in the girl's best interests.'

Fr. Eldrith scowled at the Deacon, but was quick to resume a mask of politeness. 'I do not see why exactly *I* am answerable to a stable boy, but if this expedites matters then very well, Deacon I will wait here with the boy while you go to Blanche and ask her to intercede with saints and perform this miracle.' The priest folded his arms defiantly while the Deacon took his leave through the chapel door which swung and slammed shut against the strengthening headland wind. Roger shivered.

'Inclement weather for this time of the year isn't it.' The priest commented casually. Roger noticed that he had begun to collect the spring water in small clay vessels and these were lined up, about twenty of them in the space behind the altar. 'Come and help me collect this precious water to aid your neighbours in the village. Perhaps you could take some to young Edwy so he could put some on his tongue and cure his foul language.'

Roger looked down, ashamed. Edwy could curse with the best of the boys at his age but Roger felt the priest had singled out his brother somewhat unfairly, as a slight on him. Slowly he walked over to the pile of empty vessels and began to do as the priest asked.

The chapel door opened once more and the Deacon burst in and hurriedly closed it behind him, his cape bellowing out in wind. 'Phew. It is blowing a gale out there. I think a storm is brewing out at sea.' He rubbed his hands together vigorously. 'I have asked Blanche to give us a sign – another miracle if she would. She said she would try.'

Fr. Eldrith put a stopper in the clay vessel he was filling and set it down with the others. 'We should all join in prayer. We need to be receptive to Blanche's miracles.' The three of them fell to their knees in quiet anticipation. Roger glanced at his arms again, still smooth, almost perfect skin. Whatever had happened it was truly amazing. He took a deep breath and tried to concentrate on the priest's calm voice as he recited a novena. The prayers continued, quietly yet with assured rhythm almost in defiance against the noise of the rushing winds outside. Roger stared into the spring, if anything it had gone weaker rather than stronger but the change was so slight it was impossible to tell. Either way, it didn't look like Blanche was the one who was commanding the miracles, as Roger had suspected. Roger's trance was suddenly broken by a tremendous noise. Beside him the Deacon flinched; the noise continued, it sounded like a crack of thunder but much louder. It was Fr. Eldrith who sprung into action.

'What in the world was that?' The priest's voice trembled as he raced to the door of the chapel, the Deacon and Roger closely following behind. Outside, gusts of wind had strengthened and Roger thought the noise must have been thunder or a bolt of lightening; that was until he saw that the roof and side wall of Blanche's cell had collapsed.

'No!' Roger cried. He could see Blanche's russet shawl crumpled and still amongst the rubble. The three of them rushed over, fearing the worst. The girl's pale face was unmarked as they knelt before her. Much to their delight she opened her eyes.

'My arm hurts.' Blanche whispered, her expression and pallor bore the tell-tale signs of shock.

'Thanks be to God she is alive! I thought it was all happening again, Blanche's death under my care, it couldn't happen, not again. God would not allow it!' Fr. Eldrith was hopping from one foot to another in relief. Roger stared at him.

'Fr. Eldrith! We need to move these stones from her arm at once! She is bleeding.'

Roger cleared some of the lighter rubble along with deacon, but a large corner stone remained, pining Blanche's arm to the ground. Fr. Eldrith knelt down and pulled the edge of the stone; it was stuck. 'On the count of three, let us all pull the stone in that direction'. Roger exclaimed with a nod of his head.

'One, two, three, Heave!'

The stone rolled awkwardly away from Blanche, and as it did she cried out in pain. To Roger's surprise, Fr. Eldrith hurriedly tore a strip from his black cloak and set about dressing the deep cut in Blanche's arm. When he had finished the makeshift bandage he stepped back and stared hard at Roger. 'Roger, I think Blanche will recover but I can see from her pallor that she is shocked. She needs a mug of strong ale or mead if you can find any. Quick, take your mount and ride to the manor at once and get these items on my authority. I will treat her with some of the spring water. *Hurry!*'

Roger was about to do as the priest ordered when movement behind him on the roof of the chapel caught his eye.

'Fr. Eldrith! Look out.' Roger's warning was instantly muted by a strong gust of wind that stole his words and sent them off eastwards over the headland. It seemed the priest had heard the warning, but as he turned to follow Roger's gaze, it was already too late.

It happened in an instant, the capping stone from the roof of the chapel struck the priest on the side of the head and he fell forwards, like one who had been cut down in battle. The Deacon shrieked in horror, rushing to attend his superior, crossing himself and muttering prayers.

Roger winced as he dared to take a few paces forward and look upon the priest's injuries. The capping stone which was much larger than it usually appeared in situ on the chapel roof was lodged in Fr. Eldrith's head. A dark patch of blood was already beginning to clot around the weathered limestone, and fragments of bone stark white against the bloodied flesh clung to the priest's dark hair. Roger could feel bile starting to rise in his throat, he swallowed hard and closed his eyes for a moment. He only opened them when he felt the rush of air past him. It was Deacon Christopher.

'It's serious, God help him!' The Deacon had retrieved a number of clay bottles from the chapel and was pouring their contents over Fr. Eldrith, who was no longer moving. 'I must go to the village and get help. Tell me Roger – Lord Martraver's physic, does he stay in the village?'

Roger gathered his thoughts. 'No, he lives in Dorchester, but today he may be in Wareham – the fair...'

'Of course.' The Deacon stuttered breathlessly. 'No matter, the sooner I go the better it will be for our dear priest. You stay with him, I shall make haste and be back soon with help.'

Without further ado, Deacon Christopher took off in the direction of West Lytchett, his cloak flapping in the wind. Roger's thoughts instantly went to Blanche, who he had noticed had managed to sit up amidst the rubble. Thankfully the horror of what had happened to Fr. Eldrith was just out of her view. Roger went over and knelt beside her.

'Roger, what has happened?' Her voice was weak, confused.

'You're going to be okay, the cell you were in collapsed. Your arm is wounded, but Fr. Eldrith..' Roger paused thinking of the writhing priest just feet away.

'Yes?' She eyed him curiously.

'Fr. Eldrith has bandaged it for you. You had a lucky escape Blanche.'

The girl's face crumpled in bewilderment. 'Blanche? But my name is Suzanne...'

Roger managed a sad smile for the name sounded familiar. *The lavender scented letter had told him.* Roger's thoughts were hazy; there was memory of a letter, of his bones being tired and old, a recollection of yearning to be back here in this time in the prime of his youth. He shook his head briefly, as if to clear his mind of the confusing thoughts. Then he remembered Toby and his knapsack of supplies. 'Let me get you some bread and ale. It will make you strong.' Patting Blanche lightly on her good arm, Roger rose and made his way round the other side of the chapel. Toby, sheltering from the wind kicked his hooves restlessly. Roger stroked the horse's muzzle to settle him and his eyes cast downwards to a cloth knapsack that rested by the side of the chapel. At first he thought it was his own pack that had fallen from the horse's saddle but on closer inspection he saw the rectangular outline of an object concealed within. Pulling open the flap, he was astonished to see the book that Blanche so badly needed – it must be the priest's knapsack! Excitedly he cradled the book in his arms and returned to where she was sat, still half dazed.

'Here, look what I have brought for you – as you requested!' At first she looked even more confused that she had been earlier, but as the cloth fell away to reveal the glint of Brass, a smile of recognition graced her lips. Roger smiled back. To see Blanche remotely happy again was like feeling the sun in the depths of midwinter. 'I have to confess, I don't know why you want it, but I found it in the priest's knapsack.'

To Roger's surprise, she suddenly raised herself onto her good arm, trying to stand. 'Here let me help you.' Roger offered his hand and the girl clutched it tightly.

'We must go inside the chapel.' She whispered. 'Where is Fr. Eldrith and the Deacon? Are they inside?'

Roger looked at his feet. 'No. Something terrible has happened. As the pair of them walked round the other side of the chapel, deliberately avoiding Fr. Eldrith's broken body, Roger explained about the priest's violent accident. 'He was trying to help you, he had just finished dressing your wound and that is when it happened.'

'Is he dead?' She asked.

'I think so, if not he will be soon'. Roger did not want to admit that the gory sight had turned his stomach. 'No man could walk away from that kind of injury. He lies round the other side of the chapel, the Deacon has rushed to get help.'

'In that case we must move with haste, I need to escape before the Deacon or Fr. Eldrith catches me again!'

The pair of them scanned the headland before they disappeared into the silent dark of the chapel. All was clear. The girl approached the chapel's central column, and stood exactly where the spring had rose from the ground. Roger gazed at her mystified. 'Did you really make the spring waters rise, and put healing into them?'

The girl smiled. It was a wistful smile. 'I don't know. I wish I did. At first I thought it was a folly, but I believe there is wisdom here in this chapel. An *ancient* wisdom, one that I do not fully understand. I hope to understand more very soon though.'

'Are you leaving?' Roger asked, biting his lip to prevent the moisture in his eyes pooling and brimming over.

'Yes. I have to go now. You see I don't belong here.'

'Take me with you!' Roger suddenly proposed in desperation. 'I want to be with you!'

The slender girl held out both her good and bandaged arms as best she could and the two of them embraced, tears flowing freely now.

'You are a good soul Roger. You helped me at my time of need. Go back to your duties now, for you belong here.'

Roger stepped back, the aching in his heart was immense. 'If that is what you want, Blanche, then I shall not get in your way.'

She smiled bravely at him. 'There is something you could do, when you go back to the village this evening'.

Roger looked up and she could see there was hope in his tearful eyes.

'Send Lady Philippa a message. Tell her to follow her heart. If she is certain what will make her happy, then she must strive for it. She has a brave and inquisitive soul; such a gift would be a shame to waste and these qualities will help her achieve her aim. Come now, you can help me in what I am about to do. I need you to close your eyes and kneel quietly in prayer, before the crucifix.'

Roger was uncertain, but as he pondered the message Blanche had given him, he dropped to his knees and closed his eyes. Quietly, she spoke some words of blessing, touching his head gently. 'Keep your eyes closed now.'

Roger could not resist, he opened his eyes to a narrow squint. He could see Blanche holding the ancient book, pressing the Brass against the worn stone of the column. Suddenly he remembered; what he needed to do. In a flash he projected his arm towards her, his fingertips brushing against her woolen shawl. He blinked, and in that split second she had gone, leaving no trace, not even foot prints in the dust where she had stood.

CHAPTER 52

2009

It was after 6pm when Greg and Melanie arrived in West Lytchett. Greg, who had been the passenger in Melanie's 4X4 had tried to make light conversation during the journey, but had struggled to find a topic that Melanie seemed interested in. In the end he had given up and resigned himself to awkward silence, reasoning that Melanie was the type of person who needed the quiet to concentrate on her driving. It didn't matter anyway, what mattered was that they found Suzanne safe and put their worries to rest, but as they turned into the chocolate-box village, Greg felt an uneasy feeling creep over him, a mixture of fear and excitement. He shivered a little and Melanie closed the windows.

'It can get windy up here –we are on a headland, look that's Tilly Whim on the left, and there's Suzanne's car. I'm sure she will be just fine.'

Greg looked in the direction Melanie was pointing and noticed someone was stood outside the front door of the terraced cottage, peering through the letter box. 'Who's that Melanie?'

Melanie's eyes narrowed- it seemed at first she hadn't noticed the white-haired elderly woman stood on the garden path.

'I've no idea, but it looks like she is waiting for the door to be answered. Come on, let's go and find out.' Melanie maneuvered the car into a space behind Suzanne's and they both got out.

'Hello!' Melanie called after the old woman. 'Can I help you at all? I'm Melanie, I own Tilly Whim cottage.'

As they entered through the gate and walked up the fragrant, flower-encroached garden path Greg thought he could see the tears on the elderly woman's face. He felt not only dread, but a sense of deep sadness as his eyes met hers. Without waiting for her reply, Greg spoke out with renewed urgency.

'We are here about a friend of ours, Suzanne Brookes. Have you seen her?'

The elderly woman nodded slowly and stared out into the distance, somehow disregarding the two visitors. 'Lance was with her.' She said strangely.

Greg and Melanie exchanged looks. It was Melanie who broke the short but poignant silence. 'Here, let me open the door and see what's what.'

Fumbling with her keys, Melanie turned the lock. Greg noticed her hands were shaking despite her mask of composure. Within seconds Greg and Melanie were inside the cottage, calling Suzanne's name. The first thing that struck them was the curtains were closed in the living room, which Greg interpreted as a bad sign. *Why had Suzanne not drawn them back?* Pulse racing, Greg followed Melanie into the kitchen and stopped in his tracks when Melanie let out a loud shriek. Before them on the kitchen floor, laid Suzanne, her forehead and face covered in dried blood, her eyes staring and her mouth opened a little as she made strange little noises. It was then he noticed the elderly woman who had been stood outside the cottage was now standing next to him.

'Get her an ambulance - quickly!' The woman ordered with a strength and authority in her voice that Greg hadn't anticipated.

Without hesitating, Melanie pulled a phone from her bag, dialled 999, and headed back into the living room away from the carnage to give the operator the details. At the same time, the elderly woman knelt down by Suzanne and stroked her cheek, seemingly not at all bothered by the blood and gore. 'Poor, poor dear. So brave. Just like my Lance. Poor dear.'

Greg noticed Suzanne's eyes flickered in recognition of the elderly woman. 'Lance? I'm sorry, do you know what has happened to Suzanne?'

The woman took a new packet of handkerchiefs from her pocket and put several on Suzanne's forehead at the source of the wound, and kept one to dab her eyes. At this moment Melanie returned to the kitchen with news that an ambulance was on its way. 'They've said not to try and move her, but keep her warm and as comfortable as possible until the ambulance arrives. Forgive me for asking but, who are you again?'

Straightening, slowly from the kitchen floor, the elderly woman 'My name is Margaret. I live in the village and Lance is, *was*, my wonderful brave husband who I have today just lost.'

Greg and Melanie looked at one another, bewildered. Sniffing into her handkerchief, Margaret continued. 'I have only known Suzanne a few days, whilst she has been staying here in the cottage, but she is a good person, a strong person. She can and will pull through from this! Here, let us use this sofa throw as a blanket for her.

Taking one end of the beige throw, Greg knelt down and covered Suzanne's legs which were bunched into a foetal position. Quietly he whispered into her ear.

'Suzanne, I don't know what has happened to you but we are going to get you to hospital. Is there anything we can do to make you feel more comfortable in the meantime?'

Suzanne blinked a couple of times as if trying to wake from a trance. She remained silent but raised a pale hand towards Greg. Greg took her hand and clasped it gently in his own.

'It's okay, Suzanne. It's all okay now.'

CHAPTER 53

September 2009

Dear Suzanne

I hope this letter finds you well. It has taken me a while to track you down, but regardless of this fact it is still no excuse. I should have been in contact sooner. I suppose you might be wondering where I disappeared to on that day your friends came for you? Even if you do not wonder this and do not even care now, I feel that I owe you both an explanation, and apology.

Since my Lance's funeral I have been living with my sister in Dundee. I had to get away from West Lytchett you see, after all that had happened, it was too much to bear, all the memories, getting Lance back for a short, but wonderful time only to lose him again. I'm sorry I lied to you Suzanne, about him being dead. When I first met you I did not think any of this would happen, it seemed easier for me to lie than to try to explain what happened to him all those years ago, and of course once you tell a lie like that, you can't take it back. The doctors said he had totally lost his mind, he would never recover and that the best place for him was an institution, and to me in many ways telling you he was dead wasn't a lie, for my Lance had died many years ago when the illness claimed his mind.

But a wonderful thing happened Suzanne when you came to West Lytchett- he started to improve, dramatically, over the course of just three days he not only knew who I was, but was able to wash, dress himself, recall the places we had visited on holiday together and the music we both used to dance to. It was wonderful to have my Lance back again. I had to tell him of course, about what was happening to you. I felt a responsibility towards you. I had lost my husband to such a devastating illness and stood by as it happened. But I had a feeling that Lance would know what to do, that somehow his recovery and you turning up in West Lytchett was all connected. As it turned out, my hunch was right, Lance already knew about you. He had seen you in his dreams. A chill creeps up my spine as I am writing these words, for I do not understand what happened, it is unexplained but true.

So with the agreement of the nurses at Bellemere, I collected Lance on that Tuesday morning and brought him back home for the day. I had, prior to collecting him, called round at Tilly Whim Cottage, but it was early and in the end I decided not to knock on in case you were sleeping. Under other circumstances Lance and I could have spent a poignant, reflective day alone together in our home, but Lance was very clear, knowing the trouble you were in, he asked to go to St. Alban's straight away. Once inside the chapel, Lance started acting strangely, scratching at the central supporting column with his overgrown fingernails, like he was searching for something. When I handed him the pair of tweezers he had asked for, it all became clear; one of pieces of metal sticking from the column was stuck deep within the stone, and I could see that it wasn't a pin or a coin, it was the Brass! When Lance finally worked the Brass free from the stone he turned and looked me, told me he loved me and that we would meet again someday. I rushed to him, afraid that he might somehow use the Brass as a weapon against himself but as I went to embrace him there was a strange turbulence in the air around us and the next moment he was gone. Vanished.

The rest of the story you have probably heard, Lance's body was found the following day at Dancing Ledge, he had suffered heart failure and I still have no idea how he got there. I was interviewed by the police shortly after and when I told them that he had vanished at the chapel they assumed I was a batty old lady, losing my marbles. They recorded death by misadventure, that Lance had strayed from the chapel, taken a walk and died from exhaustion. When he was buried, I made sure the Brass was secretly buried with him. It caused enough trouble to the living, I felt a responsibility to ensure it was put out of harm's way. I hope you agree with what I decided to do.

The police still continue to search for Edward Suthermount, as I am sure you are aware. He too has seemingly disappeared and has not been seen since the night of your abduction. With no living relatives and few friends to speak of, I have taken it upon myself to tend the small garden of Arne Cottage, just to keep things tidy for the sake of the village. Last week I was busy dead-heading some flowers when I came across a bundle of papers lodged in the foliage –a small manuscript. I have kept hold of this as I think you should see it first before we hand it in to the police. There is some water damage as you would expect, but most of it is legible and I'm sure you would think, very interesting given our discussions about Blanche.

Setting that dreadful business to one side for a moment, I have some other interesting news for you. When I returned to West Lytchett at the beginning of September, I found a team of archaeologists have been excavating land in proximity to St. Alban's and they have unearthed a burial – a female skeleton. There are a number of medieval items among the bones, one of which is a piece of brass, but the Kist tomb is Anglo Saxon in style which is puzzling. Scientists are carbon dating the bones at the moment so we shall see. Could this be Blanche?

Finally, can I offer an invite to come and visit me here at Encombe Cottage? If you are interested, the skeleton and other artefacts are on display for a short time in the church hall and then the skeleton will be re- interred in St. John's church yard.

Yours sincerely,

Margaret.

Seeing Edward's name in print had made her feel chilled to the bone. Suzanne noted Margaret's contact phone number at bottom of the letter and folded it pensively. A lot had happened since June, some good things, and some not so good, but at least life now seemed to be heading in the right direction. She looked up startled; Greg had snuck up beside her and was nuzzling the side of her neck. Suzanne shivered, indulging in the spontaneous moment of sensual joy.

'Exciting news?' Greg asked as he slipped his arms around her waist.

'Yes, I suppose so, although it's not the job interview I was expecting.' Suzanne leaned back further into Greg's embrace and passed him the letter.

'Give it time, the deadline for applications only passed a couple of days ago.' Greg reassured her. 'Besides, you are more than qualified for the position. It will suit you far better than your previous job. Pete Doyle says you did well to get out, the company is badly run and agreeing voluntary resignation was the best outcome. If only I had the guts to do the same!' Greg became silent for a few minutes as his eyes scanned Margaret's immaculate handwriting. After a while he turned Suzanne around to face him. 'If you need to go back, then that's fine. Do what you need to do.'

Suzanne sighed. 'Margaret says she has something for me, a manuscript. I probably wouldn't go if it wasn't for that but...'

'Hushhh.' Greg drew her closer. 'Look it's obvious to me that you need some closure on what happened. Why don't you give Margaret a call and talk to her before you decide? You can always politely back out of her invitation if you want – just tell her you are busy with your university course, that wouldn't be a lie.'

'Yes you are right. Although if I told her it is a part time archaeology course she would say all the more reason for me to visit – especially now this skeleton has been uncovered!'

Greg tilted Suzanne's chin so they were face to face. 'Just leave that little detail out.' He grinned.

Suzanne felt herself relax under Greg's easy stare. That is what she had come to love most of all about him. His ability to be serious and trustworthy yet light hearted all at the same time. Smiling back at him she felt as if her cares had melted away for a moment. 'Okay. But I'm only going back there if you come with me.'

CHAPTER 54

Margaret was waiting in the large bay window as Suzanne and Greg made their way up the neat path of Encombe Cottage. Suzanne held her hand up in a wave but when she looked again Margaret had disappeared. Greg stole a glance at Suzanne before he pressed the doorbell.

'Are you okay?'

'I'm fine, really I am.' Suzanne forced a nervous smile.

The doorbell sent out a polite chime that sounded like church bells, but Margaret was already opening the door.

'Suzanne and Gregory, welcome! Do come in.'

Suzanne noticed how Margaret had aged over the space of a few months; new lines had appeared under her eyes and her hair wasn't as neatly blow-dried and set as usual. Greg and Suzanne stepped into the hallway and were immediately shown into the front room where tea and cake were ready and waiting. Suzanne couldn't help but feel sorry for Margaret and also admired her stoic show of hospitality despite the fact she must still be grieving for her husband.

'It's cherry and coconut. I hope it won't spoil your dinner.' Margaret smiled weakly as Suzanne and Greg took a seat next to one another on the sofa.

'Thank you, you really shouldn't have gone to any trouble.' Suzanne offered.

'Oh nonsense! Plus I do believe we have grounds for celebration.' Margaret gestured towards the couple. 'I see that every cloud has a silver lining.' The amber liquid splashed a little from the teapot as Margaret set about pouring the tea.

Suzanne blushed and looked towards Greg who to Suzanne's surprise had also coloured at Margaret comments. It was Greg who replied.

'It was just meant to be. Suzanne and I have been getting along great. Moving in together was the next step and it's working out just fine.' Greg smiled at Margaret, a look of genuine happiness radiated from his face.

'Well I am so pleased for you both, well done.' Margaret took her cup of tea and sipped as she reclined back into her armchair. The room was quiet for a few moments as tea was drunk and mouthfuls of cake eaten. Margaret finally broke the silence.

'I suppose you are wondering why I wanted you to come here in person?'

Suzanne felt a pang of anxiety at Margaret's question. 'I guess one reason is to see the skeleton they've unearthed?'

'Yes, but more importantly, remember the manuscript I mentioned in my letter? Here.' Leaning towards the table at the side of the armchair, Margaret retrieved large padded envelope as passed it over the tea tray.

'As you know I happened to 'stumble' upon this in Ed's front garden. I was going to hand it into the police straight away, but I thought you should see it first.'

Suzanne instinctively looked inside the envelope before putting in her hand to retrieve the small but thick manuscript. The book had no illustrations or pictures on its cover, just the title.

'The Mysterious Saint Blanche'. Suzanne read aloud and looked towards Margaret for a cue to continue.

'Go on, there is nothing sinister about it, have a look inside.'

Reluctantly Suzanne opened the first page where Ed had begun a Foreword about his research into St. Wite, whom, she learned, was believed to be an eighth century saint, and Blanche Myddelton, an educated peasant girl who lived in the fourteenth century. The Foreword went on to explain how he had come to conclude they are one of the same person and history has confused the two.

As Suzanne was reading, a memory flashed back to her as clear as day – she was back at the chapel on that terrible night. Ed was ranting in a crazed manner; he had said something about this, his final literary project as a repentance, to honour the saint whose life he had destroyed. Suzanne shuddered and Greg put his hand on hers in comfort.

'Do you think this is a good idea?' Greg had directed the question towards Margaret but it was Suzanne that answered.

'Yes and I'm fine. Honestly. It's just, it doesn't make any sense. Why would Ed believe that Blanche was a saint from the dark ages when she actually lived many hundreds of years after this in medieval times?

Margaret shrugged her shoulders. 'I was hoping it might make some sense to you, that it would answer any remaining questions you have, about Blanche and her fate.'

Greg ran his fingers through his hair and Suzanne could sense his exasperation and desire to protect her. 'Margaret as I know you are aware, back in June Suzanne had a very nasty head injury that has played a significant part in this confusion. She herself even said the bump on her head was to blame when she was recovering in hospital. Is it wise to carry on delving into these memories, hallucinations or whatever you might call them? Shouldn't the focus be on getting justice for what that evil man did to her and then she can look to put this whole traumatic experience behind her and move on?'

'Greg, can I just say something? Suzanne piped up, her mouth strangely dry after drinking the tea. 'You're right, I suffered a serious blow to the head, but that can't explain all the bizarre things that happened to me in the days prior to that. I certainly didn't imagine them – Margaret here is my witness. She is just trying to help me piece together all the facts so I understand what the meaning of this episode is, so I, *we* can move on.' Suzanne squeezed Greg's hand in assurance. She knew he was trying to help, although he could not fully comprehend or yet possibly even believe her story. Suzanne thanked Margaret for the book. 'I will have a proper look at it later and see if it triggers any thoughts or memories. I take it there has been no further developments with finding Ed?'

Margaret shook her head. 'Absolutely nothing. I know the police seemed skeptical when you told them about the abduction, but the fact that he is on the run doesn't look good for him does it? I mean, it goes some way to verify your account of what happened.'

Suzanne looked down at her ankle where the thin white scar of the where Ed's shackles had been. 'I suppose not. I would just feel better if he was found and admitted what he did. That way people might believe my story, or at least some of it.' She hadn't expected to feel this way and as the tears that she'd tried to fight back brimmed over her lower eyelids, Suzanne let out a sob that sounded like a young child. Greg comforted her as Margaret passed her a box of tissues.

'You don't have to go to the re-interment tomorrow Suzanne, not if you are not up to it.' Margaret said placing the box of tissues on the sofa between her and Greg.

'No, I want to go.' Suzanne sniffed. I'll be fine, I wasn't expecting to get upset. I'm sorry.'

'Oh don't you be feeling bad. Now then, have you both got dinner and somewhere to stay organised?'

Greg nodded explaining that they had booked in a B & B in a village nearby.

'Well you take yourselves off there when you are ready, go and enjoy Dorset while you are here, no need to be staying while an old woman plays gooseberry!'

As Suzanne got up to leave she could see that Margaret too was tearful, but trying to hide her emotions in the way she usually did. They had both been victims in this, Margaret had lost her beloved husband and Suzanne had almost been trapped in another time, a world as foreign as one could imagine. Victims, yet survivors nonetheless.

"Goodbye Margaret, and thank you for all you have done for me."

With that Suzanne and Greg left Margaret in peace to reconcile her own thoughts.

CHAPTER 55

The day was dawning misty and humid. September had been an exceptionally mild month, and as Suzanne drew back one curtain and pushed the sash window of the B & B open, she noted that through the twilight, October was promising to be the same. Looking back in the direction of the bed, Greg continued sleeping, seemingly unware of the change to his usual surroundings. By contrast, Suzanne hadn't slept well, despite Greg's advice to put down Edward's swan-song book on the Mysterious St. Blanche, she had stayed up into the early hours reading with a morbid fascination. It had, as Margaret had suggested, triggered memories - memories that hadn't resonated since her abduction. But were these actual memories, or had Ed been playing mind games with her? Had he read extracts of his book whilst she was semi-conscious – is that why the ideas within seemed familiar?

Suzanne's thoughts were interrupted by the beeping of the alarm clock, announcing in unforgiving tones that it was 7:30am. Moving away from the window Suzanne silenced the clock seconds before Greg's flaying hand reached over to hit the snooze button.

'Morning.' She leaned over and kissed his stubbly cheek.

He looked at her with the confusion of not knowing what day or where he was and then smiled warmly, outstretching his arms in a come back to bed gesture.

'We have to get up early remember? Suzanne whispered into his ear.

Greg grunted in protest but in a few moments he had roused himself enough to swing his legs out of bed and make them both a coffee. Suzanne welcomed the bitter taste as the caffeine started to make her feel more alert. She had been dreading this trip for the past few weeks, but it was necessary. Necessary to get the closure she needed and, perhaps satisfy a curiosity that was growing within her.

Within an hour, Suzanne and Greg had finished breakfast and were heading out on the three mile journey to St. John's church. Greg was unusually quiet and drove silently until they reached the village where he stopped just short of the duck pond.

'It's not too late if you want to turn back you know. They will understand, I'm sure.'

Suzanne smiled wistfully. 'I need to do this Greg, I need to be here. Even if they don't find Ed, this may bring some closure to what has happened.'

Greg nodded in agreement and drove on the final section of the journey until they were outside the church.

They found the vicar and an officer of the local archaeological society waiting for them at the porch, just as Margaret had said. The vicar welcomed them, and re-affirmed Suzanne's interest in the discovery.

'Welcome Ms Brookes and..'

'This is Greg, Greg Jones, and please, call me Suzanne.' Suzanne offered.

'Of course. I'm Reverend McKay and this is Sidney Bolt of the Purbeck Archaeological Trust. Margaret told us you would like to view the remains and discoveries before they are re-interred as you have an interest in local history and family connections to the village, is that right?'

'Yes.' Suzanne tried to clear her throat in a bid to sound more authoritative. 'I'm researching my family history as I have connections on my mother's side. I also found something when I was a child visiting the village, an artefact. Something I should have handed in really. I heard that a similar item has been found with the remains?'

Suzanne noticed Sidney Bolt raising an eyebrow in interest at her admittance, but remained silent, prompting Suzanne to explain further.

'It was an ancient Brass, but I don't have it now, I think we lost it in a house move.' As she spoke, Suzanne thought about the Brass, the one on the front of the book that Roger had brought to her and visualised it metres below ground in Lance's grave, not too far away.

'A pity.' Sidney said, his voice heavy with genuine concern. 'It's proving to be a real puzzle this case. The carbon dating is back in and the bones are 8th century, belonging to a female, about 40 years in age. This dating is contemporary with the style of the Kist tomb, yet the grave goods are certainly medieval. No later than 14th century in their type and appearance. One possibility is that the grave was disturbed at some point in the thirteen hundreds and the items were placed there then, but there is certainly no evidence of the tomb being unsealed until we found it. Most odd.' Sidney was shaking his head as if trying to make sense of all the facts once more. 'Anyhow, you may view the items that were found with the skeletal remains here, inside the church. After the re-interment, they are to go on display in the local museum.'

Suzanne nodded and started to follow the vicar and Sidney as they walked forward into the entrance of the church. Greg had picked up Suzanne's hand and squeezed it. For the first time Suzanne wondered how Greg must feel about this unusual visit, and pondered if he felt a similar nervousness and apprehension at what they were about to see.

The bones had been placed in a standard modern day coffin that was resting on a trestle table at the end of the nave, near the altar. As Suzanne approached she could see the pale cream ruffled silk lining protruding from the top. The sight reminded her of when she said her final good byes to her Grandmother many years before. The memory created a wave of emotion within her and a painful lump swelled in her throat.

'You are welcome to look inside the coffin.' The vicar prompted. 'I'm sure Margaret told you that the re-interment service is at 10 o clock this morning, although sadly we have no way of finding out who these bones belong to, at least we can lay them to rest in consecrated ground here in the church yard.'

Suzanne smiled acceptingly in acknowledgment of the vicar's words and wondered if these remains could actually be the bones of Blanche as Margaret had suggested. Ed's book had theorised that St. Wite and Blanche had been one of the same person, an explanation for this being that Blanche had been able to access the Portal and had journeyed back and forth from the middle ages where she lived as a holy anchoress, to the dark ages staying for a short time under the tutelage of St. Aldhelm. But Ed's book had maintained that St. Wite had died in the fourteenth century, her remains most probably enshrined at the church of Whitchurch Canonicorum some fifty miles away. However this was Ed's version of events as he has planned them. It was a version where Suzanne had become Blanche, and had been locked away in a miserable cell for the rest of her life. This, of course, had not happened.

The pair were now standing over the coffin, looking inside. Suzanne stared into the hollows of the skull where once a bright pair of eyes - Blanche's eyes, might have been and she closed hers, just for a moment. She was back in the fourteenth century, as Blanche, incarcerated in the anchorite's cell that Fr. Eldrith had constructed, trying to relive and remember. It had all happened so quickly, Roger had been trying to help her escape, then the weather had turned and the capstone had fallen, resulting in Fr. Eldrith's death. What had happened when she travelled through the Portal for the last time? Had she, Suzanne gone one way into the 21st century and Blanche to the dark ages? Back to where they both truly belonged? That would at least explain the difference between the bones and the grave goods not matching in date. When Suzanne opened her eyes she found herself staring at the long limb bones which had been laid out carefully in the confined space. Something wasn't right. Blanche was of slight build and small in stature. This skeleton had belonged to someone taller, more robust. Her attention was drawn to the items that had been found alongside the bones that had been locked away in a display case. Suzanne's heart leapt when she noticed the small ingot of Brass that was in a compartment next to a medieval brooch and clasp, and a small dagger.

It did all happen. Fr. Eldrith ordered Roldan to melt down the Brass. It wasn't a dream.

It was then that pieces of the puzzle began to fall into place. When she spoke it felt as if it was not her voice but someone else's.

‘In your expert opinion, Sidney, would you say this person could possibly have been a noble, considering the quality of the goods buried with her?’

Sidney Bolt stole a glance at the vicar. ‘The goods are of high quality as you suggest. It is unclear what the Brass ingot’s purpose was, perhaps it was used as a form of coinage, but certainly the dagger and brooch are of a good standard of workmanship, typical of those carried by the nobles of the 14th-15th century. However, there lies your problem! We can confidently say that the grave goods did not belong to the skeleton as the huge disparity in the dating suggests. They must have been put in the grave several centuries later.’

Suzanne nodded, her mind was racing as the story unraveled. It didn’t matter that the Brass had been melted down – it still retained its power! For now she understood who was laid out before them.

‘Thank you so much for letting us see the bones and other finds. It has been a privilege.’

The vicar and archaeological officer smiled politely and offered Suzanne and Greg a hot drink before preparation for the reinternment service began. Suzanne thanked them both but declined their offer.

‘There is someone I need to speak to before the service, we won’t be long.’

Suzanne led Greg out of the church and breathed in long and deep, as though she had subconsciously been holding her breath all the time they were inside the ancient building.

‘What’s happening Suzanne? I thought we were hanging around here until the service commences? Greg looked bewildered and Suzanne felt sorry for him being on the periphery of events, not able to understand or believe what had happened to her during the summer.

‘I have to speak to Margaret. There is something I need to tell her.’

CHAPTER 56

It was only a small number of villagers that attended the service, perhaps no more than twelve, but there was feeling of serenity and a poignancy in the ancient hymns that had been chosen, some dating from the dark ages, and others medieval. As the small gathering clustered by the grave pit and the coffin was lowered down into the ground, Margaret turned to Suzanne.

'Your visit here was successful in once sense.' She whispered. 'You came to West Lytchett to find your ancestors and you did!'

Suzanne nodded respectfully towards the grave. If it was the remains of Philippa Martravers that they had laid to rest, she certainly had discovered more about her ancestry than she had hoped for. It was somewhat ironic that the newly dug pit was only a couple of metres away from another recent grave, one that contained Lance Martin Willows, who had also been Roger Cheney – Philippa's loyal servant. Suzanne noticed Margaret steeling a glance towards her late husband's grave, tears welling in her eyes. Discretely she reached out and touched Margaret's arm, feeling a strange sadness descend upon her. Three of the villagers drew handfuls of dirt and threw it towards the coffin. As the burial rites drew to an end, Margaret patted Suzanne's hand. Tears were rolling down her powdered cheeks now, there was nothing more to be said.

Later on that night, as Suzanne drifted in to a deep and dreamless sleep, the curtains of the B & B room bellowed with a sudden gust. Outside, some of the early autumn fallen leaves were blowing around in circles in the small courtyard garden. Faster and faster they whirled as if a small tornado had descended. Suzanne flinched in her sleep, but didn't wake. Something small and rodent like scuttled across the yard outside, its fur bristling and tiny heart racing as it witnessed the unexplained forces at work. The leaves were spiraling upwards now, towards the open window of the bedroom. If Suzanne had been on the brink of consciousness, she would have noticed the curtains bellowing once more, and a dark shadow seeping into the room like black ink into water as it permeated the air making it thick and uncomfortable. The shadow came to rest at Suzanne's side of the bed hovered and over her. Close to her face it reveled in the warm exhaled air from her nostrils as if it was gathering energy, then in a split second, it flew back out through the window and restlessly wandered the Dorset countryside until it found what it was looking for, locked away in a cabinet in a museum.

EPILOGUE

Spring A.D. 707
St Alban's Head, Wessex.

Wite knelt by her friend's grave, saddened that nothing more could have been done to help her. Weeks had passed since that fateful night where she had tended to Philippa's sickness, all in vain. The new shoots of grass and sporadic growth of forget-me-nots around the grave marker were testament to this passing of time and encouraged by Philippa's final words about her servant Roger being in good health despite the onslaught of pestilence, this seemed to bring a new hopefulness. A few paces behind her stood Ealdhelm, his head bowed respectfully.

'If only Philippa had come here sooner, before the pestilence had made her so weak, we might have saved her.'

Ealdhelm nodded. 'This is true. But Philippa had chosen her path, she was custodian of the well, and she guarded it and the Portal diligently throughout her life. Come now, I have something I want to show you, something that will bring you good cheer.'

Wite pushed herself up from the stony ground and followed her tutor to where he was now standing, at the stone altar in front of the looming high cross. Resting on top of the altar was a book, finely bound in velum, and adorned with a Brass plate, depicting Ealdhelm himself. Wite gasped at the beauty of the object, she had never seen such a fine work of craftsmanship. As she drew closer, Wite looked to Ealdhelm for approval.

'Go on, you shall be the first to examine it.' Ealdhelm smiled. 'As you can see, your work has my seal of approval.'

Wite carefully turned the cover and was astounded to see her writings and illuminations had been compiled within.

'Take it, this belongs to you.'

'But!' Wite protested.

'I know, it is of high worth as an object of beauty, but you know the meaning of the words written within and the power of the Brass, it is an object that will transcend time and place. Only you can keep it safe for now. Many will come in the future, after us and try and use the power of this sacred place, but your story will make sure that all is well in the end.'

Wite smiled. It was a wistful smile, one borne out of first-hand experience. She also sensed there was a lot more she did not yet know for Ealdhelm had spoken of other Portals, but their whereabouts were closely guarded. The sun was sinking lower in the late May sky and now she was alone, she felt able to reflect, stare out to sea and ponder the *other girl,* the one who had saved her. If it hadn't been for her, she wouldn't have escaped Fr. Eldrith's wrath. She owed everything to her, whoever she was. Wite sighed, now it was time to retreat to the sanctuary of her dormitory. When she had first come to this place Ealdhelm had explained that time was not a linear process, but more of a loop, a different reality for each one of us. Up to a point, that had helped her understand the Portal and what had happened, why she had been chosen for this new life. Wite tucked the book under her cloak and took the path down from the headland, with the wise words of Ealdhelm ringing in her ears;

'Always take care with your actions Wite, for what you do now in this life will impact on another in a thousand years' time. We are all inextricably linked.'

Acknowledgements

I am grateful to Marjorie Wallace who in 1985 put information together in the form of a leaflet on St.Aldhelm's Chapel (1st Ed. 1985 & 10th Ed. June 2012), the subject of which provided my inspiration for this novel. Also, a massive thanks goes out to all members of my family who have been involved in this project in one way or another, spurring me on. Namely mum Norma, my sister Joy, and niece Katie and of course Dave, my devoted husband and critical friend.

10565029R10122

Printed in Great Britain
by Amazon